*Heather and Gordon*

# THE PICTOU TRIANGLE

### BY

*So grateful for my bridge welcome.*

## JEAN LUCAS

*Jean*

www.trafford.com

**North America & international**
toll-free: 1 888 232 4444 (USA & Canada)
phone: 250 383 6864 ♦ fax: 250 383 6804
email: info@trafford.com

**The United Kingdom & Europe**
phone: +44 (0)1865 722 113 ♦ local rate: 0845 230 9601
facsimile: +44 (0)1865 722 868 ♦ email: info.uk@trafford.com

10 9 8 7 6 5 4 3 2

## Dedication and Acknowledgments

### For my sister, Sheila Scarr

I wish to record my thanks to my sister for the help she has given in promoting my books and correcting my proofs. Deep gratitude is also due to Lucille and Geoffrey Campey for their constant encouragement and helpful comments, and I thank Lucille especially for providing much of the research material on which the story is based. I recall my visits to Scotland and Canada in their company with unalloyed pleasure.

Many of the real characters of my first book on the topic of Scottish emigration to Canada, "An Edinburgh Lady" also have small parts in this companion novel, but Robert and Angus are characters of my imagination. Their adventures in smuggling and emigration, respectively, however, are true to the times, and I have tried, though writing in a modern idiom, to convey the problems and manners of the age as accurately as I can. Thomas Dudgeon, William Wilberforce, Sellar, Loch and Lord Stafford are, of course, featured in history.

Should I inadvertently have strayed from a true interpretation of what actually happened, this is entirely my responsibility. I hope those who enjoyed "An Edinburgh Lady" will like this second novel too.

Jean M. Lucas

# CONTENTS

# BOOK I

## Chapter One - Time to Change

The man on the deep verandah had been lounging, drenched in sweat, under the hot sun, which had been beating down until only ten minutes earlier. He was watching the slaves straggling home to their shacks from his sugar-cane fields. Now the tropical night had descended suddenly as it did in Jamaica. The blazing heat had been quenched, leaving a sticky after-warmth, and the insects round the house stepped up their dusk cacophony in appreciation.

William Mackenzie took another mouthful of planters' punch from the tankard in his hand, and resumed his pondering over the future. Stocky, broad-shouldered and powerfully built, he was not untypical of the dour Scots race that had left the glens to seek a fortune abroad. At the turn of the nineteenth century it had been a twist of fate which directed the then twenty-year old to the West Indies rather than the Americas, to the sea initially, rather than to farming. However, he had made a shrewd move and prospered accordingly.

First he had worked as Mate on a slave-trading sailing ship, bringing cargoes of miserable Africans to be sold to the plantation-owners to pick cotton or cut sugar-cane. Then, as a ship-owner himself, he had begun to amass a fortune in ready cash, which he invested in fields and property. The passage of the Anti-Slavery legislation in the British Parliament in 1807 had severely curtailed these activities, thanks to the dratted Reformer, Wilberforce, but had not stopped them completely. A run-in with the British Navy in 1811, from which he had escaped having his ship confiscated and himself fined £5,000 only by the skin of his teeth, convinced him, however, that the slave-trade was no longer worth the risk and effort. He had been minded to concentrate on building up his land-holdings instead. He had three plantations, on one of which he lived, while the others were managed under his occasional supervision.

There was not too much profit in sugar these days, although the market had held up well until 1815 and the end of the Napoleonic wars, but there was plenty of juice to be made from the molasses trade with North America, and from rum if one could get it past the Revenue hawks. The triangular trade, which had enabled goods to be exported from Britain to Africa, brought slaves in the same ships to the West Indies and carried tropical goods back to Britain, had more recently eased off and given way to the two-way Atlantic run. When the timber market opened up in an Eastward direction, many of his ships carried another human cargo of emigrants westward. He had seven ships in operation, all under reliable Captains, but each with a secret hold or compartment for the rum to be taken to Glasgow whenever possible.

William's business life might have prospered, with its mix of legitimate and illegal trading, but his social life was a disaster. Few white women would tolerate life on a plantation.. His women had been a succession of slaves, or free coloured girls, varied by the occasional Hispanic, and his male companions were the hard-drinking, heavy-gambling set who belonged to the British Club. His vacations were an occasional excursion into the cooler Blue Mountains, but the trek by mule was arduous. An occasional break in Boston or Halifax was usually business-based. He had bought books there and brought them back to study – some racy stories, but often improving books on finance and magazines on politics, so that he could keep abreast of events in the rapidly changing world of the growing British Empire. He was too canny a Scot to waste his hard-earned lucre on gambling, and while he drank rum because it was there, his real tipple was whisky, which he came by seldom.

It was time for a change.

William got up, automatically shook a couple of cockroaches out of his sandals before putting them on, and called to his house-man to serve dinner. A shower consisted of a sprinkling of water from a hand-held can, while the only fan was provided by means of another slave swishing the air rhythmically with leaves from a banana tree. Dinner as usual was atrocious – a rice concoction topped with scrawny chicken. No gourmet, even William found cause for sharp criticism as he pushed its glutinous inedibility round his platter.

He did not have to live like this.

He wondered whether he could return to his roots in Scotland, but his ties with Britain had long since been loosened, and he had a feeling he might still be a wanted man in the annals of the Navy. The New World would be better. The port of Halifax in Nova Scotia was expanding rapidly, as Loyalists, displaced from the States by the War of Independence, had drifted northward. It even had a black community into which the servants he might take with him could fit. It would be a staging-post anyway.

William's decision was virtually made. Stevenson had offered to buy this plantation and might offer a good price. He would use this evening to see if he could bring him up to scratch. Acting on his resolution, he changed into dry apparel yet again, and rode into the village of Ocho Rios.

The smoky atmosphere of the Club where everyone puffed on local cigarillos, and the noise generated by dozens of men, tongues rendered loquacious by drink all competing together, hit William forcefully as he entered from the comparative stillness outside. He was immediately hailed by acquaintances eager to talk about the latest iniquities of the British Parliament – the compulsory registration of slaves to prevent internal smuggling between the West Indian islands. It had been a watered-down proposal, less onerous than the full emancipation espoused by William Wilberforce and his coterie, but still the planters were against it to a man.

Stevenson was there and the two men tried to escape the din by retreating to a quieter corner.

"I'm willing to talk terms," William offered. "Do you want the whole outfit, Agent, overseers, slaves, house, or only some of it?"

"All I think," said the prospective purchaser. "But I'd need to look around first."

"You're welcome. Come at tea-time tomorrow and you'll see it in action. But keep our transaction between ourselves. I don't want the whole world knowing I might sell up."

"Suits me," responded Stevenson, "but you've surprised me. I didn't think you would want to deal."

"Surprised myself!" grunted William. "I'd been mulling it over, like. Didn't entirely know what I'd do instead – still don't, really. But I've been here seventeen years and it's beginning to get me down. They say "sell, and leave a bit of profit for someone else" and I reckon that's what I'll do, rather than hang on until I'm really too old to change to anything else, or until an upset like the revolt in Barbados breaks out here."

"I don't reckon that is likely. You've got a good estate with plenty of prospects yet. That's why I'm interested."

"Mind you, the price has got to be right," warned William. "I can put in a manager and walk away."

"It doesn't always work, though I suppose that is what you've done that with your other plantations. But it's this one I want as it marches with mine. Makes economic sense to run the two together."

William agreed. "I'll have some figures ready for you," he said. They parted company and joined the crush round the bar.

As William returned home, he passed the cluster of slave shacks, quiet and peaceful as exhausted labourers recuperated after their eleven-hour day, to be ready to face another back-breaking stint on the morrow. Six days a week was the rule with Sundays off for religious service, and every other Saturday to cultivate their own plots.

In the overseers' barrack-like hut a raucous party seemed to be in progress. Someone was showing off his whip-cracking skills. William did not permit flogging, except for some really heinous crime, but whips were still used to "tickle them up a bit" if a slave gave signs of falling asleep on the job.   Sugar cane was really hard work, amongst tough plants and sharp stalks, which could soon cause injury.   It made sense to give the workers a breather now and then to drink or re-bind their feet to prevent cuts.  A sick slave was no good to anyone.  He felt he treated his work force reasonably.   There were dozens of worse owners.  He hoped Stevenson would be fair too. But emancipation was coming, he was sure.   Registration was only the first step.

He unsaddled the mule and turned it loose in the paddock while he hung up the saddle in the tack-room. He had equipment here, which he could add to the inventory.

Not dissatisfied with his night's work, William crawled naked under the mosquito netting and fell stertorously asleep.

\* \* \*

Transforming himself from a plantation owner into a gentleman, even a gentleman of the New World, was no easy task, William discovered.

Halifax was a well-established society.   The Military had their Fort on the top of the hill, and streets of town houses had been built down towards the waterfront. The streets themselves were narrow and cluttered with carts and carriages.  There were shops and banks, brothels and inns, food stalls and warehouses.

Depositing his money in a Bank was a first priority, and William arranged for payments from Jamaica to be received regularly.  Cautiously, he used a different Bank from that which already handled his shipping concerns. One never knew when the damned institutions would go bust, and he did not want to be caught with all his financial eggs in one basket. Furthermore the less the tax-levying authorities knew about each company the better.

He joined the Caledonian Club as a way of meeting people and learning more about Halifax society. He also took a room at the biggest hotel while he sought respectable lodgings. He already had business premises near the waterfront to look after his shipping concerns, and he paid the clerks there an early visit. His rare appearance caused a flutter of concern, reinforced when he made it clear that he was now proposing to settle in Nova Scotia and develop a closer interest in his businesses.

He renewed acquaintance with a lady of easy virtue he had regularly visited when he had come to Halifax on business. Margery had come up in the world since he first knew her, and now presided over a larger establishment with a number of girls working for her.

Clothes were an urgent necessity. It was summer in North America, but gentlemen still dressed formally, and virtually none of his Jamaican casual wear was of use. Tailors charged the earth, but money was really no object to William, and he needed to look the part if he was to buy an estate and look around for a wife. He found the new clothes added to his confidence and decided it was money well spent. Besides, it was pleasant to be cool and to employ those fragrances and adornments without which no gentleman could be complete.

He bought the local Gazette and other newspapers, eager to glean news of the town society, and to become familiar with house prices. He haunted the Club bar until he could find out who were just garrulous acquaintances, and who were men of more substance who could be useful to him.

That he could also be useful to others did not escape him. He was free with carefully edited information about his property possessions and his shipping interests. He did not hide the fact that he was eager to settle, that he was a "warm man", that he was looking for a cultured society after years in a tropical wilderness.

He received some invitations. The dining-out ones he accepted with alacrity. As far as assemblies or balls were concerned, he had no skills in dancing, but could hold his own in the card-room.

It was there in fact that he met Judge Fogo, now retired from the American circuit and researching in Halifax a book he was writing. The Judge was holding a dinner-party and extended an invitation to the newcomer.

It proved a fateful evening. Hostess of the event for some dozen people was the Judge's daughter, Delia. William was immediately bowled over and utterly captivated by her charm, grace and beauty. Delia moved easily among the assembling guests, greeting them warmly and chatting vivaciously. William felt tongue-tied in her presence. She was quite the most beautiful female he had ever encountered. He touched her hand briefly and conventionally and she asked, with practised and easy, but demure, interest, whether he would be in Halifax long.

"I am my own master now, and can stay as long as I wish," he replied, but she had turned to greet another, and there was no time to continue the conversation.

As the wine flowed and the delicious dishes were piled on the dining table, he needed to pay attention to the fellow-guests to his left and right. They were ladies of more mature years, and conversation was limited and somewhat stilted. He did venture to ask about his hostess. Was it not singular that such a striking young lady was hostess only to her father?

"They've moved around from town to town since her mother died, I believe," said Mrs. Farquharson, whose husband seemed to be a lawyer seated on the opposite side of the table. "The Judge is retired now. That's Miss Fogo's chaperon, the lady in grey."

William studied the nondescript figure pointed out to him. With crimped hair, a lace fichu and pince-nez, the duenna was hardly a powerful personality, but he thought her further acquaintance would be of advantage.

The ladies withdrew and the gentlemen made merry with port and more unrestrained conversation. William discussed the effects of the registration of slaves on the West Indian sugar economy, which was of interest to a banker near him.

When they re-joined the ladies William made a beeline for Delia's chaperon, whose name he discovered to be Mrs. Cecily Forfar. He felt that, if he could fix his interest with her, and stamp himself out as someone to be remembered from the whole party, it would be a useful bridge towards the real object of his desire. He first complimented the lady on the excellence of the meal, the warmth of the hospitality, and eventually on the elegance of the house, which had been rented for a year, while the family looked around.

"My cousin is desirous of seeing Delia established soon," confided the lady. "We have had enough of rented homes and getting used to new societies. Boston was an experience we enjoyed, but we are Loyalists with ties to the old country, and we felt it was not for us as a permanent home. In any case I intend to return to Scotland when my cousin's daughter marries."

William's Scottish Mackenzie connections were obviously of interest to the lady. They discussed the clan as she tried her best to discover William's exact relationships within it. He pleaded ignorance after such a lapse of time, but made it clear that, as a younger scion, he had no expectations from that source. However, he was at pains also to make it clear that he had done very well for himself since emigrating. He glossed over any reference to slave ships, and concentrated on the plantations he owned, and his current shipping trade. "Wealthy merchant" was what he hoped would feature in her eventual report to Delia and her father.

From the chaperon he found out that Delia was an art-lover and frequenter of picture-galleries. William expressed his own keen desire, instantaneously manufactured, to learn more about pictures before attempting to start his own collection.

"Delia would help you, I'm sure," offered her cousin. "She is really quite knowledgeable and of course she does some painting herself."

This gave him an obvious opening  of which William took immediate advantage, begging his young hostess as he returned to the tea-tray for a second cup, to take pity on his ignorance, and help him acquire some knowledge of art before he was made a fool of by the experts.

She readily assented and made an appointment for the following Thursday for him to visit the Heraclean Gallery with herself and her chaperon.

William left the house wonderfully buoyed up by the thought of a day with this glorious creature.  The horrors of Ocho Rios were vanishing into a distant memory as he began to see an alluring future unfold – a country home, a cultured wife, a dynasty to be founded. That it might be beyond his achievement, he barely contemplated.  He would need to acquire polish and social skills to win her, but his fortune must be in his favour,  he thought, and Delia seemed ideally suited as a partner in his new career as a gentleman.

Within weeks he had sought Judge Fogo's permission to solicit his daughter's hand in marriage. The old gentleman had questioned William as to his ability to support Delia, had agreed what her portion should be, and replied that Delia was willing to receive his addresses.  She made only one stipulation.  Her father would be alone in the world if she married, and she hoped her husband would agree to the Judge living with them.

For her part Delia found William a rough diamond, but not uncongenial.  His reading, during the lonely Jamaican evenings, had enabled him to converse on a variety of topics.  He was a man who had made his way in the world; he confessed that, during his seafaring days, he had jousted with the law on occasion, but come off best.  He deferred to her opinion on manners and artistic matters.  He had the wherewithal to spend lavishly on anything she might want. He obviously admired her and he had confided in her chaperon that it was his earnest desire to win her for his wife.  She was twenty-three already – almost on the shelf – and she desired to enter the married state, to which, for a female, there was no feasible alternative.  She told herself that she was not of a romantic disposition.  This offer would do very well.  She would accept.

## Chapter Two - Delia

It was satisfying for Delia Mackenzie three years after her marriage to William, to survey the broad acres of their estate, situated some three miles outside the port of Pictou, and to realise that they were now one of the leading couples in the neighbourhood. That their wealth depended on William's business interests in the West Indies, she knew, and it had been those business interests which had taken him away from her for more than a year in 1819. She had had the companionship of her father, Judge Fogo, four years retired from the North American circuit, for much of the time. Together they had visited Paris and Madrid to view the famous paintings housed in both cities, before returning to the Malibou estate to enjoy the North American summer, and put down roots in the local community.

For the past year Delia and her husband, together with Judge Fogo, who was living with them in their spacious home, had been cultivating Pictou's small but genteel society. Money, allied with prestige, and augmented by a beautiful and lively young hostess, was a sure recipe for success. Whether the event was a Ball for twenty couples in the mirrored ballroom adjoining the house, or a more intimate but beautifully served dinner party in the main house, Delia's invitations were much prized. Nor did the couple hesitate to subscribe liberally to the Town's many fund-raising events for charity, while Delia gave her time also to the Committees which planned them. A particular currently favoured object of her charity was the plight of the tenantry of Rogart in

Scotland, who were being dispossessed of their holdings by the Sutherland family and were being championed by Thomas Dudgeon, who was appealing for funds to help them emigrate to the New World. Delia's motive was not one of pity, but she had a sincere belief that Scottish settlers were just the kind of people her neighbourhood needed to expand and prosper. She had sent a substantial subscription, and promised all the support in her power.

Delia's beauty was no pale, ethereal model, but striking, vibrant and demanding of admiration. She had luxuriant, dark hair, curling profusely from a high forehead and around her pretty ears, usually adorned with jewels. A clear creamy complexion, sparkling dark eyes and a neat nose were complemented by lips which were full and red in the best Spanish tradition, and indeed she had Spanish ancestry some generations back on her father's side. Her throat and neck displayed to advantage in low-cut dresses, and her figure, when laced in the current fashion, was perfection itself.

That she had accepted in marriage a husband who was much older, nearing forty to her twenty-three at the time of their wedding, had not been much remarked on in Halifax. It was understood that Scottish pioneers, such as William, came out to make their fortunes, and when they had succeeded, their wealth could command an arranged marriage to give them the social position they craved. The wife would be brought up to expect a marriage, which could afford her status and position. All she had to do, beyond bring a dowry, was help her husband found his dynasty, and have the social talents and skills of organisation to run a perfect home.

Delia had wanted these things too. She had been about the world a good deal with her father. She was no simpering miss, fresh from the schoolroom. She was practised in acting as hostess for her father. Through his companionship she had learned to extend her interests and inform her mind. She was ripe to settle down in comfort and luxury. She wanted children, whom she could bring up to be leaders in a new country, her adopted Nova Scotia. She herself wanted to contribute to this new land.

For the first year, she and William had an extended honeymoon, enjoying their travels and their love-making. She had blossomed under his skilful tuition into a partner as sexually aware as he was. Their artistic interests proved compatible too; she showed him the buildings, the works of art, the sculptures and paintings, which she found enthralling. Together they acquired many objets d'art for their new estate. He relied upon her taste, but was happy to learn the history and provenance of their acquisitions. They were very much in charity with one another.

For almost the whole of their second year of marriage, William had to tear himself away from Delia and return to his plantations and his business empire, leaving her in the care of her father at Malibou.

He had missed her hugely, and for a few months after his return, they re-captured the first fine careless rapture, but as time went by and the months became nearly another year, William's mood became more sombre. In company he made an effort to be normal and cheerful, when they participated as a couple in the social round, but it seemed that he might be developing a grudge against his young wife.

Delia was careful not to flirt with other men in his presence. She had lightheartedly engaged in verbal flirtations while he had been away, as a result of which she was deservedly popular and seen as amusing company, but she had never given the remotest cause for anyone to think she was other than a chaste and loyal wife. She wondered whether any malicious gossip could have distressed him. Once or twice she tried to find out, but he brusquely cut short any enquiries.

They began to meet little during the day, to be either going out to social entertainments or to be giving parties at home in the evening, and to make love perfunctorily, rather than with the first early uninhibited rapture, as a sort of expected duty, at night.

Delia had no mother with whom to discuss the oddities of the male sex, and she had dispensed with her colourless duenna on her marriage. An elder sister or close cousin would have been helpful, but there was no-one. She was herself concerned that she had not yet begun in the family way. It should have happened naturally that first year, she would have thought. Was this disappointment at the root of William's coolness?

She wanted to become pregnant, to start the expected family. What could she do, she wondered, to help matters along?

Old wives' tales from the servants suggested a number of highly improbable remedies. In any case, many of their worries were directed at stopping unwanted pregnancies, rather than starting new ones. Delia made a point of paying visits to some of the younger matrons with new babies, to take little gifts, coo over the new arrival and express envy.    No-one seemed to be experiencing any difficulty except her.    She learned a great deal about what to do when one was with child, which midwives could be hired, the layettes she would need, the nursemaids who would look after the infant. She heard many dramatic and horrid stories about child-birth itself and the suffering of its participants.    None of this put her off in the slightest; the whole world went through this process, some with more difficulty; some with less.  She just wanted to get on with it!

* * *

Eventually, somewhat embarrassed, she consulted their Doctor at his office.    She confirmed that her marriage had been swiftly consummated, that marital relations had continued with the exception of the second year when William had been in the West Indies, had resumed and continued till this day.  She submitted to an examination;  she  answered  a  number  of  personal questions.  She had never had the slightest reason to think she could be infertile.    There had never been any false alarms. Just no indication of motherhood!

The Doctor explained that it took two to make a baby!   There could be a malfunction with either partner. He could see no sign of problems on her side.   Would she like to ask her husband to consult him also?

Delia felt a marked reluctance to do any such thing. She pleaded to know if there was anything she could do herself to help, since it was not a matter, which she would find it easy to discuss with William.

The Doctor promised to lend her a manual such as he had made use of himself, which would give her chapter and verse of the process, and the problems which could arise, but he urged her once again to obtain her husband's co-operation. So Delia went home with her tome and studied the small print.

* * *

It was not easy to find the right opportunity to approach William.

Eventually, one morning after breakfast, when her father had gone for an early walk, Delia motioned to the servants to leave the room, and said, with her heart in her mouth, "William, I think we should have a little talk about our family situation."

He said harshly, "You have not kept your side of the bargain."

"I want children as much as you do," she replied. "That we have not been blessed as yet, is something I hope we can remedy."

He turned his back on her and stared fixedly out of the window across the lawn.

"Blessed!" he snorted. "The plain fact is I've married a barren wife."

She suppressed a retort at the insult, and said calmly, "I have been doing what I can to find out what might be the problem. I have had an examination myself, but nothing obvious seems wrong, and the Doctor has suggested that perhaps you also could visit him for a . . "

He turned and interrupted furiously, "I might have known you would try and shift the blame on to me."

"Well, the book says ..."

"The book says!" he shouted scornfully. "Since when has the conception of children depended on a book?"

"Age sometimes comes into it ..."

"I am not old. Hundreds of men many years older than I have fathered families!"

"Yes, I know, but it might depend also on hot climates, or disease ..."

"Disease!" he exploded. "How dare you!" He struck her a stinging slap across the face, and followed it up with a hefty push that sent her staggering into a sofa, upon which she collapsed, in fright and distress.

"It has been a disaster!" he panted. "Your mother had only the one child. I might have known you'd serve me a similar trick – but I was bewitched. I should never have married you. Fool that I was! I'm going to Halifax. Don't look for me for a sennight."

His face like thunder, he swung on his heel, took three strides to the door, and banged it forcefully behind him. William had gone.

Left among the ruins of her world, Delia sobbed wretchedly. Her instinctive fears as to his reaction had been exceeded. He had been unspeakably cruel. She had never had to face such unjustified anger in her whole comfortable existence. Should she confide in her father, who was seen even now in the middle distance, returning to the house? What could he do? Interference between married couples was a thankless and unrewarding task.

When she became calmer, she recollected that William had said he would come back after a sennight. If anything was to be saved from the wreck of her marriage, she would have to solve the problem herself, look to understand what lay beneath that explosion of anger, consider what choices were left to her.

It was a tall order for a young woman. She would have her horse brought round, and ride out until she could think clearly.

\* \* \*

With Beau Brumell saddled and attired in her habit, she left word for her father, and left the house. Her groom rode some ten paces behind, and she first let the fidgets out of her horse with an exhilarating gallop, then slowed to a walk as she reached the crest of the hill. The air was clear, the sun hidden hazily behind thin cloud. Down below and to the left lay the town of Pictou, and the estuary, with specks of ships moving towards the harbour. There were always timber ships moored and loading, and on the arrival wharf many of them would have brought passengers to Nova Scotia from Scotland or Liverpool.

Just now there were berthed three naval vessels from England. She could not distinguish them clearly from this distance, but she knew them to be on a courtesy visit. She and William had planned to go to an informal dance the very next evening, which the ship's officers were expected to attend. Should she cry off, or beg her father's escort?

Probably it would be best to strive for normality; she could always claim that William had been called away on urgent business. Besides, it would be fun to meet the English officers.

Delia's mind returned to the focus of her concern. William was determined that their childlessness was no fault of his; she was even more strongly convinced that everything was normal with her own body. There was one way to find out! Take another lover and see what happened then!

The enormity of the idea, which had come flippantly unbidden into her troubled mind, shocked her deeply. She would be betraying her marriage vows. She would risk discovery and disgrace. It was not to be thought of.

Yet, … if William remained intransigent, they would both be forever miserable, trapped in a childless, increasingly loveless union. Divorce was unthinkable. When one married, it was a life-long contract. From her consultation with the Doctor, she knew present medical knowledge was insufficiently advanced to offer help. She supposed they could adopt children, but somehow she knew this would be no comfort to William. He was a businessman, a hard man. He would give money to charity, because it was expected, but he had no reserves of compassion. He would give no succour to other people's brats … she could almost hear him saying it.

She had to acknowledge that those wounding words of his had been right in a way. He had married because he had been bewitched by her beauty and he knew that she was capable of becoming the hostess he craved for his new estate. He had expected that she would provide him with sons and daughters to inherit his wealth. Nothing so crude as a bargain, but certainly an understanding!

So far they had failed, but all the blame for the failure he was attaching to her. She felt a strong resurgence of the anger and sense of injustice caused by William's fierce attack. She had never been slapped or pushed in the whole of her sheltered life. Tears stung her eyes until she could hardly see. She tried to brush them away with the sleeve of her habit. There was a lump in her throat. But it was no time to give way to emotion. She had to fight the situation, and not give way to it.

Supposing she could find a lover! That wicked thought had re-entered her mind, and this time she considered it more carefully. It would be despicable to find him from within their own circle. That could lead to passions and feelings, which once aroused, could not be damped down again, to jealousy and intrigue. But what if she could attract, say, someone like an English officer, who would be of good family, but who would sail away even before William returned from Halifax, and never be thought of again?

These thoughts were crude and disloyal ones, but everyone knew that in royal circles, children were born out of wedlock and princes had their mistresses. The King himself, when Prince Regent, had been familiar with Lady Jersey, one of the Patronesses of Almack's itself, the very establishment which set the standards of courtesy and behaviour for the ton, --- and she had been one of many of his mistresses. In Paris too, most of the ton had their clandestine affairs. Why even England's hero, the dashing Lord Nelson, had shared a ménage à trois with the married Emma, Lady Hamilton and her complaisant husband, Sir William. She had borne Nelson a child too!

Delia's groom rode up and suggested that the horses were straying too near the edge of the property where the land dropped away quite steeply. She thanked him, turned Beau inland, and resumed her musing while the groom dropped behind once more.

How could such a liaison be achieved? She could offer a day's riding to one of the officers, which could appeal to someone who had been on board ship for months. That would give her an opportunity to know a new friend better, to play some flirtatious tricks. She would have to play the part of a lady flattered by the attention she had aroused, and subtly eager for a romance, but not be blatant, or she would invite disgust. At least a couple of meetings would be needed, after an initial introduction.

Delia began to contemplate her wickedness with some satisfaction. The more she dwelt upon the idea, the more she found benefit in it. She loved this park and her home; she saw no future in the disintegration of the stability she had achieved. But she could not respect a husband who hit her and shouted at her. She believed that she had correctly identified the cause of his anger – rage and disappointment that they had not started a family, vented on her, but perhaps mingled with an underlying suspicion of his own inadequacy. She could imagine his joy if she could announce that she was with child. He would be happy again. He would fuss over her instead of accusing her. It began to seem a positive advantage that she should cuckold him. In comparison with some of those royal scandals, her own plans were modest and intended for the family good. If a child ensued, her own fertility would be assured; if it did not, then nothing of value would have been damaged, for their marriage was obviously already undergoing a powerful strain. She would then have to think again.

If she succeeded, William must never discover what she had done. That would be a secret never to be disclosed to a living soul.

She returned to the house, pleased that she had not given in to weakness cravenly, or told her father what had happened. The judge's training of his daughter had been justified. She had not lapsed into feminine vapours. She had brought a dispassionate logic to bear on the problem, and she congratulated herself that she had achieved a pragmatic solution. All she need do immediately would be to seek her father's escort for the dance tomorrow and gloss over to him William's abrupt departure.

\* \* \*

William, meanwhile, flinging himself on his horse, and with a saddle-bag containing only a change of raiment, rode at a canter along the long road to Halifax. In a furious temper, partly directed at Delia, and also partly at himself for lack of control in giving way to violence against her, he spurred his horse to put the maximum distance as quickly as possible between his home and his destination. He was already beginning to regret the violence of his rage. You hit slaves or recalcitrant sailors. You did not hit cultured and intelligent women! Had he poisoned his relationship with Delia for ever? Even in his anger, he did not want that.

An overnight stay along the road at a hostelry near Truro was needed to rest the horse.. On reaching the provincial capital of Halifax the following day, he sought out an inn of repute at which to lodge, and went on foot to find his own old familiar, Margery. She lived near the harbour on one of the side roads off Water Street, and near Constitution Hill, where she carried on a brisk trade to meet the needs of those who had been at sea for months.

She was somewhat more blowsy and stout than when he had last seen her three years before, but greeted him with warm hospitality, and began her practised blandishments. There were a few old flames Margery was eager to keep as her own prerogative, but most of her customers she now passed on to her "girls" at the rear of the parlour.

"I thought you was married and settled with a beautiful young lady in Pictou. Indeed I came to take a peek at your wedding," ventured Margery when William was comfortable on her chaise-longue with a drink at his elbow. In reply he boasted about his house, his parkland and his place in Pictou society. "What troubles you then?" she asked more directly, sensing he would not be with her at all if matters were as well as he claimed.

"My wife is not in the family way after nearly three years," he said bluntly. "We wanted children; she's not frigid; we started off in a capital way, but it's all going wrong, and I don't know why."

"Give it time," urged Margery. "Babies don't come to order, and some folks are in too much of a hurry.

Though I've spent my life avoiding brats, I must be the last person to help you get them ..."

"She has no mother or close female relative to advise her, and that's a difficult situation when much of the knowledge is handed down from generation to generation. She's been to her Doctor; he says there's nothing amiss. Now she's accusing me!"

"Aha," said the Madam. "Sits the wind in that quarter? You men don't take kindly to suggestions like that. Well, it could be. You've been a lusty lad in your time, I don't doubt. We've had some sport ourselves, and I don't suppose I'm the only one. You was in the West Indies for years, wasn't you?"

"Yes. There were plenty of women there, of course. Spanish and African mainly. I wasn't celibate!"

"I wouldn't expect it of you," concurred Margery. "You could have got an infection, I suppose. There's many a nasty little germ around. Noticed any problems yourself?"

"Absolutely nothing."

"And you're how old now?"

"Forty-two."

"And looking thirty-two," she said, with an automatic compliment. "They say there's less power as one gets older, and that's a fact. But you're a lad in your prime. Can you find your little wife a female friend or two to give her some hints? But give it time, I say."

"You're a good pal, Margery." William felt reassured and, refusing her offer of a luscious brunette as an evening companion, promised to call again the next night instead

He had merchants to see and shipping business to transact while in Halifax. Perhaps he might contact a medical adviser as well, but his instinct told him it would be a pointless exercise. Probably Margery was right. He must make his peace with Delia and give it time. But for this one problem, she was everything he had ever wanted in a wife. He must not wreck it now.

Before starting out on the two-day return journey to Pictou, he visited a jeweller he had previously patronised. Delia had tutored him into accepting that elegance lay not in flashing gold nor sparkling diamonds, but in shape, style and form. He rejected, therefore, the sunburst pendant presented to him, but chose instead a necklace of local amethysts with but a single diamond displayed in its clasp. It would look magnificent against her creamy skin. He hoped it would win him back the favour of the clever and beautiful woman he had made his wife.

# ChapterThree - The Affair

Delia, meanwhile, had gone to the younger Mortimers' dance under the escort of her father, whom she established in the card-room while she sought the company of other young matrons of her acquaintance.

Prominent among the guests were the men from the English naval ships, a tall Vice-Admiral, hair flecked with grey, whom she learned to be Richard Gordon commanding the three-ship mission, and a small group of other naval-uniformed men. The most handsome, decided Delia, surveying them from under her eyelashes and behind her fan, was undoubtedly the fair-haired, animated First Lieutenant, youngest by a few years, she thought. How to be introduced?

She went boldly up to her hostess. "I'm partnerless tonight," she confided. "William's away to Halifax for a sennight. Who can you find me to dance with?"

Her gaze was directed towards the sailors, and, securing two more unattached damsels, Mrs. Mortimer took her bevy of ladies over to perform the introductions.

Richard Gordon was courteous in the extreme. He bowed over her hand, and engaged Delia in conversation about Pictou. They took part in a country dance, and he returned with her to where the naval men had again congregated, introducing her in turn to Gregory Farebrother, the handsome lieutenant.

Lt. Farebrother might be about her own age, Delia thought, or perhaps a year or two older. She asked him about their previous port of call. Hearing that it had been

Boston, and previously on the West Indian station, she first chatted about Boston which she knew well, and then confided that her husband had extensive property in the West Indies.

"He's not here tonight," she added, "or he would have been exceptionally interested to meet you."

"Does he trade there?" asked Gregory.

"Not so much now. He owns plantations of sugar cane, but they are all managed by others. He lives now more retired, although he spent nearly a year there recently, so you can hardly call him an absentee landlord, and he was settling all the leases and legal arrangements."

"And you?" queried Gregory. "You are no colonial farmer's daughter!"

Delia acknowledged this appreciation of her sophistication. "My father is Judge Fogo, lately retired from the circuit. He is here tonight in the card-room. I have been his hostess since I was sixteen when my mother died. I have lived in England, Spain for a while, Boston, Quebec, and now here since my marriage."

"Why are all the most beautiful ladies married?" asked Gregory rhetorically.. "They are all snapped up by the time they are twenty while we poor fellows are languishing lady-less at sea!"

"I thought you kept a wife in every port," she teased.

"No such luck! It's six months at sea, then a few hours ashore, then off again. By the time we get back home, the damsels have got tired of waiting."

"How long will you be here this time?" she asked.

"Till Saturday only. Then a month or more at sea as we head back to Portsmouth."

"Then we must find you some amusement in Pictou," suggested Delia, as they joined the dance. Conversation was spasmodic until the tune ended and they were stranded at the far end of the long ballroom.

"It's so hot," complained Delia, unwilling to let this promising young man disappear. He possessed himself of her fan and plied it briskly.

"We could take a turn on the balcony," he suggested. She preceded him through the glass door onto the covered balcony where cane chairs and plants offered opportunities for a discreet tête-à-tête.

"How long till supper?" she wondered.

"One more dance, I think. Shall we sit this one out, and then go in to supper together?" he replied.

They sank on to the available chairs. "Amusement in Pictou is limited," said Delia. "But I could offer you some riding while you are here. We have an extensive estate just three miles away. Would you care for that?"

"I certainly would," he enthused. "But of course I have no horse or equipment."

"Both can be arranged," she said. "We do not keep a big stable, but I can send word to McAndrews who have a livery stable in Harbour Road to have a horse ready for you. I will meet you at our gates and show you our park."

"I will need some directions."

"Assuredly. Tell McAndrew you want the road to Malibou and he will point it out. Follow it until you come to a cross-roads. Turn right and up a slight hill. Our gates, complete with lions couchant, are on your left. I'll wait for you there at twelve noon tomorrow."

"This will be a great treat," responded Gregory. "But don't disappear. I want to beg for another dance."

"Just one more," Delia assented, and kept her new admirer by her side until supper, where they joined a table, and she introduced him to others of her acquaintance. After one more dance, she relinquished him to one of the wallflower girls before tongues started wagging. Her own carriage was ordered for eleven o'clock as she knew her father did not care to be out too late, but she left highly satisfied with her night's work. Whatever the morning brought, she had achieved the first part of her plan.

* * *

The next morning Delia dispatched a footman with a note requesting McAndrew at the Livery Stable to provide Lt.Farebrother with a good horse and riding clothes. She enclosed money to cover the hire charge, then instructed that her own horse, Beau, be brought round. The groom would not be needed, she added.

The housekeeper was next summoned and questioned about opening up the summer-house. Her father had expressed a wish to use it now and then, she explained mendaciously. "I wish it to be aired and cleaned and the cushions and chairs prepared," she instructed. "We may as well have it ready for William's return from Halifax."

There was little time to waste before their 12 noon rendezvous, but when Lieutenant Farebrother reached the park gates, Delia was waiting, an ostrich feather curling from her modish hat and a plum-coloured riding-habit outlining her trim figure.

She and her new companion galloped side by side over the newly-greened turf. Winter had given way to summer, and the browned earth was springing back to life. The sky above was blue, with only a few puffs of cloud and the sun's warmth was reaching its peak at the middle of the day. Delia reined in her horse, and Gregory brought the hired hack alongside so that they could converse. She had taken care to ride where the undulations of the ground kept them out of sight of the house which William had had built near the top of a modest hill.

They approached a small copse of trees, mostly spruce, but with a sprinkling of birch, bursting into leaf.

"Shall we rest a while?" she suggested.

Gregory dismounted easily, and came to lift her down from the side-saddle, looping both reins over the branch of a tree so that the horses could not stray.

Delia chose a sunny spot and seated herself on the grass, patting it invitingly to suggest that Gregory join her. He looked doubtfully at the pale fawn breeches he was wearing. "The grass will leave a stain," he feared aloud.

In mute reply, Delia unhooked the plum-coloured wrap-around skirt of her habit and spread it wide so that he had no excuse not to join her. The movement revealed more than a hint of white cambric petticoat and be-ribboned underwear.

Gregory first knelt beside her, then ventured to undo the ribbons of her hat and remove it before lying on his side close beside her and gazing down into her face.

"You are being a true temptress," he murmured. "Are you quite sure we should be doing this?"

Delia met look with look. "We shouldn't, of course," she agreed demurely. "But it would be a pity to turn one's back on such an opportunity. . ."

He needed no second invitation, but began to kiss her, first gently and then more fiercely as his kisses were returned with interest. Passion flared between them, fed by Delia who used all the wiles she knew to excite her new lover further. The riding skirt became a cloak for disarranged clothing as flesh met eager flesh. Breathing heavily and with beads of sweat gathering on his lip, Lieutenant Farebrother enjoyed the dalliance to the full.

"I had no idea Pictou would hold such pleasures," he said eventually, gazing down into her flushed face.

"It was wonderful for me too," she responded in a low voice. "It's a shame you are sailing away so soon. Can you visit again before you go?"

"Not tomorrow, sweetheart, for I have to take charge of the ship. Perhaps Friday .."

"Then please tell McAndrew you'd like the horse again. I hope to have our summer-house in use by then. We can be more private and more comfortable."

"Your habit has suffered, I fear. Give me your hand, and when you're standing, I'll brush the grass from your skirt."

She allowed him to lift her up and hooked back her habit. Her hair had escaped the confining comb, and she attempted to twist it back neatly. "How does that look?" she asked.

"Charming," he murmured, "but not very convincing. You look like a giddy girl and not the mistress of a mansion."

"I feel like a giddy girl, and it's a lovely feeling," Delia confessed.

Gregory turned her round and flicked his handkerchief over her velvet habit, kissing her lingeringly before she pinned her hat back over the disarranged hair. He brought Beau over and lifted her back into the saddle. She waited until he was mounted, and they walked the horses back to the gate.

"I'm glad we decided not to have a lodge and keeper," she said. "William wanted to build a proper Scottish estate, but I think this is quite smart enough for Pictou. One doesn't want to overdo things. I couldn't persuade him not to have the lions, though, and he was disappointed it had to be a wooden house and not Scottish granite."

"I see you have a clock tower in the best estate tradition," he commented. It was all they could see of the house behind its screen of trees.

"Do you live in a big house?" she asked.

"My parents do, in Wiltshire, but I'm the third son, and it was either the Army or Navy for me. My eldest brother will inherit the property."

"Till Friday, then," said Delia, turning Beau's head back towards the long drive.

"Till Friday," Gregory promised. "Same time?"

"Twelve," she agreed, and turned in her saddle to watch him trotting away.

\* \* \*

38

Throughout Thursday Delia was in a fever of impatience to see Gregory again. She was thrilled that her plan was working, and yet apprehensive that it might not yield the desired result.

She was firm in her resolve not to become emotionally entangled, and yet she could not help feeling the heady excitement of tasting forbidden fruit. The contrast between William's brutal treatment of her, which still caused burning resentment, and Gregory's flattering caresses was stark in her mind. The latter could only be part of a fleeting interlude, but sweet nonetheless. It was all happening so quickly. Friday would see a climax if she could achieve it, for by Saturday her newly-acquired lover would be gone, and William would soon return.

By evening the housekeeper reported that the summer-house had been prepared, and handed over the key at her mistress's request.

"I shall want to check it before Saturday," Delia told her casually. "We may need to order more chairs or fresh curtains if we are to entertain there this summer. Now, let me run over tomorrow's menus with you. I shan't need anything before evening, but the Judge will want luncheon." She knew that Judge Fogo would be occupied with the book he was writing, but needed to make sure also that he was expected in to lunch. Really, illicit affairs required the minutest attention to detail!

\* \* \*

On Friday at noon, Gregory was a few minutes late, and Delia waited in a fever of impatience until reassured by seeing his horse turn the corner at the foot of the hill. She rode a short way to meet him.

"I thought something was preventing your coming," she said directly.

"Nothing could prevent me coming," he answered with emphasis, leaning over to kiss her hand. "Yesterday was quite the longest day of my life, and I've been aching to see you again."

By unspoken consent, they turned their horses, not towards the ride, but along the path leading to a summer house, fronting a small lake. The horses safely hitched to railings round the building, Delia unlocked the door, and they shared a passionate embrace just over the threshold.

Neither was shy or nervous. The assignation had been made for one purpose only and they lost no time in fulfilling it. Delia had provided drinks for refreshment, and they talked a little during the respite.

"Are you very unhappy with your husband?" asked Gregory, perhaps seeking a logical explanation for their sudden tempestuous affair.

Delia hesitated only a moment. "You must not imagine that I am unhappy," she said firmly. "We have a marriage which is convenient to us both. I do not doubt that my husband will have affairs, if he has not done so already. I will only say that I do not think I shall mind, even if I know about them. Perhaps I am not of a jealous disposition. Naturally, I would not expect quite the same attitude to me. I don't expect him to condone everything I choose to do, but there it is. I know how to be discreet. I shall make the best of my marriage."

Gregory was silent.  "But you will think of me sometimes, I hope," he said.

"Of course!"  She leaned on one elbow and studied his face with care.  His hair was almost fair, in contrast to her own, and his eyes were hazel.  His nose was a dominant feature, high-bridged with eyes set well apart under straight brows.  His mouth was wide,  firm and straight, and there was a dimple in his left cheek.

"I will treasure your face in my memory, even though I have no likeness to remind me," she replied.  "But we shall not meet again. It is not to be expected, with each of us on a different continent and the whole Atlantic Ocean in between."

"You forget that I've crossed that same Atlantic Ocean three times already and tomorrow will be my fourth crossing.  It's not impossible we shall meet again.  Can I write to you?"

"No," she said with finality.  "I should not reply."

"But I must leave you my direction --- in case there are consequences of our friendship that you cannot handle.  I can't just walk away …"

"Most would," she declared flippantly, but she looked at the piece of paste-board he extracted from the card-case in his jacket pocket.  "Grove Park, near Petersfield," she read.  "I can remember that.  It must be near where my favourite author, Jane Austen, lives."

"Ten miles or so," he concurred.  She handed back the card. It must not be left around to excite questions.

"It has been a magical interlude," she said.

"I shall not find it easy to forget you," he murmured regretfully.  "Making polite conversation with a simpering miss is not likely to appeal after a red-blooded affair with you. Why had it to be so short?"

"I have to return to my role," was all she said. She had not wanted to trifle with his affections nor make him fall in love with her, and yet she had to make him want her just once more. "We don't have to say goodbye for a while yet. The day is young," she urged.

* * *

William arrived back dog-tired at Malibou following his visit to Halifax. He wondered whether to seek to see Delia immediately. Although she had retired, he thought she would not yet be asleep. Keen to make amends, he trod up the pair of stairs to her room and tapped lightly, entering at her "come in."

Delia lay to one side of the big bed, her dark hair cascading over alabaster shoulders, reading by candlelight. He thought she had never before looked so beautiful. He sat down on the edge of the bed and slipped the pouch containing the necklace into her hand. "I'm so very sorry," he said humbly.

To his surprise, she pulled his face down towards her, as if to kiss him. He had not expected her to be so complaisant. "It must not happen again," was all she said. "If we have problems, we must talk about them."

"We will," he assured her fervently. She examined his gift and was clearly pleased at its good taste. "Lovely," she murmured. "Are you very tired? Would you like to stay?"

William needed no further prompting, but shed his clothes with alacrity and climbed in beside her. She embraced him warmly, partly glad that he had returned when he said he would, and partly not daring to defer their love-making if a credible pregnancy were to follow as a result of her liaison with Gregory.

When, after a while, he fell asleep, Delia remained wakeful, mulling over the enormity of her betrayal, yet hopeful that its outcome might resolve the incompleteness of their marriage. The deed was done. It was no good regretting what had taken place, nor even dwelling on the delirious enjoyment of it. The cracks in her marriage had been repaired tonight. She would take every step to strengthen it from now on.

The affair had been so swift, so tempestuous; she thought it unlikely that it would ever be discovered. William had been received back with such unexpected amity that he would suspect nothing. The groom had not been with her, and that was often the case when she rode within the grounds. The summer-house she would visit again in the morning, to check that all had been left clean and tidy. She would order new cushions to justify her visit to it. None of the gossips in their circle would be likely to remark to William that she had spent too long dancing with one man, for she had been circumspect there, and her father had never even seen her in Gregory's company.

The only danger was if she herself were to reveal by any change of behaviour that there had been an event to disturb her equilibrium. Self-controlled as she was by nature, and through the influence of her father, she resolved to become even more so, never allowing herself the luxury of thinking of the incident again.

## Chapter Four - Secrets and Suspicions

At the end of February 1821 Delia was brought to bed of a son. The intervening months had passed pleasurably for the most part. William had been triumphant and delighted at her news, attentive for her welfare, and eventually worried about her health as her condition approached its climax.

It was a long and difficult labour, and there had been warnings about the outcome for both mother and child. When at last strident yells were heard, and the nurse carried an indignant baby downstairs to be shown off to father and grandfather, there was relief all round. William would have gone immediately to Delia's room, but was stopped by the Doctor.

"She is not well and must rest," he said. "I am afraid there may be fever. I will return again soon. In the meantime the midwife will stay with her to keep her cool and calm. She may see the child if she asks for him, but so far she is too distressed and confused."

Judge Fogo, overhearing this, was beside himself. "Her mother was just the same," he said. "It took months for her to recover from Delia's birth. You don't think she could die? ..." he added fearfully.

"She is a young woman with a good constitution and most women in this situation will recover quickly once the birth is over," the Doctor answered. "But she seems unnaturally flushed and feverish. We'll know more in a few hours if she can rest and sleep."

Delia had found the whole process more excruciating, exhausting, seemingly unending and a ghastly torment.  Her mental state was badly affected. She saw herself being punished for her wickedness by this long drawn-out torture.  Her body was reaping the pain for her illicit pleasure.   Little red devils with pitchforks seemed to be prodding her to make her scream.  There were flames and fires consuming her and she could not escape.  Her thoughts became rambling and chaotic, and she only dimly heard the midwife's instructions, while obeying them were beyond her powers.

She was barely conscious even that the torment had ended.  Hot and cold in turns, she suffered for another two days hovering in and out of consciousness, before taking a turn for the better, and lying limp and wan in a more natural sleep.

When her son was brought to her, she was reassured that he had fuzzy dark hair, that he had the right number of fingers and toes, and that his lungs seemed none the worse for his rough delivery.  But as for taking charge of the infant, the effort was too much,  and he was relinquished to the care of the wet-nurse and his nanny.

William told her over and over again how pleased and delighted he was, what a courageous and clever wife he had, how much he doted on them both, but to no avail. Delia remained depressed,   pale and lethargic for many weeks.

They had to decide names for the child.  Gilbert for the Judge, William for his father, and Austen were the three chosen.  William could not understand the logic for this third choice, but was too concerned for Delia's spirits to object when she said it was to honour her favourite author.   That it was also, once removed, a reference to the part someone else had played in the little boy's creation, was her secret alone.

She could trace in little Gilbert, tiny though he was, the eyes and eyebrows, the dimple in the cheek that she had so carefully observed in Gregory.   She was sure no one else in Pictou would notice, for the naval officer was out of sight and out of mind, but there was no possible doubt in her own conscience, that he was, in fact, the product of those rapturous, illicit moments.

William, on the other hand, was finding similarities with long-distant Mackenzies, and the Judge was convinced that there were distinct likenesses to his own father.  They were happy in their pursuit of his lineage, and she was delighted for them.   It had been her intention throughout to provide for the inheritance, but she became more and more convinced that this child was to be her last as well as her first.   Apart from the danger to her health, which would serve as the reason, she could never risk such a deception again.   Moreover, it seemed extremely likely that William's hotly-denied infertility had been the problem all along.

As she grew stronger, Delia began to attend the Presbyterian Church with much greater regularity.   She had sinned and she must expiate that sin.   The child was baptised into the Church and she promised that he would be brought up to belong to it.   At the same time, she would see that he would be worthy to become a good citizen of her adopted land, Nova Scotia.

\* \* \*

Thrown more upon their own resources while Delia was ill, William and Judge Fogo were discovering that sharing homes, even large and palatial ones, had drawbacks. The two men had little in common, the younger hardened, wealth-seeking, forceful; the elder reserved, artistic, analytical. Conversation languished without Delia to keep up the flow.

The younger man began to suspect the older one of sneering at him in subtle ways for his twenty years in the wilderness, of denigrating his earnest attempts to learn about art and antiquities, of thinking his money and the way he spent it verging on vulgarity.

For his part the elder began to suspect that his daughter's future with William might not be all he had wished for her. He actually admired William's efforts at cultural improvement, but he found him bombastic and self-opinionated. He deplored William's capacity for drink, although he granted he could usually hold his liquor.

Drink came into the house by the keg, and he suspected that the *Mary Ann* when she was in port with her molasses cargo from Jamaica was the source. On the only occasion when he had seen William the worse for wear, he had more or less admitted a recent shipment, thinking nothing of smuggling it in. The Judge felt there were hidden depths to the man, which he was normally at pains to conceal. There were gaps in his history, referred to obliquely, but which he was unwilling to explain. The Judge did not think William could have amassed all his undoubted wealth from a West Indian plantation, or even three of them.

William had more than once in his hearing criticised the British introduction of slave registration. He was vigorously opposed to full emancipation and thus naturally he would have been opposed to the ending of the slave trade in 1807. Those willing to take the risk had amassed even greater profits when ships had been engaged in slave-running against enforcement by the Navy. Judge Fogo had once tried and sentenced a Ship's Captain who had been caught at it. He wondered if William had been in the slave-running business.

The Judge knew that William owned seven ships – maybe not the same ships that had run the blockade. Among the present ships were several belonging to an ocean-going fishing fleet, the *Mary Ann*, for instance, which was a frequent caller in Pictou. Why had William settled in Pictou anyway? Was it because the little port, though busy, was much less seriously policed than Halifax? Supplying fish to Glasgow, which was William's legitimate trade would be lucrative, but was it lucrative enough to sustain this lavish life-style? Perhaps he was supplying other cargoes too.

Judge Fogo was far too acute to question William directly, but he knew something of investigative methods, and as a former prosecuting Counsel he could spot the witness who told you just enough of the truth, while obscuring the rest, and he could evaluate such statements. William made no secret of his diddling the Inland Revenue with the odd keg of rum. Was he perhaps a smuggler on a much more serious scale also?

In England free-trading, as it was called, was regarded as something of a sport. French brandy was

48

regularly landed on the south and east coasts, avoiding the Revenue cutters and the coastguards, and was purchased by gentlemen, clerics and magistrates alike. But trans-Atlantic smuggling, if that was what William was engaged in, would be in another league entirely, well-camouflaged no doubt, in planned, deliberate deception.

Perhaps this was all in the past. Evidence might be possible to come by, but did he really want to find out? Disgrace for William would bring social disaster for his daughter too. Best to leave well alone if it was all over now, but he would keep a watchful eye on Master William's activities in case the temptation to start up again ever reared its head.

* * *

That winter Judge Fogo spent in London, researching his book from the archives of the British Parliament. He also wanted to meet William Wilberforce if he could, and find out more on Delia's behalf about the work Francis Dudgeon had been engaged in on behalf of emigrant Highlanders.

His absence was a welcome respite for William who at last had his family to himself.

Delia was attempting a water-colour likeness of the child – a difficult task since he was like quicksilver, crawling in all directions and never seeming to be still for a moment. She could capture his features, of course, when he was asleep, but she needed his expression and the look in his wide brown eyes as well. The fuzzy birth-hair had come off, and a fairer silkier version was taking its place.

William himself had discovered hunting. A party of local men was in the habit of organising an expedition into the hills in search of moose. Among the party were Alexander Thomson and his younger brother, Robert, a well-built young man of twenty-three. William thought Alexander a sober-sides, a pillar of the Presbyterian Church and a lay preacher, as well as a prosperous local merchant, but with whom he had little in common. However, young Robert was like a restive colt, game for any mischief. William liked the cut of his jib, the image of himself at the age of twenty. They were paired together and he thought he might be able to use Robert one day in one of his enterprises.

For his part Robert wanted to be anywhere other than on his father's farm, looking after pedigree cattle. He begged William to help him get abroad. He was desperate to leave Pictou and would do anything, he said, to work his passage to Scotland or the Indies.

William used him once or twice on errands to Halifax when he didn't want to go himself. The youngster proved his resourcefulness on one occasion, escaping footpads with the money he had been entrusted with. As a result he was invited to Malibou, introduced to Delia, and finally offered a job on William's brig on the Scottish run with fish from Newfoundland to Glasgow.

Over a generous measure of rum William took Robert into his confidence. "We do a circuitous route," he said. "There are reasons for this. You will need to keep your mouth shut about where you go, and whom you see. Can you do that?"

Robert swore eternal silence and the methods were outlined.

"I've been doing this for ten years," said William. "I've been producing molasses from the West Indian plantations, and I also own a rum distillery in Jamaica. Molasses is much in demand in Cape Breton among the Scottish Highlanders, but there's no profit in shipping it there, unless we can do a subsidiary trade. So I became the sole supplier of molasses to Cape Breton, using the same boat then for the short distance between Ingonish and Port-aux-Basques. I also bought a small cod fishery at Port au Basques and there's a Highlander called John Campbell in charge of the fish processing business. That's all perfectly above board, and actually makes a profit in its own right. Campbell's under instruction only to employ Scots. That way I can trust them. You're a Scot too, and that's why I'm trusting you!"

Robert muttered his appreciation.

William went on. "So we load bulk sugar and molasses and rum in Jamaica, the latter two in barrels marked "molasses". This is a regular run, and each ship sets off for Newfoundland. The sugar is off-loaded at St. John's, where the customs checks are known to be perfunctory, and no-one's ever discovered the rum. In any case some of the barrels are genuine molasses, which go on down to Port-aux-Basques. In fact all the molasses barrels go to Port-aux-Basques, where John Campbell sorts them out -- molasses on to Sydney, Cape Breton, and the rum transferred to the bottom of an ocean-going fish cargo-boat, secured with large stones and small pieces of cut timber which looks like ballast. The lower deck has been specially framed, so that anyone peering down the hatch will think it is ballast, and we then pile dried cod in the hold on top of it."

"How do you get it out?" asked Robert, enthralled by the tale and honoured to be entrusted with its secrets.

"Well, this ship goes across the Atlantic to Greenock, where Simon Bennett, who was once in the Navy, meets her. He's a major fish importer, and he offloads the cod on to his regular wharf. He then moves the vessel to his own ship-building yard, to a quieter wharf, on the grounds that she needs a minor re-fit. He gets out the rum, knows where to sell it on, and back comes the money with the ship, of course, all ready to do another run. Except that it's not always the same ship. I ring the changes among them, to avert suspicion. The Captains are in the know, of course, and everyone gets their cut. You'll get yours if you go along with it."

"Of course I will. Everybody benefits, as far as I can see, except the British Government."

"Oh, I'm a universal benefactor!" said William sarcastically. "But you have to be sworn to secrecy. If my respected father-in-law ever found out, we'd be in real trouble. He's a retired Judge, as you know."

\* \* \*

Gradually Robert Thomson became more and more drawn into William's business ventures. His father, William the Pioneer. and his elder brother, Alexander, were apprehensive. Although on the surface Robert's familiarity with such a well-to-do family as the

Mackenzies was flattering, Alexander in particular felt that his younger brother needed to have a care.

"Pooh!" retorted Robert to this well-meaning advice. "Just because you never go anywhere or do anything, there's no reason for me to be a stick-in-the-mud. I want to travel around a bit, see something of the world, and in any case I'm more than old enough to take care of myself."

"You might remember that Nat and I spent years re-building our farm after Father's release from that mistaken spell in prison. The least you can do is put in your effort to keep it prosperous now."

"There's plenty of the family to look after Maple Tree Grove, and I'll do my bit when I'm here. But if I don't get out of Pictou, I'll bust! I want some adventures. You talked me out of enlisting when I was 18, and I'll be damned if I let you talk me out of going to Scotland when I've got the chance."

So Robert went, and Judge Fogo came back, and all went merrily until 1825 when Robert returned from an Atlantic trip on William Mackenzie's behalf and reported a narrow escape. A revenue vessel had intercepted them well out to sea beyond the Firth of Clyde. It had made a cursory examination, but suspicions had obviously been aroused, and it had followed them in to the port. A more detailed search had followed, once they were berthed, and the captain questioned for hours. They had judged it best not to attempt to unload the hidden cargo, but disposed of the top cargo of dried fish, and the captain had the brilliant idea of buying fishing nets which were to form a return cargo. They pleaded the need for a quick turn-round, and the nets were loaded at the same time as the dried fish was unloaded, so that the ballast remained covered.  Then they set sail back within the day. Admittedly the valuable rum cargo remained unloaded, and they would have to try and run it another time, but the secret hold had remained undiscovered.

William and Robert were closeted in William's study, drinking rum for an hour or more, while this tale was unfolded, and they emerged just as Judge Fogo crossed the hall.

"You did well to get away with it,"  William was saying.  The younger man,  flushed with the drink and somewhat unsteady,  was boastful.

"I'm not afraid of the excisemen,"  he said. "They've got to play by the rules, but we don't have to ..." he caught sight of the Judge and stopped abruptly.  "I'll see you tomorrow, then," he added.  "My respects to Mrs. Mackenzie."  He left quickly.

Judge Fogo looked enigmatically after him and said, "A word with you, William."

William turned on his heel and the Judge followed him into the study.

"What exactly are you smuggling?"  he asked.

"Smuggling?" queried William, putting on an air of innocence.  "Why, you know I don't pay duty on a barrel or two I get here."

"I'm not talking about a barrel or two.  You are employing that young man on a more or less regular basis. My suspicion is that you have a major illicit operation going on,  probably into Britain.  I've wondered about it for some time, and that unguarded conversation has more or less convinced me."

"You've no proof," declared William, his defence mechanisms forced into action.

"No proof, true, but if I lay information it will be for others to find the proof. The names and registration of your ships is known. It shouldn't be difficult to apprehend one of them and find proof."

William knew this to be true. His ships would pass a cursory inspection, but not a well-informed search. The trick with the netting could not be played again, and all his other ships would be suspected if one cargo was uncovered.

"I would advise you not to lay information," he responded, injecting a tone of menace into the words. "It would make life very uncomfortable for Delia – not that I'm admitting a thing."

"I'm aware of that," returned the Judge. "I shall sleep on it. I thought you had given up the illegal side of your business and were concentrating on legitimate trade."

"I do trade legitimately."

"I'm aware you have some healthy businesses. What I don't understand is why you have to put everything at risk by engaging in underhand deals too."

"It's only your disordered imagination, which is suspecting something illegal," flashed William, beginning to bluster and show his anger.

"You have a wife and son to consider. What you once did in the Indies as a single man should be no guide to your conduct now."

"Don't lecture me! I know what I'm doing. Your well-being is tied up with mine, so if you're wise, you'll keep your nose out of business which doesn't concern you."

"A duty to uphold the law is every man's concern – and mine especially. Will you promise to stop?"

"Stop what?" William prevaricated.

"Stop whatever you're doing illegally. Not that I think I could trust your word."

William laughed harshly. "You take my hospitality, but you don't trust me. Well, so be it. Are you still coming on our expedition tomorrow?"

The Judge hesitated. He was looking forward to a day out in the hunt for deer.

"Yes, I'll come," he said. "But I want you to think carefully over what I've said, and I'd like us to discuss it again when you have given it serious thought."

William agreed smoothly. "Yes, I'll do that. Good-night."

They went their separate ways, William to consider furiously and frantically what urgent measures he could take to thwart the Judge. He had no doubt that the Judge would put his public duty over his personal wishes. He could persuade Delia to take Gilbert away and then set about accusing his son-in-law.

William knew he would have to stop Robert Thomson's mouth too. The young man had been careless, crime enough, but he knew too much, and what he might be forced to tell under pressure would give the Judge his evidence and ruin William's whole existence.

Rapid action was needed.

# Chapter Five - The Accident

Judge Fogo had expected the next day's shooting-party to be five or six strong, but Alexander Thomson sent word that he was expecting a consignment of goods for his store, from a ship which had arrived and would be unloading, and so he could not come. There were, therefore, only a couple of loaders and beaters in addition to William, Robert and the Judge. However, the Judge felt no apprehension of danger.

They toiled up the hill near the East River, spotting a herd grazing in the distance. The terrain was uneven and pocked with rabbit holes. Despite a strong stick to help him and the loaders carrying the party's weaponry, the elderly Judge fell behind the other two.

"He heard what we said, you know, and tackled me immediately afterwards," William confided to Robert as soon as they were alone, referring to their meeting the night before.

"I'm sorry. I should have shut up once the door was opened. What did he say?"

"He said he ought to lay information against us. I reminded him that this would react badly on Delia, and he said he'd sleep on it. But I can't be content with that. He's highly dangerous. He wants me to promise to stop the trade, but then said he couldn't trust me to keep such a promise."

"Would you stop?" asked Robert.

"I don't think I can – there are too many people in the chain, depending on the trade. I could phase it out over time, I don't doubt, and perhaps that is what I'll do, but I couldn't stop tomorrow even if I wanted to. And why should we for the sake of one old man's scruples? I say 'we' because you're involved too, as deep as I am."

"Then what can we do?"

"I'll think of something. Stop. We must wait for the old fool. But just remember, if I solve the problem, I'll want your unquestioning support."

"Of course, you can count on me," said Robert, as they turned, waiting for Judge Fogo to catch them up.

William was cordial and pleasant to him. "It's a mighty pull up this hill, but I hope our sport will be worth it," he said. "Do you want to rest a while?"

"No, I can manage," replied the Judge, "as long as I take it steady."

They went up in line abreast, not talking to save the Judge's breath. Then William suggested the beaters stop and make a base camp.

"No need for you to come further just yet," he said. "We shall have to tread warily once we reach that copse up ahead, or the herd will get wind of us and be off. Take the left-hand sweep, Robert, and creep round until you're in sight of them. Go through the middle, Judge, as the distance will be shorter and you'll get nearer to take a good shot, and I'll take the right-hand loop. We must keep very still and quiet, and no-one start shooting till I give the signal."

"What is the signal?"

"An owl-hoot, or as near as I can mimic it. You'll be the furthest away, Robert, so keep your ears tuned. Both barrels, of course."

The herd of deer was feeding peacefully just beyond the small group of trees and seemed not to have sensed any unusual activity.    The three men trod carefully, keeping as low to the ground as they could, and using the trees as screens.   To tread on a twig or small branch would be dangerous, as the sound of a crack would carry a long distance, and they moved from tuft to tuft of grass wherever possible.   Stalking their prey successfully was the main excitement.

Suddenly William gave the pre-arranged signal. Three shots rang out; the herd scattered instantaneously, one of their number wounded and fallen.   Two more shots followed, in pursuit of the speeding animals,  but seemingly having little effect, as the targets grew rapidly smaller.   Finally there was one further shot a couple of seconds after the others.

Robert had broken out of his hiding-place and raced across to the fallen deer.   "I got the buck!" he shouted excitedly.   He drew his hunting-knife with which to finish off the animal, unaware that his companions had not joined him.

William stood motionless at the edge of the copse. He seemed to be bending over something on the ground. As Robert looked up he shouted, "Come over here!"

Robert left his now dead trophy and ran back to the tree-line. "What's wrong?" he asked.

"The Judge! He's been shot."

"Shot!   Surely not!   We were in line abreast, shooting forward.  He couldn't have been."

"He's dead," said William unemotionally.   "Look, there's the bullet-wound, oozing blood."   He lifted his gaze, and looked into Robert's anxious face. He spoke deliberately, and with emphasis. "You need to get away. Escape while you can. I'll say it was an accident."

"But I didn't shoot him," protested Robert, bewildered. "It must have been your shot, not mine. I shot the buck. There were five shots first, then one later."

"You see what will happen? There'll be an inquest. They will ask us both questions, and we'll tell stories that are slightly different. It will end in confusion, suspicion. They might accuse us of murder, or manslaughter at least. They'll look for motives. But if you go, the explanation will be clear. It was an accident and you've fled."

Robert looked appalled. "But …but I don't want to go. It wasn't my fault."

William's face assumed its grimmest expression. "I shall say it was your shot," he warned. You agreed a minute ago that if I could save us, you'd unquestioningly do what was needed. Now you're arguing, when you have to trust me and obey. Dead men tell no tales. That's my solution to our problem. But we have to keep ourselves out of jail. The "Mary Ann" leaves at three on the afternoon tide. Get down to her unobtrusively; you can make your way down the far side of the valley. I shall cover you by saying you headed inland. The ship will take you to Jamaica. You can work as overseer on the Blue Moon plantation. I'll put a thousand pounds a year in your bank account until you get back in a few year's time. Do it, Robert," he added forcefully.

Conflicting emotions chased themselves across Robert's countenance. He looked at William's set and unyielding face. William was in deadly earnest.    There was no doubt about that.

"I can see I'll have to," said the younger man, slowly.   "You've got it all worked out. I had no idea you meant to kill him, when you said you'd find a way of dealing with him.   I could never, and would never, have done that, and I'm appalled that you have.    What ever will Delia say – her own father!"

"I've got the more difficult task," said William. "I've got to make it right with the authorities, and cope with Delia's grief too.    I can only do it, if I've got a scapegoat. But I pledge that it will seem an accident.    I'll do what I can to make things right with your family, but they mustn't know where you've gone, or someone will scream 'collusion'. You must simply disappear!  Drop the gun and go. Here's money to start with;   you'll earn more at Blue Moon, and you'll have capital to come back to.  I'll always be in your debt, Robert,  for doing this."

The younger man took one last incredulous look at the corpse and stumbled away.  He had been totally dominated by William in the past three years, and he could not think straight at all, much less suggest any alternative.   There was not much time to spare if he was to get on board the *Mary Ann*.   He began to run until his figure was only a speck in the distance.

William watched till he was out of sight, then switched his own gun with Robert's, wiping the stock of each with his handkerchief.   Leaving the Judge where he had fallen, he went back to the servants waiting below.

* * *

"There's been a dreadful accident," announced William to the two loaders. "You heard the shots. Well, one of them hit the Judge. He'd dead, I'm afraid. I've left Robert Thomson with his body, while I came down to get you to bring the litter up for him. We killed a stag too, but we'll have to leave that, and adapt the sling to carry the Judge."

The two men looked at one another in alarm.. "How could that have happened?" asked one.

"It's a bit of a mystery," lied William. "But I think probably Robert decided to move his position after firing the first barrel. There was a bit of a pause before the last shot. and maybe the gun went off before he could sight it properly. The Judge had both barrels fired but I don't think he hit anything, unless he stumbled and was shot with his own gun. I missed both times, but then I'm a rotten shot. Someone will have to find out whether it was a near shot or a distant one when they look at the body. It's a terrible tragedy, and I can hardly believe it."

Together the small group climbed back up the hill. "I can't see Mr. Robert," said one of the loaders.

"I left him there," confirmed William. "We tried to see what we could do for the Judge, and that took a few minutes, and we tried to fathom out what could have happened, but Mr. Thomson said he'd wait. I think the Judge should be over by the trunk of the silver birch, which he was using for a screen."

Indeed the crumpled body was where he had left it, but of Robert there was no sign.

William shaded his eyes and scanned the distance. "Where's he gone?" he asked. "I know he was upset, but ...oh, is that him making for the Halifax road?"

"I don't see no-one," said the loader, looking to where William was pointing.

"No, he's just jumped down somewhere, but I think it was him. Duncan, you take his head, and we'll lay the Judge in the animal sling. See! There's the buck Robert got with his first shot. The Judge won't be as heavy as the buck would have been. What a terrible thing to happen!"

The little party wended its sad way down towards the Town.

Needless to say, Pictou was in a ferment over the accident. The officer from the court-house came out to Malibou to interview William and the loaders. Robert Thomson's whereabouts were endlessly discussed.

He can't have got far," said the officer, "without a horse, and on foot. A search-party should soon catch up with him."

"But why run away if it was an accident?" said others of the town.

Delia was shocked to the core by her father's death and kept to her room, sobbing with grief. She also was concerned by implications of the accident. "Why has Robert gone away?" she asked William. "Surely he should be here to explain what happened."

"He may fear a manslaughter charge," suggested William. "That would be very serious for his family. I know it was a pure accident, but the courts are sometimes zealous to accuse somebody if there's been a death."

"What evidence can you give to prove it was an accident?" she asked.

"I'm absolutely sure it was. What possible motive could Robert have had for it to be anything else? I thought at first your father might have tripped and his own gun gone off accidentally, but it seems there were no powder burns and the gun must have been fired from some distance away. That can only have been Robert's gun. I fired in quick succession and missed both times. As you know I've only taken up the sport recently, and I'm not a brilliant shot. Robert hit a buck with his first shot, and perhaps fired wildly with his second, or tripped and spoilt his aim. You've had a great shock, my dear. Why don't you lie down and rest?"

"I just keep seeing his dear face," she wailed. "We have been so close, he and I since Mother died, and now he won't see his book published, or watch his grandson grow up!"

William put his arm comfortingly around her, and held her close until her distress eased. All the time his mind was racing. Was there any detail he had forgotten? What would they do about the funeral? Presumably it would have to be postponed until after an inquest. What if Robert hadn't got away on the *Mary Ann*?

His interview with the Thomson family was very difficult. Robert's father, William the Pioneer, refused to believe that his fourth son would have run away.

"He wouldna do a thing like that," he said. "I've brought up my seven children to believe you own up and face the music."

"Robert has changed lately, it seems to me," commented the eldest brother, Alexander. "He's come under other influences. I only wish I'd gone shooting with them yesterday. Accidents will happen, and I don't say I could have prevented it, but perhaps we could have been more careful."

"We were careful," insisted William. "We each had a route, and none was ahead of the others; we moved forward in line abreast. You know how we usually work when we're a larger party. You've been with us often enough. Well, we did exactly the same yesterday."

"Mebbe he'll come back when he's thought it through," said the old man. "Where could he have gone to, anyway?"

"He set off in the direction of the Halifax road," volunteered William. "I first asked him to go down for the loaders, but he said he would stay with the body while I went. Perhaps that was when the idea of going missing occurred to him. I was away a good ten minutes, perhaps a bit longer, and I thought I got a glimpse of him away down the hill nearing the road, and then he seemed to jump out of sight. Duncan didn't spot him."

"Perhaps you ought to go and look for him, Alexander. Persuade him to come back," suggested William the Pioneer.

"I'll go if it will ease your mind, Sir," agreed Alexander. "He may not get far if he's neither spare clothes nor money."

"Shall I come with you?" offered William.

"No, thank you. You have your wife to console. I'll enquire at cottages along the road."

William took his leave. While he was confident Alexander would find no trace of Robert along the Halifax road, he wondered what would happen when he failed. Would they turn to consider the shipping alternative?

As it happened, luck was with him. Several ships had left Pictou on that afternoon tide, and there was nothing to single out the *Mary Ann* from the others. It had been a high risk strategy, thought William. Quickly conceived and boldly executed. He deserved his luck. He thought he had not lost the ruthlessness of his early days on the slave ships. If a slave was sick, you pushed him overboard quickly, so that he did not infect the others. The Judge had been unwise to threaten him, and even more unwise to give him notice of the threat.

The court hearing was comparatively easy. William repeated his oft-told tale; the loaders corroborated it to the best of their knowledge. The officials offered no alternative, after a cursory investigation. The verdict was 'Accidental Death.'

Robert had no way of knowing that, however. He found himself marooned on a hot, steamy West Indian island, with no escape in prospect.

* * *

Meanwhile, in Pictou, Alexander, Robert's eldest brother, found himself forced to play the detective. In the absence of any organised police force, the little town had few resources with which to investigate a complex crime.

Acting on William's glimpse of a figure jumping down a bank into the Halifax Road, Alexander saddled one of his father's horses, and set off to try and discover where Robert had gone.

From the rough road, he constantly looked back at the copse of trees on the hill where the fatal shooting had taken place. He kept it in sight until high scrub trees and an undulation in the ground obscured his view. Then, leading the horse, he retraced his path, searching for broken branches, or crushed foliage where a man might have burst through. He found nothing significant, nor any scraps of clothing caught on a hedge or twig, nor any heavy footprints in the dried mud at the side of the road, where a man might have sprung down.

For almost a mile he trudged, then turned and walked forward again, hoping that the opposite vantage point might reveal something to assist. There was nothing.

Alexander remounted and trotted forward along the road again until a farmhouse came into view. He shouted a "hallo" and a trim woman came round the side of the timber building, with eggs gathered in the scoop of her apron.

"Have you seen a young fellow pass by – tall, reddish-brown hair, on foot, about noon-time or a little later?" he asked.

The result was a shrug of non-comprehension and so he asked again in the Gaelic tongue. This time he was understood, but the woman said she had seen nothing.

Alexander rode on until he reached a couple of shacks, not substantial enough to be called cottages, but neat for all that. An old man, who spent most of his time in the small garden in front of the house, straightened his back and did his best to be helpful.  He described a pedlar calling, and a man galloping past on a black horse, and a couple in an ox-wagon, carting tatties, but no-one on foot save the eleven-year old boy from the farm above.

It was a mystery.  Either William had been mistaken, and Robert had not come this way at all, for he would have passed the old man,  or perhaps he had kept to the edge of the fields, rather than risk using the road.

Alexander was not the man to give up easily, and he rode on for another five miles, asking where he might, but the trail was non-existent, and he turned for home reluctantly as both he and the horse were tiring.

"I doubt whether William saw what he says he did,"  Alexander reported to his father.

"He said it was only a fleeting glimpse.".

"The only other way out, Sir, would be by sea. Tomorrow I must ask at the harbour, which ships set sail, and whether he was seen on the quay."

"If  Mackenzie's testimony is unreliable, we have no proof that he tried to run away.  Why couldn't the young fool come home?"

"Precisely because he is young and foolish – and over-influenced by Mackenzie," judged Alexander. "But a further thought has occurred to me.  William made no attempt to search for Robert.  Could he have come by an accident, himself. I think,  perhaps we should search the copse, even before we enquire down at the harbour.  I could take a couple of men with me at first light."

"Say nothing to your mother about that!"  warned William the Pioneer.  "But, yes, it should be done."

# BOOK 2

## Chapter Six - The Urge to Emigrate

Nova Scotia and Cape Breton in the early nineteenth century continued to be populated by emigrants from Scotland and Ireland. The poverty of people there created an urge to emigrate in order to better their lot. Since the historic arrival of the *Hector* at Pictou in 1773, the little port had become a gateway for immigration from Europe. The economy in the mother country was worse in some years than in others, but periodically there came a surge of emigrants, and there was one such surge between 1819 and 1822 from the Sutherland estate in Ross-shire. It was a time when land-owners, eager to see a better return on their land, were turning their acres over to the grazing of sheep.

Angus Ritchie, a nineteen-year-old under-groom from the Kilcalmkill estate, had developed just such an urge. His father, Denis, had survived the changeover from croft-farming and had become a well-regarded shepherd, who worked on the sheep-farm owned by the Kildare family, mostly resident in Edinburgh.

Angus and his younger sister, Elizabeth, and their much younger brother had attended the Church School locally, the elder two shining at their lessons. Leaving school at thirteen, there had been a lack of suitable work for Angus, but by good fortune his father secured an apprenticeship for him in the Kilcalmkill stables. He did well as a stable-boy and rose to become a groom.

Sometimes the country-folk, who worked on the estates of the aristocracy, were taken by the families they served into their town houses, and Angus found himself at eighteen as a groom in Edinburgh with a billet above the stables. He was responsible for seeing that the horses were well turned-out for the carriages in which the family drove round the city. His main jobs were the daily trips to take Miss Camilla and Miss Gertrude to the Seminary, and to fetch them in the late afternoon. In the meantime, with the coachman driving, he had to hold the horses' heads while they were kept waiting as the mistress of the household went shopping or calling on her friends. He let down the steps or put them up as required, and was sometimes rewarded with a coin for his trouble by friends of the family as he performed this service.

If the young ladies went riding, it was his job to mount them, make sure the stirrups were comfortable, and follow on another horse, some three or four lengths behind to ensure that they came to no harm, and eventually to help them dismount.

Angus was also able to place his younger sister, Elizabeth, in a household nearby. In the servants' hall, he heard gossip that a nursery governess was needed for the three and four-year olds, to teach alphabet, sums, drawing and reading, and he begged the neighbouring house-keeper to recommend his sister to her mistress. When an interview was granted, he rode night and day back to Kilcalmkill to fetch Elizabeth and school her in what she needed to say and do. Miss Ritchie secured the post.

Elizabeth's quiet, calm good sense and her recent advanced schooling, for she had stayed until fifteen as a student-helper at her local Church school, helped her to fulfil the position satisfactorily. Brother and sister were able to spend their half-days off together, exploring the historic city of Edinburgh, visiting its museums, and enjoying its fairs. Elizabeth also set about acquiring other fashionable skills in which she was deficient, the music, painting water-colours, French and embroidery which would be required as Governess to older girls.

All went well until about a year later when Miss Gertrude Kildare, one of the young ladies of the Kildare family, started practising her arts of flirtation on their good-looking, red-haired groom. High-spirited, rather silly, and still at the schoolroom stage, the young ladies were not yet "out" in Society. Miss Gertrude, the younger, was the bolder of the two.

She would beckon Angus to ride abreast with them, and first sought his opinions on the horses and fashions of their acquaintances.

"Do you not think Miss Murchison's bonnet is a becoming colour?" she would ask. "'Tis a pity she's so plain. It would suit Camilla better, don't you think?"

Glancing at the older girl's pasty complexion, Angus responded, "It's not for me to say, Miss."

"I must say, you look after our horses very well, doesn't he, Camilla? Does it take you very long?"

"Not too long, Miss. I like to see their coats well-brushed," he replied politely.

"I shall come and watch you one day," she said, shooting him a roguish glance.

"You'll be welcome, Miss, if you and the Governess care to step round."

71

"Perhaps I shall come without the Governess ..."
She ventured a wink.

"I don't think your Papa would like that, Miss," he
muttered, flushing red with embarrassment.

He knew he must not become too familiar with
either of them since their position in Society was vastly
higher than his own. Unfortunately, he was not
experienced enough to turn off their attentions without
causing offence.

"We fancy to go on a midnight ride," suggested
Camilla one day. "Gertrude thinks it would be fun to
choose a night with a full moon, and go out towards the
Fair on Rough Common, and see what sport the
townspeople get up to."

Angus kept silent, but was chivvied also by
Gertrude.

"You could get the horses ready and meet us by the
garden gate. Wouldn't that be exciting? We could wear
our cloaks, and scarves round our throats, so that people
would not recognise us. You would have to wear
something other than your livery."

"It wouldn't be fitting, Miss," Angus replied after a
moment's hesitation.

"Fitting!" his tormentor exclaimed. "Who are
you to tell us what is fitting? You must do as we ask."

"No, Miss. I cannot do that. You should be in
your beds at midnight, not gallivanting round the town,"
he said bluntly.

"Camilla, this bumpkin is telling us what we may
and may not do. Did you ever hear such cheek!"

Angus was well aware that he was in trouble and had caused offence, and dropped behind the sisters into his usual servant's position. When thy arrived back at the mansion, he dismounted and assisted the girls as usual, but Gertrude flounced into the house with her head held high, while Camilla gave him a rueful glance.

The next happening was a summons to the house to see their father.

His Lordship was probably quite well aware that his daughters had a flighty streak. Nevertheless he had to take their part against an "uppity" servant. Miss Gertrude had said that the groom was too forward in his attentions. A man of medium height, his Lordship's figure showed a tendency to corpulence. His superfine coat of dark blue was well-cut and worn tightly across his chest, as was the fashion. It would hardly last another season if he did not curb his indulgence in good living, thought Angus, conscious that most of his Lordship's tenants existed on potatoes and oatmeal. Layer upon layer of a snowy necktie supported his Lordship's chin, which thus pushed up, added to his air of arrogance.

"I am sending you back to Kilcalmkill," he said. "You are obviously not suited to wait on us in Town. Coachman says your work is good, but I have to have someone who is acceptable to the young ladies. Take a letter to my Steward, and ask him to send a replacement."

Angus felt a surge of anger at the injustice of the punishment. He resented the power his Lordship had over him. It was useless to argue; useless too to claim that he had only been trying to protect the girls. Nevertheless he felt he ought to try and explain. "My Lord, I have only done my best to prevent the young ladies doing something I thought imprudent," he stammered.

His Lordship's eyebrows rose. "My daughters' conduct is not for you to criticise," he declaimed grandly. "You presume above your station, and that is why you must return."

They could tell any lies, say what they wished, and they would be believed. Still seething with resentment, Angus returned reluctantly to Kilcalmkill, his chances of a good reference diminished, and his demotion obvious to his fellow-workmen on the estate.

Elizabeth had been heartbroken at his departure. "I shall miss you so much," she said. "All my pleasure in being here will be destroyed."

"You must make other friends," he urged. "And you have your studies. At least one of the family is set for a brilliant future," he added bitterly.

"Would that it were you, instead of me. It is so unfair." Elizabeth responded with sympathy.

Angus indeed felt badly used, but he did not intend to let this disappointment thwart his ambitions or ruin his life. He resolved to escape if he could the unjust society where an accident of birth and the inheritance of wealth could give some men absolute domination over others.

\* \* \*

When the news reached the Ritchie family that Thomas Dudgeon, a farmer, was holding a meeting to help Scots to emigrate, Angus Ritchie was one of the first to pick up his bundle and stride over the hills to find out what he could.  He had to believe there was more to life than horses and stable work.

The Dornoch Firth lay calm and placid, mirroring the pale blue sky that June morning in 1819, as Angus joined others wending their way to the Meikle Ferry Inn. A busy coaching and ferry hostelry, the Inn, together with its landlord, John Gibson, was at the centre of local activities.  Angus fell in with whole families who were fearful of losing their homes, and desperate to emigrate. The McAndrews, father, mother and six bairns aged from ten to two were among them.  Angus hoisted the four-year old, who was loitering and lame, on to his shoulders and walked alongside the family.

"It's a terrible life we be havin'," complained the man.  " Wha's the sense in planting the tatties if we're no sure to be here when they're ready to grub up?"

"Ma ain brother says we should find our ain land in Cape Breton. "'Twill be better than Scotland forebye," added his wife.  "'Tis mortal cold there in the winter, but nae so damp, he's telling me, and the summers is warm and the crops grow fast."

"But whaur to find the brass, there's nae sayin'" chimed in McAndrew.  "I've heared they might get up a subscription to help us get away."

Angus enquired more about their circumstances, and it seemed that they were from the Sutherland estate. All the tenants had been offered land at the coast as the straths were being turned over to sheep farming, but they were reluctant to go.  It seemed odd to Angus that the family was contemplating a hazardous three thousand mile voyage to an unknown continent just because they were afraid to move only thirty miles down to the shore. However, there was more to it than that.

"'Tis for the babbies' sake," explained Mrs. McAndrew, who seemed the more determined of the two. "If the lairds want the land for sheep-grazing now, they'll be wanting it for summat else in twenty years' time. I've got no trust in them. There's no hope of gaining any freedom, and we want to be our own masters and not beholden to the lairds."

This chimed in exactly with what Angus had been thinking.

"As it is now," continued her husband, "all that our boys can do is take the King's shilling and go for a soldier. They might come back alive, or we might get word they died bravely in some part of the world we've ne'er heard on. And the lasses will get nae husbands when the men are gone."

It was despairing talk, and Angus could offer little comfort. His own prospects were dim enough, for Lord Kildare had offered no reference to help him get another post of the standard that he had lost, but just expected him to go back to the estate from whence he had come, till he learned to behave himself. To a proud Highlander, that was worse than dismissal. He had a job, true, but no prospects now. He wondered if his mother and father could be persuaded to go to North America. They had a little money saved, as he had himself, to afford the fare, while the poor McAndrews were utterly dependent on charity. He could go alone, of course, but his family might take the same view as the McAndrews and want to improve prospects for his younger brother, Matthew.

He resolved to learn all he could at the meeting, and for a young man with health, strength and ambition, the opportunity might be just what he wanted.

* * *

While the tenants had reasons for desperate action, the landlords also had their worries. The Big Sheep were being introduced on more and more estates, and as early as 1817, James Loch, Commissioner to Lord Stafford, had been discussing the trend with Patrick Sellar, Agent to Stafford's wife, the Countess of Sutherland.

"It's not as if we'll ever see a satisfactory financial return from the present rent ledger, particularly after this disastrous winter," he argued with Sellar in the book-room at the turreted and imposing Dunrobin Castle. The Commissioner had been called up to Scotland by the Sutherlands to advise, in the wake of Sellar's own notorious trial for murder, in the course of an eviction in Strathnaver. Sellar had eventually been acquitted, but only after experiencing confinement in prison, while awaiting trial.

Nor was the verdict a popular one, being ascribed to the influence landlords had over the workings of the law.

Patrick Sellar wholeheartedly agreed with Loch, but uttered a cautious warning. "If we continue to turn Sutherland over to sheep, there will be a-many evictions from the crofts," he said. "And that will cause trouble."

"The Countess wants the improvement and the happiness of her people," insisted Loch, suave, clean-shaven and very much the City gentleman. "In inducing them to adopt more industrious habits as well, she wants as little as possible to be done to hurt their feelings, both for their sakes and for the success of the measures themselves."

Sellar snorted. "Her ladyship should try telling that to tenants like the MacAndrews. It's impossible," he declared, with vehemence born of his own experience. "The people are obdurate. Though the crofters can only scratch a living, barely enough to pay a grudging rent, they won't go willingly."

"It has to happen." Loch stated with finality. He again covertly assessed his companion, but already he was determined that Sellar, with his rash and uncompromising attitude, had to leave the estate's employ. "The re-settlement approach, whereby we offer them better land near the coast, where they can gather kelp or take up fishing, and still keep a cow or a pig, has to be proceeded with. His lordship has set his face against either forcing or encouraging emigration."

"I'm coming round to the view that emigration is the answer," Sellar replied, slowly but with growing conviction. "Lord Selkirk's venture in taking the 1813 contingent to Red River did pay off. Their letters back to Scotland are encouraging kinsfolk to follow them, I know. Besides, I doubt if I'm the man to undertake this softly, softly approach you're talking about. Mud sticks, and though I was acquitted, my name is widely hated."

"Unjustly," agreed Loch. "If they knew they had you to thank for arguing in favour of the winter meal relief, they might take a different view. Nevertheless, work for the estate demands that due notice to leave be given to the tenants, and if they resist, the force of the law has to be applied."

Sellar perforce concurred. His keen brain was convinced that the old order was changing and could not, in fact, be sustained. He thought it would be in the best interests of the crofters to move down from the bleak hills to the more fertile coastal strips of land, where, apart from farming, there were harvests to be won from the sea by fishing. He foresaw that in building village communities families would support one another and share in the development of new skills, which would lead to their greater prosperity. The villages would promote more inter-dependence, replacing the fragmented, family-based life in the straths. But he was despondent about success in achieving such moves voluntarily. It would mean wielding the big stick of force yet again, and his own experience proved that it was a dangerous strategy.

By mid-1817 Sellar's position as Factor had been terminated, and the estate was run by Francis Suther, who had been Agent at Lord Stafford's successful Lillieshall property in his place. Sellar, who had feathered his own nest astutely while he served as Factor, retired to manage his own considerable property. He had borne the opprobrium for the re-settling policy, which it seemed would be continued, despite his reservations.

The new Agent had perforce to be heavy-handed. Duress and the arm of the law were the instruments to compel people to move, as many could not be persuaded to move voluntarily. Some tenants resisted to the bitter end.

One of Suther's early tasks in Spring 1819 was to take a group of men to Rogart to enforce the removal of a crofter household. Nothing like this had been necessary on Lord Stafford's estate in Lillieshall, which he had managed, and he had to rely, not only on the law itself, but on the traditional tactics used to enforce it.

"Ye'll have to dismember the roof," recommended the bailiff.

Suther was horrified at such wanton destruction, but realised, as Sellar had done before him, that he had to be seen to carry out the notices of eviction. Otherwise every other crofter would perceive the benefits of resistance, and copy those who held out against the law.

A crowd of women, with heavy shawls draped round their shoulders, and stiff, mud-encrusted skirts, gathered round the doorway to the threatened croft. They hissed in unison as the posse of men on horseback cantered towards them and pulled up with a flourish. Suther dismounted, and began to read the Licence to evict. A rough countryman emerged from the shack, and answered to his name.

"Your notice to yield up and leave the tenancy of this dwelling expired yesterday," declared Suther.

"Nay, I'll not leave," said the man truculently. A ragged cheer went up from the mostly female audience.

"I'll give you one last chance to go quietly," replied Suther. "Otherwise I have law officers here, and you can be arrested and taken to jail."

Two of the posse had by this time seized the man by the shoulders and were pulling and pushing him away from the croft. He dug his heels into the turf at each step, but they were stronger than he.

Then a frail figure with a black kerchief over her head, appeared, wailing in dismay as she saw her guidman thrust away. The women began to clap and encourage her.

" I was born in Rogart and my father afore me, and it's in Rogart I shall end my days," she cried.

The Factor paused. He could not forcibly remove the woman with her sisterhood gathered round. So he called forward the Sheriff, who made it clear that she would find herself in the County Jail if she persisted in her defiance.

"My good woman, you must give heed to the law. This is a proper legal document and you can be sent to prison if you disobey it." With top-hat and greatcoat, he presented a formidable figure. The Sheriff advanced another step. "The disgrace and despair of prison is a terrible thing," he added awfully.

Weeping and throwing her apron over her head, the woman was urged reluctantly down the hill after her husband, the crowd of women following, and wailing also.

The estate men entered the humble home, and threw out all its contents into a heap on the ground outside. The occupants would come back and gather them up later, they expected, and if, in the meantime, they became sodden and useless, that was hardly their concern. Unless the home was rendered uninhabitable, it would be re-possessed by its former tenants and the whole operation would have to be undertaken again. The men therefore took bolt-cutters and severed the pins holding the roof timbers together.

The rough-cut beams crashed to the ground, but unfortunately the central fire had not been fully doused, and its still smouldering embers sparked off the roof timbers, already well-dried by the warmth of the home. They flared, and caught well alight, the flames leaping skywards, to be greeted with howls of anguish from the crowd on the hill below.  The hovel was gradually reduced to ashes.

The tale lost nothing in the telling.  Every witness embroidered the story with her own blood-curdling remembrances.  An atmosphere of fear was created in the neighbourhood.  No hamlet-dwellers knew whether they might be likely to be the next in line for clearance, and rumours abounded.

One of the people who got to know of it first-hand was Thomas Dudgeon, a farmer in a modest way, who came across a bedraggled group of evicted people congregating in a churchyard, with blankets on the ground, suggesting they had been sleeping rough.  He was appalled by the misery endured by these people, and he determined to write to Lord Selkirk who had organised the earlier party of Sutherlanders to go to North America. There was no assisted emigration and many families were too destitute to scrape together the money for the passage on a ship,  food for the journey, or the tools to start farming when they got to their destination. He wanted to ask Lord Selkirk's advice on how he could go about helping people to emigrate.

Thomas Dudgeon took it upon himself also to write to the Countess of Sutherland's husband, Lord Stafford, proposing that firstly, tenants should have a say on where they were to be moved, and secondly, those who wished to emigrate should be allowed, and even encouraged and supported, to do so.

Francis Suther took Dudgeon's letter in to his Lordship. James Loch was also there on one of his periodic reporting and advisory visits, pacing thoughtfully between the walls of the book-room.

"What is this fellow up to?" queried Lord Stafford, playing with the silver, sword-shaped paper-knife on his leather-tooled writing desk. "What does he mean that people on my wife's estate are reduced to penury? I thought we were offering alternative, better accommodation to those who are being moved."

"Indeed, we are," replied Francis Suther, the estate factor. "The new villages offer three acres of land, and help with building new homes, as well as a greater variety of occupations for the tenants."

"The policy remains as we have always agreed it should be," interposed James Loch. "A policy of re-settlement near the coast where the ground is fertile, and the rents much easier for the tenants to earn."

"Then why should we pay £20 a head or more to assist our own people to emigrate?" asked Lord Stafford. "Isn't that what Dudgeon is suggesting?"

"I think he is saying that people should have a choice," explained Loch smoothly. "Either we should give them money to emigrate, or offer them a new tenancy in Scotland, not necessarily in a prescribed area – in short, where they want to go, rather than where we want them to go."

"It's not in our interest to lose people to North America, where they'll only miss their families and become homesick," responded Lord Stafford, with some petulance at his supposedly generous terms being rejected.

"Precisely. We should also find ourselves short of labour on the estate for wood-cutting and harvesting, and there would be fewer young men for recruitment into the Regiment when needed," cut in Suther. "I think you should indicate that you feel this is an interference in your management of your estate."

"Perhaps you should take it a step further, and accuse Dudgeon of a gross criticism of an enlightened policy that has stood the test of years of experience," added Loch. "Should you wish me to draft such a reply, I should be happy to do so."

"Yes, yes. Tell him to mind his own business," agreed his Lordship.

Thus, by return of post, Thomas Dudgeon received a dismissive reply.

* * *

This was probably a mistake on the landlords' part. It merely served to convince Dudgeon that there were wrongs to be righted, and when he eventually heard from Lord Selkirk that his lordship advised him to start a fund-raising operation to assist people to emigrate, he was convinced that this was what he should do.

He called a meeting in the large, black-beamed bar of the Meickle Ferry Inn, near Dornoch. The landlord,

John Gibson, a burly forty-year old, who made a handsome profit through his busy property, had listened many times to the grumbles and complaints of customers in his Inn, and readily agreed to host the meeting. Word spread rapidly and people flocked to the inn in their hundreds, including Angus Ritchie and the MacAndrew family he had befriended on the journey.

A local reporter from the Inverness Courier was assigned by his Editor to attend the meeting. Alastair McGowan, young, ambitious and clever with his pen, personally had some sympathy with the people's complaints. He had witnessed distressing scenes and interviewed many of the victims of eviction policies, while writing for the Courier. However, his Editor's word was law, and the Editor naturally did not want to alienate the powerful Countess of Sutherland, and her husband, Lord Stafford. His paper's policy therefore was not to offend the influential landed gentry.

McGowan bought a few drinks for the tenantry, and heard all about the firing of the cottage. He wrote what he hoped was a fair summary of the situation:

"Simmering discontent about land tenure in the Highlands bubbled to the surface on Wednesday, 21st June at a gathering called to consider assisted emigration," he began. "There was a great press of people such that the bar could not hold them all, and Mr. Thomas Dudgeon, farmer from Ross-shire, addressed them outside in the stable yard, struggling to make himself heard by shouting through cupped hands.

The meeting first paid tribute to Lord Selkirk, who had led parties of Scots to the New World. A letter of encouragement was read from his Lordship. He advised that a fund-raising organisation be formed to attract subscriptions from sympathetic members of the public to pay Atlantic shipping fares. He also suggested that an additional sum would be needed for the settling-in costs to help people without funds who wished to emigrate. The organisers gave a pledge that those who donated more than £25 would have their names recorded on a stone monument at Bonar Bridge. Many people spoke up in favour of the scheme.

Although many of those present were tenants of the Sutherland estate, there was little direct criticism of estate policies, except for a quoted instance of a recent fire at Rogart when a croft was burned down as an eviction was in progress. It was claimed by the Factor that the fire was accidental. Several of the estate managers maintained a watchful presence on behalf of the Countess, but did not intervene in the proceedings.

The outcome of the meeting was the establishment of The Sutherland & Transatlantic Emigration Association, with Mr. Thomas Dudgeon as President, Mr. John Gibson,, the publican of the inn, as Secretary, and a teacher at the Tain Academy, Mr. Denis Scott, as Treasurer. Other Committeemen were elected also. They set up a detailed Constitution, with the aforesaid aims, and said they would hold another meeting at Dornoch on 26th July, when all those present and their friends and neighbours would be welcome to attend."

Despite Alastair's fair account, suspicions about the Association spread. The intentions of the movement became misrepresented by its many critics, who spread rumours that it was subversive, that the organisers would be feathering their own nests before anyone saw a shilling of the subscription money, that Dudgeon was settling an old score with the Sutherland family, and so on.

For those attending the meeting there was little immediate satisfaction.. The facts they were looking for were few and far between. The meeting was chaotic because of the sheer numbers pressing into the yard of the inn, and half of the audience could not hear nor understand what was said. Much time was spent in agreeing a constitution for the Association, rather than dealing with practical matters. Angus paid his sixpence to be registered with the newly-formed body, but not everyone had the wherewithal to do so, and left grumbling with disappointment. However a decision was taken to form a Committee and launch an appeal for funds. Angus learned that ships would be chartered when the funding was in place, and he also gleaned some useful information about prospects in North America from the people he talked to in the yard, some of whom had relatives who had emigrated earlier.

There was land and to spare for those willing to work, he gathered. Each man would be his own master, and if communities went together, they could help one another until they had built cabins to live in, and cleared enough land to grow crops. It would be hard, pioneering work, but there would be no high society and no under-class. Everyone would start from an equal base. Towns were growing up, it was true, where the first settlers had landed up to fifty years ago. Such a place was Pictou. But there was still plenty of untamed forest to lay a claim to, or cleared land to be acquired cheaply if one had the money to buy it.

When he had tramped back to his father's croft with his information, and retailed it with enthusiasm, it seemed that the older man shared his keenness for the new venture, but Angus's mother was less willing. However, with her three male family members all arguing in favour, she began to warm to the idea.

"The voyage would not be very comfortable," acknowledged Angus. "We would each have a berth, but we would have to go steerage. We would have to find for ourselves, apart from fire and water, and it might take anything between four weeks and six before we land. We would have to take provisions to last us, and there wouldn't be much light between decks, or much to do."

"I've never been on the sea afore," said his mother doubtfully.

"Nor I," agreed Angus, "but hundreds of people do travel now, quite safely, so the journey would be worth it in the end."

"I wouldn't like to go and leave Elizabeth behind," his mother added.

"I think she might follow us," Angus suggested. "She is well situated and liked by the family she works for and so she had no need to move yet awhile. But perhaps when the bairns have grown in a couple of years, and gone from the nursery into the school-room, it might be the right time for her to follow us. She could perhaps save enough money to buy a cabin passage, which would be better for a lady travelling alone. I can see that teachers will be in demand in such a new country. I would not want to be separated from my sister for ever, but we could write long letters to one another."

Margaret Ritchie voiced her doubts again about leaving the estate they knew, and their friends and cousins. "It's a great step we'd be taking." she worried. "There'll be nae Kirk for worship on the Sabbath and mebbe nae school like this for Matthew."

Her eleven-year old son scoffed at that. "I don't care about schooling," he piped up. "I'd rather have an adventure, and get to work and earn some siller."

"I don't think you'd be earning much silver to begin with," warned Angus. "Mostly we'd be tilling our own land, and growing our own food, until we could expand and sell the produce. Maybe I could get work in a town in the winter and buy some of the tools and the extras we'd need, but you and Mam and Dad would have the stock to feed and look after. The big difference is that it'd be our own. We wouldn't have to be obliged to any overlord, and you'd inherit the land and then you'd be your own master."

"'Tis true enough that I see no future here," agreed his father. "While I was thankful to get the job of shepherd when the estate turned over to sheep, it's a one-skill job, and I'm good for more than that. There's three months of lambing out in all weathers, and gathering and driving the flock to shearing or to market is another task that means ye've got to be spry and nimble. I wonder how many years I'll have left in me to do it. After that it's the scrap-heap, with Matthew stuck in the same rut, most like."

"We give our lives to their lordships for a pittance," complained Angus, "and then a change of farming fashion, or a family's whim can overturn it all. Even if I went down to London and sought work as a groom, I'd still be in servitude." He sprang to his feet, and spoke passionately again. "There's nothing for us here except kow-towing to the Lairds. In the New World, we'll be Mister Ritchie, and not spoken down to by our surnames, or even fellow! Bowing and scraping to our so-called betters -- I've had enough of it! I want to start a new life in a new country. We'll make our own house with proper bed-chambers and a parlour for Mother to sit in at the end of the working day – and I want you all to come with me."

"I'm backing Angus all the way," shouted Matthew.

"Reckon you're right, lads," agreed Denis Ritchie.

"We'd best take the plunge then," his wife concurred. "As long as we all stay together."

" It may take time for Mr. Dudgeon to hire these ships, but I think we should be aboard them when they do sail," concluded Angus.

They were to wait for a considerable time.

# Chapter Seven - The Landlords Counter-attack

Thomas Dudgeon was greatly encouraged by the huge gathering at the Inn.

"This proves we have a popular cause," he told John Gibson.

"No doubt about it," the beetle-browed publican replied, as he polished his glasses and hung up his clean tankards. "Now it is up to us to spread the word that at last there's some hope of a new life. I declare I've more than a fancy to go myself."

"We've done the spade-work and established a proper Association," agreed Dudgeon. "Now we need publicity, and I'll have to get down to writing it, I can see. Leave it to the Committee and they'll argue all day about this word or that. Leave it to me."

But like many amateurs in the world of publicity, his natural enthusiasm for his argument boiled over into inflammatory language:

"The Scots are treated like serfs, if not slaves," he insisted in a letter to "The Scotsman" and other papers. "Their wishes are not consulted upon. They are engaged in no dialogue, but their masters invoke the force of law to dispossess them of the little that they have."

Furthermore, he thought to engage the sympathies of the acknowledged leader of the fight against slavery. One such letter was sent to William Wilberforce, the humanitarian and true Christian, who was nationally and internationally applauded for the success of his work in ending the slave trade. Wilberforce was becoming more plagued by ill-health and was quite frail, but still maintained a vast correspondence.

He responded with sympathy, but it was perhaps a pity that Dudgeon had not gone personally to London to persuade him to lend his weight to the campaign, rather than relying solely on a letter.

The landlords feared that Dudgeon's words and the cause they described was just the sort of movement that would engage the sympathy of Wilberforce. Such was the great man's potential influence with the Establishment, together with his power of oratory in the House of Commons, should he care to use it, that James Loch was dispatched post haste back to London. Loch did not rely on letters, but sought an interview with William Wilberforce, aiming to reassure him on matters, which might have caused him concern.

Loch walked with William Wilberforce in the garden. The coat pockets of the man known as "the conscience of the nation" were stuffed with books. His gait was unsteady and he and his companion paused frequently to rest on the bench-seats, strategically placed at the intersections of the paths.

William Wilberforce's strong libertarian and Christian principles were at that time engaged in thinking through a further stage in the progress towards the full emancipation of slaves. Although the bartering and transportation of slaves had officially ended in 1807, those already on the plantations in the West Indies and America were still for the most part not free men and women.

Wilberforce confessed that his sympathies had been touched by Thomas Dudgeon's appeal.

"Your work on slavery is widely respected and endorsed by Lord Stafford," pursued Loch tactfully. "But I venture to suggest that an intervention in the House on the Scottish land question would lead to much controversy. It is a complex matter, where right and wrong are much less clear. Emigration, which seems to some to be a solution, would nevertheless denude our country of worthy people who are needed here on the estates."

"Mr. Dudgeon seems to think that their situation in Scotland is akin to slavery," commented the great man.

"Then Mr. Dudgeon mistakes the matter," responded Loch. "Contrast the punishing regime which you are rightly trying to overthrow, with the undoubted rights of free Scots in the Highlands. They could accept the very improving offers made by the Estates, or they could maintain their existing independence. What is not possible to deny is that economic progress will affect them and they need to move with the times. If I might respectfully suggest it, allying yourself with this confused equation might even damage your integrity on the main emancipation issue."

"My own life's work and my major desire is to continue my progress towards full slave emancipation," agreed Wilberforce. "Everything else is secondary. Nor can I undertake to campaign on behalf of everyone who seeks my help. I do my best to support and influence the Government privately, but I do not involve myself in other campaigns, however worthy. It is too distracting."

Before they parted, Wilberforce did promise not to raise the matter in Parliament, which Dudgeon had besought him to do, but this was all Loch achieved, as Wilberforce said he had already replied to Dudgeon that he would support the Association's charitable aims by raising money in Edinburgh and India to help them, even if he would not actively campaign.

* * *

A crisis meeting at Dunrobin Castle followed Loch's report.

"We have been tolerant too long," was James Loch's conclusion. "This man, Dudgeon, is a rabble-rouser, who has set the press on us, and I cannot foresee an end."

"We have to counter-attack," suggested Francis Suther. "What do we know to Dudgeon's discredit?"

"I think we can call Thomas Dudgeon's motives into question, and complain that, far from raising money in subscriptions, his meetings are costing those who attend a small fortune to register their interest. Money is also going into the publican's pockets through the consumption of liquor by people who go to the meetings," said Loch. "I am surprised that John Gibson lends his support. He has a good business at Meikle Ferry with all classes of folks, and would be a fool to compromise it.

"Such accusations, if they are made, must not come directly from us," insisted Lord Stafford..

"They don't need to. I wager there will be no shortage of people willing to make any type of accusation in order to support you, my lord," opined Loch. "Mr. Suther here can find an argument to set against every one of Dudgeon's letters, I've no doubt, and someone to sign them too."

"I blame a lot of this on Lord Selkirk," complained the Lord Stafford.. "His crazy emigration schemes have become a sort of plague, unsettling our tenants throughout the county. His type of unworldly theorist is a sheer nuisance to those of us who try to get the best from the land."

"Milord Selkirk is more concerned about the New World than ours here," agreed Suther. "But what about our Presbyterian Ministers? The Presbyterian Church has been very slow to send Ministers to the New World. A good rant from the pulpit on Sunday would be worth much in turning people against Dudgeon."

"Your Chaplain could be brought in to encourage that line of thinking," suggested Loch to Lord Stafford, who nodded. "Let everyone do his bit to silence this enemy."

"What is the legal position of this Association?" queried his Lordship.

"I know just the man who can advise us," replied Loch. "It is probably not enough to attack Dudgeon without causing the organisation he has set up to collapse as well."

Thus James Abercrombie, an attorney from Edinburgh, was to be commissioned to advise, and the Estate's "dirty tricks" campaign meanwhile was set in motion.

* * *

Loch's intervention with William Wilberforce might have staved off Parliamentary action for the moment, but there were always other Members of Parliament who might intervene. To whip up public opinion against Dudgeon's movement was deemed the next tactic. The "inspired" correspondence sent by the landlords' supporters to the Inverness Courier described Dudgeon as a dangerous rogue, and some Presbyterian ministers agreed to lash out at him in their sermons.

The farmer, however, aided and abetted by John Gibson, displayed remarkable tenacity. Emboldened by his Scottish press successes, and by now assisted by Alastair, the young reporter, he enlisted national support for his campaign by writing another strong letter, this time to the Times, which brought reporters from various London papers to the Highlands to write up their sob-stories. Gibson welcomed them to his Bar, for journalists were good customers. There was no shortage of tenants lining up to give heart-rending interviews about their hardships, and the publican pointed out various hard-done-by tenants who would be glad to tell their tale to the newspapers. Privately the Times Editor saw the burgeoning story as a useful stick with which to beat the Government.

As a result of this widespread and emotive publicity, big donations came in from supporters as far afield as Delia Mackenzie, wife of one of Pictou's most prestigious merchants in North America, and Mrs. Phillipa Allen, wife of a prominent ship-owner from Leith, who pledged her husband's help and that of her Church fund-raising Committee. Mrs. Mackenzie had written, "I am proud of our country here in the New World. It provides great advantages, and a new society is growing here. Still the country needs new people, such as those of good Scottish stock, to enable it to expand and to flourish." Far from scotching Dudgeon's movement, the landlords' counter measures had succeeded in securing even more adverse publicity and the emigration movement appeared to be spreading.

When the leading Edinburgh QC, James Abercrombie, joined the fray on the landlords' side, tactics changed from those of the bludgeon to those of the rapier. By a stratagem and in roundabout fashion, Abercrombie contrived for Dudgeon to be "reliably informed" about a new scheme for emigrants to get money from the Government if they pledged military service. It was known that soldiers from the American War of Independence had been helped to obtain land as a reward for their service, and this seemed a very plausible rumour. Thomas Dudgeon naively saw this rumoured scheme as an opportunity for his needy emigrants, and he and his friends in the Transatlantic Association published an advertisement addressed to "Loyal Highlanders" which was printed in The Inverness Courier" and signed by Thomas Dudgeon. It called on

"LOYAL SUBJECTS to rally round the CONSTITUTION of our country. Highlanders from 18 to 40 years of age are invited to attend a MEETING of the SUTHERLAND AND TRANSATLANTIC FRIENDLY ASSOCIATION," it announced. "Which is appointed to be held at GOLSPIE in Sutherlandshire, on Tuesday, the 4th of January at 10 o'clock a.m. for the purpose of evincing their firm

attachment to His Majesty's present Government, by an offer of their services in a Military capacity."
Thomas Dudgeon, Secretary
Fearn, December 20th, 1819

Mr. Dudgeon had swallowed the red herring trailed before him. Alastair MacGowan was contacted, and he wrote a piece in the Courier, amplifying Dudgeon's advertisement. But Francis Dudgeon was treading on dangerous ground. The Lairds had always been responsible for raising militia in their areas. In the wake of the Cato Conspiracy, the last thing the Government wanted at this time was Mr. Dudgeon's help in recruitment. The Editor of the Courier on the advice of the Lord Stafford's henchmen warned in a leading article of the dangers of insurrection.

The Law was invoked and Robert Nimmo, Sheriff Substitute for Sutherlandshire, took prompt steps. He issued a Public Notice on New Year's Day, signed by himself and twelve Justices of the Peace, one of whom was Patrick Sellar, warning the people that the meeting called by Dudgeon was illegal, and that his Society was suspected of dark aims beyond those it openly expressed.

The Notice went on:

"We therefore consider it our duty as Magistrates of this county to warn the loyal and peaceable Inhabitants of this jurisdiction of the impropriety of their being participants of such a meeting, or of the consequences thereof. The Address of the county of Sutherland is already before His Royal Highness the Prince Regent, offering the most cordial support in defence of our King and Constitution; and the people know well that, as on every former occasion, they will be called upon whenever their services may be required, and that in a legal and proper manner, and without the interference of men of doubtful principles, totally unconnected with the county."

This seemed to have thwarted the meeting. The pugnacious publican, John Gibson, argued fiercely that it was all a hum, and they should take no notice, but other members of the Committee were of more timorous persuasion and feared conflict with the law. Two weeks later the Courier reported that the Transatlantic Association was at an end.

Thomas Dudgeon was deeply upset that he had been accused of having seditious motives. He wrote to Lord Stafford, denying that he had ever sought to act contrary to his Lordship's wishes, but was solely motivated by the desire to help those tenants who wished to emigrate.

Lord Stafford did not deign to reply.

* * *

Though the Transatlantic Association had collapsed, the work it had done and the money it had raised ensured that the voyages of the *Ossian* in 1820 and the *Ruby* and the *Harmony* in 1822, sailing from Cromarty, were supported by voluntary funds. Thus poorer emigrants, such as the McAndrews with their six children, could be taken to the New World without cost.

Lord Selkirk, who had done so much to promote emigration to Prince Edward Island, Boldoon and the Red River had died and was buried in France in 1820, but his inspiration lived on. Thomas Dudgeon also kept faith with those in whom ambition to emigrate had already been aroused.

In the event it was 1822 when the good ships *"Ruby"* and *"Harmony"* left Scotland bound for Pictou. The *Ossian* had sailed earlier but had been over-subscribed before Angus got to hear about it. The ships had been provisioned by the funds of the Association, but as the Ritchies were leaving voluntarily, and were not destitute, they provided their own fares. Nails, spades and saws were part of the cargo, also having been provided by the generosity of the subscribers. Over 250 people left Scotland, of whom many might otherwise not have been able to go.

Thomas Dudgeon was on the quayside when the ships left, ticking off all the passengers' names, including Denis Ritchie, Margaret Ritchie, Matthew Ritchie, (now aged 14) and Angus Ritchie.

Elizabeth had promised to follow a couple of years later when she had finished her training and could see her present occupation coming to an end. She had sent a sampler embroidered with a saltire to demonstrate her new-found skills. It was to be a symbol of the link between the auld country and the new.

## Chapter Eight - Man Overboard

When Angus Ritchie received word that two more ships were being commissioned by Thomas Dudgeon to set sail for the New World, he enlisted as much help as he could from fellow-workers on the Kilcalmkill estate to help transport his family to the coast at Cromarty.

An old Highland pony was "borrowed" to carry the luggage or provide a respite from the long walk for his mother. Treasured objects from their home were wrapped in bundles convenient to carry. The fire-irons which had been a marriage gift to Denis and Margaret were to go with them, as were a variety of cooking pots and cutlery.

Many things had to be left behind. Their wood piles were divided among their grateful neighbours – by all accounts there was little except timber in the land around Pictou. Hens and piglets were sold cheaply, or eaten, or salted for the journey. They would need some bedding, which Margaret hung on the line to be beaten and aired before compressing into as small a compass as possible, packing it into clean sacks. The family Bible was parcelled and wrapped safely in a bundle of clothing. Small tools were cleaned, wrapped and placed with candles and other valuables in a small wooden chest. They believed pickaxes and spades would form part of the ships' cargo.

A farewell feast was held with kinsmen and friends. Keepsakes were exchanged, and the family set off on its four-day trek to the sea. They had been warned not to be late, so allowed a couple of spare days in case of unexpected hindrance.

As their little party passed through various hamlets on the drove road, they received good-will gestures as farmers' wives pressed milk or whey upon the travellers.

There was no sign of the ships when they reached Cromarty and made overnight camp near the shore. Others had been this way before, as rough shelters had been erected with poles and hessian and left in place. Among the waiting throng was a piper from one of the glens who rendered some stirring tunes to buoy up their spirits. Some of the younger men and girls joined in a reel, but many of the emigrants were both weary and sad as they contemplated the hills behind the coastal plain, gazing their last on the land they were leaving for ever.

Next morning two ships were spied on the horizon, and the *Ruby*, closely followed by the *Harmony*, drew closer. Their stately sails billowed as they steered into the harbour, and were then lowered while they rode at anchor. Boats would ferry the passengers and their belongings to the ships. The *Ruby* was a brig of some 128 tons, and the *Harmony* a snow of 161 tons, both built in Aberdeen, and neither in their first youth. Possibly they had been whalers in a previous existence. Classified as E1 on Lloyds Register for insurance purposes, they were stout, ocean-going ships, under the command of experienced captains, particularly George Murray of the *Harmony*. While not built for the passenger trade, they had been adapted to carry people westward and timber back again to Scotland.

Angus thought they were small enough, in all conscience, to tackle the huge distance and the uncertain elements. However, it was June and a good month for the voyage and his main feeling was one of excitement at this new phase in his life. Some two hundred and fifty emigrants had gathered for embarkation and Thomas Dudgeon was bustling about, enquiring anxiously about a family he believed to be missing. After the traumas of his Emigration Association and his battles with the Duke's henchmen, to say nothing of the money-raising activities in which he had been involved, it was a triumph for him that the ships and the people had come together for this significant exodus.

Angus spotted the McAndrews with their six children, all grown bigger since he last saw them, and suspected, with some concern, that Mrs. McAndrew was not far from producing her seventh.

It came to their turn to be marshalled into a ship's boat, rowed by the crew of the *Ruby*, and they took their final farewell of Donald McDougal, who had accompanied them, and would take his old pony home again. Angus saw his father and mother safely stowed in the stern, while he and Matthew handed their bundles and baggage in to them before leaping into the boat themselves. Their sailor oarsmen crammed the boat as full as it would hold before pulling away from the jetty towards the ships.

Angus introduced himself and his brother. "We're willing to help," he offered, "If extra hands are needed."

"Lord love you," responded the sailor. "We'll have you up in the crow's nest, given half a chance. Have ye been sea-faring afore?"

Angus confessed his ignorance but said he was eager to learn. However, even the limited movement of the small boat was giving him an unwelcome sensation in his stomach, while his mother, he noticed, was becoming remarkably pale.

"It'll take you a while to get your sea-legs," commented the sailor. "We're used to it, but the motion turns most folks queasy."

"Like riding a horse, perhaps," suggested Angus. "At first you feel you'll never get used to the changes in pace, but you do."

"Mebbe! Hosses don't come our way much when we're apprenticed to sea before we're fourteen."

"But you must have visited many interesting places," ventured Angus.

The sailor exchanged a look with his fellow oarsman. "If you mean the docks in Eastern Scotland or America, they're all alike," he said. "Now in China or India, that's a different story. All them yaller and brown girls …" His companion guffawed, and Angus, a rigid Presbyterian by upbringing, thought it best to let the conversation die.

The family clambered up the rope-ladder, hanging down the side of the ship, and then down another ladder through the hatch into the hold. Their berths were planks roughly planed and nailed on to struts along the sides of the vessel. Cramped into a two-foot distance from the berth above, and just long enough for a man to lie, they promised little comfort for the next four weeks or more. There were a few fish-oil lamps here and there to lighten the gloom. He dragged the small wooden chest over to one, upended it to form a makeshift desk, and took out a half-finished letter to his sister, Elizabeth.

"We are aboard at last," he wrote. "There is a great crowd here from the Sutherland estates as well as other parts of Scotland. Mama is tearful, as you would expect, but Matthew and I, and I think Dad too, are cheerful. Matt has gone exploring already, but I wanted to finish this letter and hope to get it conveyed back to shore. We pray to God to watch over us on this great adventure.

This ship is called the *Ruby*, a brig I am told, and squat in design. She is smaller than I expected, and the wind will no doubt buffet us mightily once we leave the shelter of the harbour. We are to go in convoy with another ship, the *Harmony*, and I believe both the Captains to be experienced mariners, as are the crew. The passengers seem very agreeable, and we have a piper aboard. I've also seen a couple of fiddles among the families' baggage. No doubt we'll make merry once we get used to the ship's movement. I will write to you again when we reach America, but do not expect to hear for two months or perhaps three. In the meantime, Mama and Papa send their love, and hope you remain well and happy. Your affectionate brother, Angus."

He sealed the missive, having crossed it to get the last few lines on the one sheet of paper, and went up on deck to see to its dispatch. Captain Brodie used his loud-hailer to announce that any letters or luggage not needed should be brought to him, as the last boat was now leaving for the harbour.

Thomas Dudgeon had come on board to see his protégées safely bestowed, and was now returning. He took Angus's letter, and the young man thanked him warmly for his help in arranging the sailing.

"I wish you God Speed," the farmer replied. "I profoundly hope that most of you will prosper, though I expect there will be some who won't."

It was a prophecy that would be fulfilled sooner than he knew.

* * *

The first few days proved to be a kind of hell. The passengers were seasick, and the hold became a stinking heap of moaning humanity. Among the few who escaped was Angus's younger brother, Matthew, who was so engrossed in the workings of the ship that he spent most of his time on deck, badgering the crew with questions. He was particularly enthralled by the ship's bell, which was rung sharply every two hours to signal changes in the watch. Angus himself, realising that fresh air was the only answer, joined him as soon as he felt able.

He discovered that the Captain maintained quite a library of books, which he was welcome to borrow. While many of the passengers were not literate enough to be able to take advantage of this amusement, soon they heard that a concert would be held, and in that most could take part. There was an inter-denominational service on the Sunday morning, shared by all. As soon as most of the passengers recovered, the hold was hosed down and the ship made clean and tidy. The swabbing of decks was a twice-daily chore, and the sailors were in the habit of finishing the routine with open-air baths, tipping water over one another to get rid of the dirt and sweat. The water ran out through the gunwales. Some of the male passengers thought this such good sport that they joined in too. When the sun shone the voyage was pleasant enough as most people crowded on deck, but when rain squalls overtook them, the wind howled and the sea was choppy, they had to go below for safety, and the hatch was closed.

Water was provided, and for the first week was fresh enough, but later had to be boiled, or have vinegar added. The cook's job was to feed the crew and the few cabin passengers, but there were little stoves for the steerage passengers to use, apart from the galley. Some of the women found it best to pool their resources, and make a vast stock-pot which they took it in turns to stir. Oatcakes, in hard form, or flattened and filled with various mixtures, were a popular alternative.

A chicken coop on deck was raided once a day for the cabin meals, and a lamb was butchered too. Two goats were milked twice daily. Salt beef and bread formed the staple diet, but the Highlanders were not used to this, and mainly used the food they had brought with them. The men trailed a fishing line, which was occasionally successful in catching a fish to make a welcome change.

One of the crew had the extra job of sail-maker, and was often to be found, squatting in a corner with his needle and thread, patching up the canvas. What had appeared white and shining at Cromarty in the sunlight, proved on closer inspection to be grey and coarse, but the sails were the ship's only power and had to be strong and durable and mended immediately if they showed signs of wear.

The carpenter was another craftsman on whom the ship depended. Apart from his harbour work of fitting up the ship to carry the steerage passengers, he had constantly to inspect the ship for damage, and was called upon to repair deck timbers if needed. But in the early part of the journey, he had time to spare to whittle sticks as toys for the children, who crowded round him, listening to a fund of stories.

It was not compulsory to have a Doctor on board at this time, but the Second Mate had some first-aid training and was able to assist if the passengers' combined wisdom could not solve their problems. Cleanliness was the first essential if disease was to be prevented, and the Captain was adamant that all the emigrants play their part in keeping good hygiene -- not too easy as a series of buckets provided the only means of relief.

Roughly half of the two hundred and fifty souls were travelling on the *Ruby* and the remainder on the *Harmony*. Sometimes the ships were in hailing distance of one another, and then were barely in sight, as the Captains tacked against the prevailing westerlies at different times.

For Angus and Matthew it was a completely different world, and they enjoyed the magic of the seascape and the atmosphere of adventure. The seaman who had rowed the boat from which they embarked proved to be called Jem, and he was a source of information about the ship and the way it was operated.

The Newfoundland Banks, with their misty eeriness, were reached after three and a half weeks. Sea-birds, which had been scarce in mid-ocean, now flew around companionably, sometimes landing on the rigging or perching on the rails. One bird in particular would not go away. From its self-selected perch it would occasionally emit a mournful squawk, but mostly stayed silent and watchful. The carpenter was concerned and tried to shoo it away. He muttered that it was a sign of ill-fortune when a solitary bird stuck to a ship. The sailors, who were a superstitious lot, could each dredge up a tale to prove the ill-omen.

A number of fishing vessels were now sighted, and when the fog descended, there was a cacophony of sounds as klaxons sounded their warning notes.

They had passed the Banks, and were entering the Gulf of St. Lawrence when they saw the heavy black clouds of a threatening storm. The wind was rising and the Captain ordered his passengers below. The *Harmony* had been a mile or so ahead and was already shortening sail. Perhaps thinking to catch up, Captain Brodie held on to his sails a fraction too long. A ferocious gust almost spun the ship round, and she dipped dangerously to port.

Down in the hold everyone's possessions went skittering down to end in a heap against the ship's side. The passengers clung on for dear life, and a few started praying. Thankfully the ship righted herself speedily, and the chattels were hurled to the opposite side as the *Ruby* surmounted a big wave, and plunged down into the chasm beyond.

The storm lasted for over an hour of screaming winds and tossing turbulence. Most people were ill again, and some thought their last hour had come and fell to praying. But gradually the noise abated somewhat. Although the timbers were still creaking, the wind seemed less loud and the ship's motion smoother. The passengers began to sit up, rather than lie, and surveyed the melée.

Then disaster struck.  Up on deck, the sailors had furled the sails, and the ship was drifting under bare poles, but the storm had brought her closer, both to the *Harmony*, now to starboard, and to the shore on the port side.  The shore was rocky, and it was necessary to hoist some sail to use the wind to get away from it.  Rain was still falling, but less heavily, and the sailors strained mightily to raise the sodden sails.   The look-out shouted "Rocks ahead," and, as the ship veered away from the shore, her stern scraped on a submerged outcrop, and the Captain knew there must be some damage.

He sent the carpenter and his mate below, and sure enough, water was beginning to seep into the hold from damaged woodwork on one side near the stern.  It would become a flood unless it was speedily secured.  Mattresses were grabbed and planks nailed across them, while the passengers were told to carry what possessions they could and assemble on deck.  Two other sailors descended to man the bilge-pumps.

Captain Brodie signalled to the *Harmony*, "Hold damaged.  Can you take some passengers?"  Captain Murray answered:  "Yes, how serious?"

He did not know, as yet, but ordered the ship's boats to be crewed and made ready.

The *Harmony* would not be able to cope with all the emigrants, but he thought he should send the women and children with food for safety's sake.  The two boats could not take all, and already families were wailing at being split up from their menfolk.  Denis and Margaret, as an older couple, were kept together, and she kept crying for Matthew to join them.   "He's only a child," she kept saying. The Captain relented. Fourteen was a borderline age. "But you must stay," he told Angus. "I need hands to save the ship, and already the crew is half strength, what with the boats and the pumps and the repair team."

Angus fell back, waved to his parents, and was sent down into the hold to man the pump and release a sailor to come back up and raise more sail. The sudden storm was abating, and the boats were able to row across the short distance to the *Harmony* and return for a second load of passengers.

Meanwhile Angus pumped as if his life depended on it, which it probably did. Eventually another couple of passengers were sent down to relieve him and when he went back on deck, it was to find the main-sail filling out and the wind lessening. However, the seamen were having difficulty raising the sail on the mizzen mast. One of the guide-ropes had snagged, and they were short-handed. They called Angus over.

"Can you climb up and release the rope," one asked.

Angus looked doubtfully at the rigging, but his keen eyesight spotted the snag, and he thought he could manage the climb. His heavy tweed jacket had been discarded down below, but he now removed his boots, in order that his feet in thick socks could feel the frail ladder, and donned the thin oilskin handed to him.

He set off, hand over hand, and reached the rope, tugging until it came free. Then he looked down, and felt dizzy almost immediately. He had climbed further than he thought, but the rope rungs were still beneath him. He had taken one step down when a sudden gust of wind caught the now rising sail. The boom swung around and knocked him sideways. He crashed with his left side into the mast, and felt an intense pain in his arm, which hung uselessly from his shoulder. With only one arm, he could no longer climb down, and he shouted for help.

The seamen heard, but could not help him immediately, as their sail had to be made fast first. Angus hung on grimly with his right hand, the left one crippled and making him feel faint with pain.

The sea was still rough. Although the worst of the storm had passed over, the heavy sea swell remained. The *Ruby* pitched to starboard. Still Angus clung on with all his might and main, but when the inevitable dip to port happened, he could stand it no more. His grip loosened and he plunged towards the deck. The angle of the list to port made his body miss the deck, his head struck the ship's rail and his inert form hit the water.

"Man overboard," shouted the seaman who had watched with dismay. The First Mate rushed to the spot. At first he could see nothing, then thought he saw a dark shape just beneath the surface. He flung a line towards the shape, and made sure the rope ladders were in position. The boats had still not returned from the *Harmony,* but he hoped one would come back shortly to pick up the passenger if it proved he could not swim. More than that he could not do. He had insufficient men to sail the ship and he himself must be on the bridge.

The ship lurched again, and when it righted itself, there was no dark shape to be seen.

The Captain, emerging from the hold where the pumps seemed to be gaining on the water level, and the emergency repairs were holding so far, was sad, but philosophical. "Right, we've lost a passenger," he said. "A decent young man, but it can't be helped. We nearly lost the lot! I must stand well off the shore, and we must wait for our own boats to come back. Ask them to look out for him before we haul them aboard."

The First Mate followed the instruction, but despite taking a wide sweep to port, the ship's boats found no sign of Angus. The tide was running strongly, they reported, and would have carried him shorewards. They had spotted a small fishing-boat, probably lobstering, among the rocks. Perhaps they would pick him up.

More likely find the body, thought the Captain. Albeit with a heavy heart, he ordered the boats to be swung aboard, and Angus was left to his fate.

As it happened, there were two factors in Angus's favour. He was without his heavy jacket, discarded as he pumped water from the hold, and without his even heavier boots, taken off to enable him to climb the rigging. Furthermore, he was somewhat buoyed up by the oilskin cape, which spread around him. He was deeply unconscious from the blow to his head, and immobilised by the shattered arm, and so he floated, borne by a strong tide, towards the shore.

Had he been conscious, no doubt he would have struggled as he did not know how to swim. But the current carried him inert and motionless, half in and half out of the water, with just enough air to sustain him, willy-nilly away from the *Ruby* and towards the land of St. John, since re-named Prince Edward Island.

# Chapter Nine - Landfall

Unable to help their missing passenger, but aided by a brisk wind, the two Aberdeen ships sped westwards, and then turned south towards Pictou. The little harbour was seen lying along a sheltered estuary through which Pictou's three rivers reached the Gulf.

There were many buildings near the shore, and rising up the hill beyond. Matthew, who still supposed his brother to be safe on the other ship, counted three white churches, and a number of other large and imposing buildings. Two jetties accommodated ships loading timber and disembarking passengers. Other ships stood out in the harbour, either waiting their turn, or riding at anchor, having unloaded. There were other smaller stages built out into the water, possibly serving a fishing fleet, or local traffic, but the little port was busy as it served as the first port of call for much of the cross-Atlantic trade.

The *Harmony* berthed first, as she carried the bulk of the human cargo, and the Scots streamed ashore, gazing around at the little town and the hills behind. The steeply wooded slopes of the hills behind the town were not unlike those they had left in Cromarty. It would be easy to feel at home here.

The voices that greeted them had something of the Scottish burr too. Some kinsmen were meeting their fellows; some Pictou residents had come out to offer help. Among them was Alexander Thomson, the owner of the local store, whose father, William the Pioneer, had been an early settler, and now farmed beef nearby.

While the townsfolk enjoyed the bustle and excitement of the arrival of an emigrant ship, and frequently gathered to watch it come in, the more genteel were apt to stay aloof. It was the more unusual therefore, to discover, lingering in her carriage a fashionable lady, accompanied by a nursemaid and child. Delia Mackenzie, having subscribed generously to Thomas Dudgeon's Emigration Association, had come to welcome the settlers herself.

It was not to be thought of that she should expose the infant to any risk of infection from the new arrivals, but she alighted from her carriage, elegantly dressed in a green morning gown, and approached Alexander Thomson, whom she knew. "I hope they have had a good voyage," she said. "There are about two hundred and fifty, I am told."

"It's a bigger contingent than we have had recently," he replied. "Thomas Dudgeon has been busy. The journey seems to have taken about four and a half weeks – a fair crossing for this time of year. Do you have anyone special to meet?"

"No-one... except ..." she hesitated a little. "I could offer work to a maid-servant, or a young couple, perhaps. Just until they get settled."

"Most will be looking for land, I expect," Alexander responded. "They'll need to get working while the weather's good and before the winter sets in. The new allocations are over beyond the West River. But if I see someone suitable, I'll point them in your direction. There may be someone glad of the chance."

The crowd from the *Harmony* was gradually dispersing, and after some manoevering the *Ruby* also came alongside. A small group, consisting of a middle-aged couple and a teenage lad, had been waiting anxiously for its arrival. They were scanning the figures alighting, but seeing no sign of Angus. Then the First Mate, who had been directed by his Captain to break the sad news, hurried across to them.

Delia's attention was aroused by a loud wail and frantic sobbing from Margaret Ritchie. Her husband, Denis, looked stunned and bewildered. Young Matthew seemed incredulous, but on the verge of tears also. Observing their distress, Delia drew closer. She had been talking to a family from Rogart, who were thankful to be on dry land once more. She had not meant to intrude, but the First Mate took Denis and Matthew back to the ship, presumably to pick up their goods and chattels. Margaret crouched, weeping, over the bundles they had brought from the *Harmony*.

Delia took her hand in a comforting clasp and bent to hear the sad tale.

"My eldest son is missing, and they think he has drowned," muttered the older woman, through choking sobs. "They said he fell overboard. It was Angus who urged us to come. Whatever will we do without him? Oh, I wish we'd stayed in Kilcalmkill and been satisfied with what we had. It wasn't much but we'd been happy there..."

"You can be happy again here," suggested Delia. "I can assure you this is a wonderful country. I am deeply sorry about your son. In every tragedy there's a silver lining somewhere. Perhaps he isn't drowned. Perhaps a boat picked him up."

But Denis and Matthew, returning from the *Ruby*, were not too optimistic.

"There was a small fishing boat, the Captain told us. But it's likely it was too far inshore," said Denis heavily. "Captain Brodie has given me Angus's coat and boots, as well as the rest of the luggage we left behind."

"We should never have got separated," bemoaned Margaret.

"It couldn't be helped," sighed her husband. "Captain Brodie said Angus was a great help with the pumps, but he fell when he climbed the rigging to release a rope that had snagged. He was a sort of hero, he said."

Matthew responded to this. "Angus would always give his best," he said. "But what will Elizabeth say?"

"Elizabeth is our daughter, a teacher in Edinburgh," explained Denis. "She and Angus were always close friends with only two years between them, closer than most brothers and sisters, I daresay. You'll have to write and tell her," he said to Matthew. "You've got the schooling I never had."

"Could she come out to be with you?" asked Delia. "I would gladly pay her fare if you want her to come." Margaret shuddered, "I want no more of my children on those dratted ships."

"It's very kind of you, madam," said Denis, "But I think we had agreed that Elizabeth would stay in her position until later when we got settled. My problem is that, without Angus, we shall find that more difficult."

"You've got me!" Matthew said stoutly. "I can work from dawn to dusk if I have to." His father flung an arm around his shoulders. "Ye're a good lad," he said.

Well, the offer stands," said Delia. "Why don't I "introduce you to Alexander Thomson, to see if he can help?"

The little family trailed off desolately in her wake.

\* \* \*

Letter from Matthew Ritchie to Elizabeth Ritchie
Pictou

Dear Elizabeth,

Dad says I must write to you, and I do so with a heavy heart, for we have lost our Angus at sea. He fell over the side of the ship when the sea was very rough. It was in the Gulf of Saint Lorance. Mam feels it very much and keeps crying. So are us all very upset. Captain Brodie said Angus was almost a hero cos he was trying to get the sail up when the crew was short of men. Angus stayed behind when they rowed us to the *Harmony*. The *Ruby* had scraped on a rock and there was some water coming in. They have said Angus is missing, beleeved drowned. It is terrible.

A kind lady here says she will pay your fare if you want to come. Dad says best stay where you are. You can rite to us care of Thomson's Store in Pictou. We have a piece of land already to build a house on. Dad says he can do it if I help cut the wood. The town here is nice. I like it. McAndrews have the next piece of land to us. The Emigration peeple paid for it, so it is now ours. It is quite hot and the midges are worse than Scotland.

Mam and all send love and keep well.

Yr affect brother,

Matt.

Elizabeth Ritchie received her younger brother's letter in place of the promised one she had been expecting for weeks from Angus. Stunned, she read and re-read the bald details, and her heart ached with the need to comfort her mother and be comforted. She felt so remote and alone. Handsome, upright, trustworthy, affectionate Angus missing and probably drowned! She could not bear it.

The news must already be six weeks old. Was that when the goose walked over her grave? She remembered a shuddering fit, which had come upon her a few weeks ago. It had been so acute, and she had felt so cold and frightened that she had had to call for a maid to look after the children in the schoolroom while she went to her chamber to recover. Perhaps she was fey. Kneeling, by her bed in the attic room, she prayed for Angus's soul, and asked the good Lord to care for her family far away.

She wondered if she should go to Pictou to see if she could get some news of him. The task seemed too insuperably difficult, and her father would make all the enquiries he could, she was sure. Perhaps it would be better to wait until the *Ruby* returned to Scotland and hear what the sailors could tell her.

She sought the shipping news in the Scotsman. The *Harmony* had an anticipated arrival date, but the *Ruby*, if she was badly holed, might have to stay for a repair before undertaking a timber-laden trip back to Scotland. She wrote to Captain Brodie, care of the ship's owners in

Aberdeen, asking if she might see him whenever he should return to Scotland.

She wrote also, of course, to her parents in shared affliction.

* * *

Delia Mackenzie in Pictou found herself strangely haunted by the disappearance of Angus Ritchie. She could readily imagine how she would feel if a similar tragedy overcame her own son, Gilbert. She was in fact over-protective towards the precious toddler and hardly let him out of her sight. She shuddered at the loss suffered by Angus's mother. Imagine having nurtured a child until manhood, and then having his life snuffed out.

She visited the Ritchie family in their new homestead the following year, having ascertained its address from Alexander Thomson at the store. Riding with her groom in attendance, she packed some small luxuries from her own kitchens in a pannier attached to the saddle. It was quite a journey, but at last she came to the simple home, built in a newly-cleared section of the forest.

"Have you any news of your missing son?" she asked, when she had congratulated Margaret on the homely touches she had brought to the dwelling, and offered her own gifts.

Margaret's face, which had brightened at the sight of her visitor, clouded over again.

"Nay," she said heavily. "I am afeared we never will. My daughter, Elizabeth, has talked with the Captain when the *Ruby* finally got back to Scotland, and he says

The Pictou Triangle

they threw a life-line and searched with boats, and couldna find him."

"My husband has some fishing interests near that area. I will ask him to make some enquiries," offered Delia. "Is your daughter intending to come over here?"

"Not yet awhile," replied Margaret. "She has a good position teaching the children of an Edinburgh family, and we can offer her nothing like it here."

"I may need a Governess for my little boy one day," said Delia. "In the meantime I could see if there is a suitable post in any of my friends' households."

"It's very good of you, ma'am," responded Margaret. "Elizabeth does write to us often, and she's really settled where she is."

"Well, let me know if she decides she wants to come. Perhaps she has a young man she's loath to leave."
"She's written nothing like that," said her mother. "And I believe she would tell us. She doted on her brother, you know."

Reaching home again, Delia recounted details of her excursion, and discussed the Ritchie family's loss with her own menfolk. She urged William to ask his shipping contacts if they had heard news either of a body being washed up on the shore, or of a man being rescued.

William promised perfunctorily to make enquiries, but promptly forgot about the whole affair. The Judge, for it was before his own demise, said "It's very proper of you to be concerned, my dear, but while few immigrants are lost, I believe, accidents do happen." The remark, alas, was a foretaste of his own imminent loss of life.

\* \* \*

Her own bereavement took Delia's mind off the loss suffered by the Ritchie family. After the accident, the Judge was buried with due pomp and ceremony. His book was virtually finished and a publisher had been secured. It was published posthumously to wide acclaim. For months after her father's death, Delia had neither time nor inclination to think of the Ritchies. Deeply sorrowful, she mourned in misery, with little support from her husband. Gilbert reached his fifth birthday, and joined other children from the neighbourhood in a Dame school in Pictou. Delia came to the conclusion that, as an only child, it would be best for him to have the company of other children, rather than a governess at home. Here again she had an argument with William. Uncharacteristically, it was he who gave way.

"Do as you will," he said shortly, and shut the door of his study so hard that the silver rattled in the cabinet alongside.

Delia buried herself once more in her charitable Committees. She had taught her child the rudiments of the alphabet, but, with him now at school, she had time to spare for wider interests.

In the summer of 1826, Delia was introduced to Isabella Liddel, who was visiting Pictou from Scotland. Recently widowed, Isabella was staying with her cousin, Helen, to try and retrieve some debts owed to her husband, a timber merchant. She soon met William the Pioneer and his son, Alexander, leading lights of Pictou, and spent a week exploring Cape Breton. She had determined to build Presbyterian churches for the Gaelic-speaking settlers on that island.

Delia was deeply impressed by Isabella. Her devotion to the Presbyterian faith was profound, and her declared intention to devote her life to the cause she had made her own, wholly admirable. Delia's own faith had been strengthened in recent years, and she promised to support Isabella's crusade with money and any influence she had.

She invited Isabella to spend a day with her at Malibou, and they played with the six-year-old Gilbert. Isabella disclosed that she had had a little boy who had died at the age of five, and Delia felt a cold hand clutch at her own heart. "I cannot imagine what a horror that would have been," she sympathised.

"It was indeed," agreed Isabella, "But when my husband also died, I felt that I must try and achieve something with my life – something beyond marriage and the family. That is why I shall work till I drop to persuade people in Scotland to give generously to support our religion in the New World."

"I think our churches here should help in that endeavour," said Delia, "And I will, too. However, I think my own main interest is to support the creation of an enlightened society here. "I have not really put it into words before, but it is important that we should build a society, which thinks not only of material things, but of beauty and of culture. Education is vital, and your husband's partner, Edward Mortimer, achieved a great deal in establishing our Academy. He was also very involved with the politics of this part of the world. I know women are not supposed to be interested in politics, but that also is important in building a good country."

"We may not have the vote," said Isabella. "But in Scotland, no-one could say we women did not have influence. My husband and I would talk about politics, and I believe that he respected my opinion, and would sometimes follow my advice."

"Yes, but William is not really political," sighed Delia. "He is all for business and for making money. Perhaps my son will have more of a social conscience."

"You'll have some time to wait," commented Isabella, looking down at the small Gilbert. "Yet the example you set him, and the knowledge you can impart may well shape his interests as he grows older."

They parted and promised to keep in touch by letter.

\* \* \*

Delia's marriage had become ever more semi-detached. William, when he was at Malibou, and often he was not, would shut himself away in his study, writing innumerable business letters, and he would be away for months at a time. Their conversations were only at meal-times, and as long as the house ran like clockwork, which Delia ensured that it did, William had very little interest in his wife's affairs.

He was very proud of little Gilbert, however, and would hoist him before him on his horse and take him riding, eventually buying his son his own first pony. He wanted Gilbert to be tough and strong, would shadow-box with him, and had no patience with tears or tantrums.

The child progressed well at school; he was quiet and studious, and at home took most of his pleasure from riding his pony. His father also took him down to the harbour, and encouraged him to explore the ships when they berthed at Pictou.

William also wanted to teach him to shoot, but this led to a fearful argument with Delia. The tragic death of her father made her adamant that her son should go nowhere where there were guns. Battle raged for weeks, William arguing that every man needed to learn to hunt, and to defend himself, Delia insisting that guns were dangerous, and she wanted no more shooting accidents in her family. With his own guilty knowledge of the circumstances of Judge Fogo's death, William eventually had to surrender to her decision for the time being. As a compromise, they set up an archery range in the grounds, and Gilbert's eye was trained in the less aggressive sport.

Delia taught him to paint, and longed to take him to the Art Galley in Halifax. It was only practical when William was away, when she had the carriage prepared, and set off on a clothes-buying and cultural expedition. To her delight her son enjoyed the outing and played the part of her escort in an incipient grown-up way. They bought books and some paintings and attended a concert. They pored over the Halifax newspapers together, and walked near the Fort, although she judged it wisest not to go down to the Harbour, a somewhat seedy environment.

Letters arrived for her from Isabella in Scotland, outlining the progress of her campaign to raise funds for Cape Breton. Delia knew that Alexander Thomson was also in correspondence with Isabella, and indeed had seen her both in Scotland and London when he had been investigating and giving evidence to the Select Committee on conditions aboard his ship, *The Lovely Nelly*. It was no real surprise to Delia when she knew in 1931 that Alexander and Isabella were to be married here in Pictou, although they would be making their home in Quebec as Alexander had become the Immigration Agent there. She and William were guests at the wedding.

Delia found an opportunity to ask Alexander whether they had had any news of his brother, Robert, who had disappeared on the day her father died.

"Not from that day to this," he replied sadly. "As you know, I failed to find any trace of him along the Halifax Road. I think he may have doubled back somehow, and perhaps got on board a ship at the Harbour. I cannot understand, however, why he has not written to contact us."

"He would have wanted to be here at your wedding," she suggested. Overhearing, William put his hand under her elbow and steered her away. "Why bring that up?" he grumbled. "The rascal's escaped. That's all there is to it -- and good riddance."

"I still think it's sad when people are missing from their families. It was the same with Angus Ritchie, who fell overboard from the *Ruby*. Did you ever find any trace of him?"

William bent his mind to a half-remembered request. "No, " he said shortly. "They're probably both dead. It happens. Silly to get sentimental."

Delia sighed. Their attitudes to life's problems were as different as chalk from cheese.

# BOOK III

## Chapter Ten - Angus in Limbo

Meanwhile Angus Ritchie found himself in distressing limbo. He did not know who he was, or how he had come to languish in this plight. He had to re-learn his life, as if the previous nineteen years had never been. He did not even know he was nineteen, nor when his birthday was. He did not know his name. All memory of his past life, save that of recovering consciousness in a boat full of fish, had been wiped clean away.

His memory was working again, but only from that moment, when he had been miraculously rescued from the sea by three French fishermen. He eventually learned that they, having taken almost all the catch they needed from the prolific waters, were thinking of heading home, when they vaguely heard a commotion from the two sailing ships standing out to sea. They kept a sharper look out than usual, and spotted Angus's inert body among the waves. They had steered towards the body, and one of the men, leaning out with a boat-hook, had managed to hook the end of it in part of Angus's clothing.

It had taken two of them some time to roll him over the side of their boat and tumble him on top of their fish catch. To their credit they took turns to pump away at Angus's back, turning his head leftwards and working rhythmically until they were rewarded with a spluttering cough, and a gulp of air from the man they had rescued. He opened his eyes and a healthier colour began to replace the pallor of his face, but all the time he uttered no word. When they tried to haul him into a sitting position, his face became contorted with pain, so they realised he had a major injury to his arm, as well as the gash on his head. They removed his wet clothes, and rubbed his limbs to restore the circulation. Then they wrapped him in sacking and the oilskin and left him to recover as best he could.

All this Angus learned when he went back to thank the French community, taking with him someone who could speak their language.

Unfortunately the boat had come, not from the nearby Prince Edward Island, but from the tip of Newfoundland's southern peninsula. Consequently it had taken the French fishermen the rest of the day and through the night to get back to their base, by which time Angus had a raging fever to add to his other problems.

The tiny French community near Newfoundland's Port au Basques consisted of only half a dozen shacks, but the womenfolk fussed over him kindly enough. They made a rough pallet bed near the fire, and fed him broth and water, and washed and bandaged his head wound. There was no Doctor, but they got a farmer who was good with horses, to look at the broken arm. A splint of sorts was fashioned, and they dosed their patient with neat rum while the bone was set.

Angus tried again to speak, to thank them for their kindness, but only an unintelligible babble resulted when he tried to do so. Neither could he understand their language.

The Frenchmen dried and examined his clothes, but there was no clue to his identity, only a single penny in his breeches' pocket.

"They were British ships, I think," one of the fishermen had volunteered. "Maybe he would understand if we could find someone who speaks English. I'm sure that coin is a British penny."

"Maybe that blow on the head has confused him," one of the women had suggested. "It would be better if we could get him to his own people, to the cod-drying place. Perhaps they would know what to do."

Angus remembered them bringing him to this British fishing outpost at Port au Basques. His only possessions were the socks, breeches and shirt, which he had worn when rescued, together with a British penny in one of his pockets. John Campbell, manager of the cod-drying plant, gave him an old Harris tweed jacket as a protection against the cold, and he was issued with the protective boots that all the workers wore. Gradually his arm mended and he gladly learned to work in the fish-drying shed. They gave him a bed in the bunkhouse. The other men tried to talk to him, but although he understood what they said, he could at first only reply by nods or a shake of the head. He tried to practise saying simple things like "thank you" or asking the time, but while his brain could frame the question, his tongue could only garble the words.

He felt so indebted to them that, when they first asked him to go out on a fishing trip, he accepted, but as soon as he neared the boat, panic gripped him. He felt an overwhelming dread of the water, in which he had so nearly been drowned, and in the stress of the moment his voice at last obeyed his brain, and he shrieked "No, no, no!"

They let him stay on land after that, but he reasoned to himself that if he could say "No, no, no!" he must equally be able to say "Aye, aye, aye!" He practised till he could do so, and also added "please" and "thank you" to his vocabulary. The gash on his forehead and temple had healed also, but there was obviously some internal damage to his brain, which had resulted from a blow or a fall, or whatever had preceded his rescue from the water.

The big breakthrough did not come until over a year later, when an Officer of the Militia one day rode into the yard. Angus was the only worker in sight, and when the Officer dismounted, he called to Angus to hold his horse. The beast had been ridden hard and was sweating and thirsty. Automatically Angus got hold of the bridle and led the horse to the water-trough. Then he picked up some straw and began to rub down the creature's flanks. "Whoa!" he said, as the horse shifted its position. "Stand still, you beauty!"

The horse nuzzled his neck and chest, and he added, "I know what you want, but I've no sugar to give you." The words came out normally and naturally, and as he realised what had happened, Angus became delighted, though shocked at the happening. He walked the horse up and down; he looked at and identified the bit, the bridle, the girths and the saddle and spoke their names. He knew about horses! It was as if he had discovered some small segment of his former life.

He had worked with horses; he knew it in his bones. When the Officer had gone, Angus went to see John Campbell.

"That horse!" he said. "I know I used to work with horses."

John Campbell stared at him in amazement. It was the first connected sentence he had heard the man speak. He shook his hand warmly. "This is a miracle! he said. "You're talking again. How do you remember that?"

"I don't know. It's all I can remember," Angus replied, as the fog of the past closed in again. "I just knew what to do for the horse. I didn't have to be shown – and I could remember the names for the bridle and saddle."

"Instinct, I suppose! Well, it's a great advance. Keep trying. Maybe you'll remember more soon."

Angus did keep trying, but it seemed his brain needed another trigger, and for the time being that was lacking. To be able to converse, however, was a major step forward. Slowly, and gradually with more confidence, he began to talk with his fellow-workers and felt less isolated. Through the chit-chat he began to feel a whole person again, though still with this troubling memory gap of early years.

He earned money and was able to buy more clothing and a pocket-knife. He learned to play cards with the lads. He took to walking and exploring the country at the weekends. He decided he must also have been a countryman. The woods, the hills and the streams were not strange to him. The sky at night was familiar, and he knew he had spent time in the open air, under the moon and stars. He used the knife he had bought to fashion a stick to help him on his rambles. He made a tall stick, and bent the top of the wood to a rounded end.

"That's like a shepherd's crook," commented his friend, Donald.

Angus looked at it with new interest. Had he been a shepherd, then? No, he did not know what to do with sheep in the same way that he did with horses. Perhaps someone he had known was a shepherd.

He thought he might have been a Scot. The burr of the Scottish speech among the Port au Basques workers was more attuned to his ear than the accent of the Irishmen or the Englishman. In particular, he found John Campbell, who was rather more cultured than the others, easier to understand. Mr. Campbell pointed out that he had the Scots colouring too, the fair to reddish hair, and the keen blue eyes of the Highlander.

More than anything he wanted to know his name. He went through the alphabet, Alexander, Andrew, Archibald ...through to Zackariah without success. Nothing seemed right for him. Of biblical names, Matthew, Mark, Luke and John, only Matthew had some resonance with him, and yet he didn't think his name was Matthew. The nickname, Barney, began to irritate him. He wasn't Barney; he was ..... !

Physically he had not only regained his strength, but his frame had filled out as he grew older. There were substantial meals in the bunkhouse. Fish predominated, but the cook kept chickens, pigs, a cow and a few lambs in the paddock, and the men's diet was varied and the food plentiful. He realised that he was lucky to have landed here.

As year succeeded year, he awarded himself a birthday – 1st July to commemorate the month when he had been carried ashore on Newfoundland. He promised his mates to throw a celebration of the ten years he had lived there. Cook entered into the spirit of the occasion and made a christening cake, with the name Barney spelt out in currants. One of his friends played the fiddle, and there was dancing. He was thrilled to discover he could remember some of the steps. He had done this before! It seemed to confirm that he was a Scot. For a surname he adopted Macdonald – they said it was a proud and famous clan.

\* \* \*

As summer slid into autumn in 1834 Barney Macdonald, as Angus was now known, extended his rambling as far as the Codroy Valley. Walking north-west along the coast, he came to the mouth of the Little Codroy River, and turned inland, by the river's south-east banks.

The foothills of the Long Range Mountains were on his right, richly wooded, and brightly coloured as the early autumn leaves were glowing on the deciduous trees, the birch, maple and witchhazel, set against the dark green background of spruce, fir and pine. The floor of the valley had been partially cleared, and as he walked further into the upland, there were scattered farmsteads and stock grazing in the pastures. A profusion of wild flowers grew on the banks of the river, some golden rod and mare's tails he recognised, although the names would not come to him. The river was home also to salmon and trout. He trailed a line and caught two trout, which he gutted and grilled over a small fire, and he feasted on wild raspberries and marshberries which grew in profusion in the fertile land.

He saw some hares and a rabbit or two bobbing about, and there was a chorus of birdsong, with swallows and swifts gathering in huge flocks to depart on their annual migration, and blackbirds and robins in plentiful supply. Ducks and snipe populated the marshy borders of the river, and he had to be careful not to get too close, for the marsh was treacherous and it was easy to step from a tussock of grass into a boggy patch. His shepherd's crook enabled him to probe ahead and check whether the ground was stable enough to walk on.

The valley was peaceful and perfect. He spent the night in the lea of a barn, some thirty yards away from a farm-house, and in the morning was woken by a cock's crowing, and the lowing of a couple of cows waiting to be milked. He put distance between himself and the farm-house as he resumed his ramble. Perhaps there would be somewhere further on where he could buy milk at a more reasonable hour.

He had walked for another two hours, still following the river, when he came to a minute village, consisting of three homes quite close together, wood-piles neatly stacked beside each, and land stretching south, east and north belonging to each farm. There was a boy pulling turnips on to a barrow, ready for the root cellar, and he asked if he could buy some milk. The boy pointed to the nearest farm, and Angus walked towards its iron-hasped door. A girl came out in response to his knock, and he repeated his request. She nodded and led him to a lean-to dairy next to the house, pouring the fresh milk into a mug for him to drink.

She was young and pretty, with fair hair tied back in a ribbon, and a dress made from some dark material, topped with a bibbed pinafore of pink and white.

He gave his name, Barney Macdonald, and asked hers. "Alice Gale," she replied. "That's my youngest brother, John, named after my grandfather. Ma and Pa have gone to St. John's to the market, and my older brother is up in the fields."

He discovered that the MacLellans lived next door, and the MacArthurs at the third house. They were Scottish Presbyterians, and had farmed along the Little Codroy for twenty-five years.

"I don't remember it, because I wasn't born then, but my family came from Canna in the Inner Hebrides," she confided, "And my father found this beautiful piece of land, which he says is ten times as good as where he started farming."

He asked her if she didn't find it lonely. "Not at all," she said. "We have a tiny church further up the Valley, and I went to school there. We know everyone in this Valley and some in Grand Codroy too. Where did you go to school?"

He coloured and remained silent for a while. "I don't know," he said eventually. "I think I must have been reared in Scotland too, but where I'm not sure. I had a bad accident ten or more years ago, and my memory for everything before that has gone."

She looked concerned. "So you don't remember Scotland either! I always feel out of it when Ma and Pa start talking about the old days. They were determined to leave and find their fortune over here, but they are always on about Canna, sort of homesick, I think, even now."

John had come in by then and asked for his tea.

They went into the house, originally a single-roomed structure, but divided into two by a partition two-thirds of the way across. They sat on stools to drink the hot beverage. "We've only molasses," apologised Alice. "Ma should be getting sugar in the town, together with lots of things for the winter. She's going to get some stuff to make a new dress too. I'm really excited!"

"All you girls want is clothes," grumbled John.

"You'll get a new shirt too!" his sister reminded him. "And as I'll have to do most of the seaming and button-holes, you'd better be nice to me."

"I'm always nice to you," he retorted. "Have you cleared the root-cellar to make room for the turnips?"

"Yes, I have. I did that yesterday. But I've got to do the dinner for you and Euan, don't forget, as well as feed the hens and do the milking. Where are you going to get your dinner?" she asked Barney.

"I don't know," he answered. "I grilled a trout last night, and perhaps I'll do the same again."

"You could have it with us," she offered. "Ma and Pa won't be back, so there'll be us three, four if you want to stay."

"Then I must work for it," replied Angus. "Do you want me to help with the turnips or chop wood, or anything else?"

John brightened at the offer. "Turnips, please," he said. "I've got another fork!"

Thus Angus spent the day in the field, instead of walking forward. He liked the two members of the family he had met so far. John provided him with two buckets – "Turnips in one and stones in the other," he said. "We may as well do two jobs at once."

It was back-breaking work, and Angus head ached with the strain, as did his back

At the meal, he met the older brother, Euan. He seemed to be in his early twenties, which would make the girl seventeen or eighteen, he thought, and John a year or two younger. They were friendly and put him at his ease. He supposed a visiting stranger was quite an event in their rural lives, and it was the tradition to be hospitable.

Angus asked about the valley. There was a cart-track, they said, to the next group of houses. "And if the Minister is there, you must ask him to show you our little Church," suggested Alice. "After that, the track goes on until it meets the road to St. John's."

"Some road!" scoffed Euan. "You can ride a horse along it, or pull an ox-cart, but that's all."

"It's better further on," contested Alice. "It's wide enough for a carriage then."

"If you had a carriage," said her younger brother. "Have you been to St. John's?" he asked Angus.

"No. I've spent the last ten years at the fish-drying sheds."

"Do you go fishing?" John did not wait for a reply. "I like salmon-fishing best. It's really exciting watching them leap. And Ma smokes them, so we have plenty for the winter."

"You seem to have found a land of plenty," commented Angus.

"We do very well in the summer-time, but Newfoundland winters are long and cold, as no doubt you've found."

"Euan, we ought to give Barney a bed for tonight," suggested Alice. "He can't go walking now; it's too late."

"A barn will do for me," said Angus, not willing to impose on their hospitality.

"No need," said Euan. "We've bunks enough for three in there," pointing beyond the partition, "And Alice can have the parents' bed."

Angus felt warmed and excited by his welcome. It was wonderful to be in a family home. He said as much to his hosts.

"Can you really not remember what your home was like?" asked Alice. "It must be very difficult, if all you can remember is life at the fish factory?"

"I know I worked with horses," said Angus. "Instinctively I know what to do with a horse. I can do practical things but it took me nearly two years to learn to talk properly again. Most words have come back, and I get by, but I don't think I can read a book or write a letter."

"You don't think?" asked Alice. "Have you tried?"

"I don't need to try. Only John Campbell of the other men, can read and write. I can count and I can gut fish. I play cards, and dance to the fiddle. I like walking, but daren't go near the sea. That is my life now."

"But that is not the whole of life," said Euan. "I'm courting a girl and we'll be married next year in the

The Pictou Triangle

church. Then I'll want a farm of my own, and there'll be bairns to look after, and I need to read and write."

Alice had got up and fetched a little book. "This is my primer," she said. "Let's see if you can read it." She sat down close to him and opened the book. "We can see how much you remember," she urged. "Do you know the alphabet?"

"Yes, I know that," he replied. "I went through all the names my friends and I could think of, beginning with each letter to see if I could remember my own, and I couldn't."

"Then you're not really Barney MacDonald," said John.

"Yes, I am. My friends christened my Barney, and I added MacDonald, since I believe I'm a Scot." He turned the book over in his hand. "It's a long time since I held one, but this feels familiar. I think I may have read a lot."

He opened the first page and a mass of letters swam in front of him. He put his finger on the first letter.

"Tee" he said.

"Very good," encouraged Alice. "What's next?"

"H and E. The cat sat on the mat."

"Perhaps you looked at the picture."

"No, I didn't. I read it. But it's a very simple sentence."

"It's a sentence anyway. It has a subject and a verb and a predicate."

Angus was not sure what a predicate was, but he assumed it was the rest of the sentence. He went on, very slowly. "It was a ginger cat, with a long tail."

"There, you can read," Alice said triumphantly. "Let's try something more difficult."

She brought over a prayer book, and both heads bent over it. He stumbled over the first word she pointed out. "Whosoever " they finally made out between them.

"That's a silly word," said Alice. "It's not one we would use today."

Angus was becoming disturbed. The girl's proximity was exciting him. Her arm was touching his. It was brown on the outside from working in the summer sun, but creamy white on the inside of the elbow, and her skin was plump and smooth. Her fair hair had become a little loose from the ribbon and was curling into the nape of her neck, where the high-necked dress was finished with a little ruffle. She had discarded her apron while they ate the excellent meal.

It was getting dark outside, and candles had been lit. In the dim light it was becoming hard to see the page.

"We should go to bed," suggested Euan. "You can try again in the morning."

* * *

In the morning, there was work to do. Alice cooked a substantial breakfast. There were eggs and bacon and potatoes and mushrooms, which she said she had picked yesterday. She would go out and get some more, she said, for they sprang up overnight. Angus felt reluctant to resume his trek, but he must go on. The longer he stayed, the more difficult it would be to leave.

John asked if he was coming back this way, or going over the hills?

"I hadn't decided," was Angus's reply.

"Come back this way," suggested Alice. "And I'll find a book to lend you, and we can practise writing too. Ma and Pa will be back probably, and I'm sure they'd like to see you."

"I'm scything corn in the top field," said Euan. "You can stay and help with that, if you want."

They were very hospitable and lovely to be with. He decided with difficulty.

"I'll go on up the valley," he said, "And call and see you on the way back."

He was glad he had made that decision. Further up the lane, the tiny Church was open and he went inside. He felt he should pray, but he could not remember the words to say. He just knew the Church had been part of his life. The white-painted walls, the altar and its cross were familiar to him. One knelt in Church, so he knelt on an embroidered hassock. There were two things now that he wanted most. They were to remember his name and his past, and now to be able to be with Alice for always.

He prayed that he might be granted both these.

The Minister had seen Angus enter the Church and came in to greet him. An elderly man, he had come across the Atlantic with his flock twenty-five years before and together they had built up their little community. He had christened and taught the children, and buried the dead, and blessed the living in holy matrimony. He had consoled the bereaved, and preached the Presbyterian faith in order that his congregation should have order and rules to live by. He sensed that this stranger might be troubled, and he offered help.

"Can I be of assistance?" he asked.

"I do not know who I am," answered Angus. "An accident has left me without any memory except for the last ten years when I have been at the cod-drying factory at Port au Basques."

"That is a grave handicap. They call it amnesia. It is unusual, but not unknown. Do you feel this Church is familiar to you?

"Yes, I think so," replied Angus. "Not this exact building, but something very like it."

"Do you recall simplicity like this, or do you have any sensation of smelling incense, or a service in Latin, or clergy with gold-laced robes?"

"No, none of that. I think I knew plain surroundings only."

"Then probably you were of the Presbyterian faith. Did you go to school?"

"I cannot recall. But when Alice showed me her primer, it was not difficult to read it slowly."

"Ah, you have met the Gales – a delightful family! Do you know if you have a family?"

"I must have had. It is a great disappointment that I cannot remember them, even their names, or where we lived. People think I must have fallen from an emigrant ship, but how it happened, or why we were on a ship, I cannot tell. But I know I worked with horses," he added.

"You are doing very well. Little by little, things may come back to you. It can happen suddenly, I believe, or very gradually. With some it never comes back, and so you should make the most of what you have. Be of good courage. You are not old; there is much of life before you. Can you not be content with that?"

Angus sighed. "I think I shall have to be. But it annoys me to be called Barney MacDonald, when I know it's not the name I was born with."

"As Shakespeare said, 'What's in a name? That which we call a rose by any other name would smell as sweet" quoted the cleric. "You may miss your family, but they will equally certainly miss you! Perhaps they are searching too. You should ask everyone, go anywhere, and perhaps you will yet be united one day. I wish you good-day."

He paused with his hand for a moment resting on Angus's shoulder, and then left the Church.

Angus suddenly began to think of, not what he wanted, but what he had to be grateful for. Kneeling again, he said softly,

"I thank you, Lord, for the life you have spared. Help me to value it and look to the future with hope. Allow me to do good to others, as good has been done unto me. In the name of the Saviour, the Power and the Glory, for ever and ever, Amen."

He did not know where the last words had come from, but they seemed right, and he went out into the sunshine strangely comforted.

* * *

He spent a couple more days in the hills above the valley. It would not do to return too soon. But when he went back to the Gales' home, Mr. and Mrs. Gale had arrived back and were as welcoming as their children had been. At least she was welcoming, but Angus thought he detected some slight caution in Alice's father's manner.

He resumed his reading lessons with Alice. She had found a magazine, which had been part of a newspaper, which she had been given a few months before. Together they read the text of a story, and then Alice found a poem by Lord Byron, which she quoted in a soft voice:

"There be none of Beauty's daughters,
 With a magic like thee;
And like music on the waters,
Is thy sweet voice to me:
When, as if its sound were causing,
The charmèd ocean's pausing,
The waves lie still and gleaming,
And the lull'd winds seems dreaming."

"I know Lord Byron was a very wicked man," she said, "But I think that is so beautiful!"

Angus seized her hand. "I know that you are beautiful!" he said breathlessly, and the magazine slid unheeded to the floor, as they shared a kiss.

Mr. Gale became even more cautious. "You don't know where you came from," he said bluntly. "I'd want my Alice to wed a man with a proper name, and of sound stock. And you hardly know one another. I won't stop you coming to see her, if that's what she wants, but it's too soon to be talking of more than that. Besides, there's many a young man for twenty miles around, who'd like to hitch up with Alice. But it's what she wants that counts."

"I know, Sir," replied Angus. "But the Minister said I was to look forward, not back. If Alice is willing, I'd like to keep on seeing her whenever we can, and perhaps next summer we can talk about it again."

On the way back to the bunkhouse, he called in to see the French fisher-folk. As usual they welcomed him, but it was difficult to converse when he had very little French and they had very little English. Perhaps because of the language, perhaps because of differing religions, the two small communities at Port au Basques kept themselves apart from one another.

To go on seeing Alice throughout the winter was not easy. Angus learned to snow-shoe. Despite the distance, he doggedly used the snow-shoes whenever the weather permitted to go over to the house in the Codroy Valley to see Alice. They practised writing together, and his skills came back gradually, so that he soon became confident in using words to express his ideas and feelings. Back at the cod-fishing base, he borrowed books from John Campbell to improve his reading too.

"Be of good courage," the Minister had said, and Angus determined that he must conquer his fear of the sea. Newfoundland was an island, and if he was to venture anywhere it had to be by boat. He must also give thought to the future. He could not ask Alice to live in Port au Basques. He must consider whether he could acquire land and build a farm, as Euan was doing. In the meantime he must save money and prove to Mr. Gale that he was worthy of his lovely daughter, and hope against hope to find out more about his background

# Chapter Eleven - Robert's Resolve

The man on the deep verandah was reading a letter from home – not a letter from a sweetheart or a mother, but one of a series from his business mentor and partner in crime.

William Mackenzie had kept faith with Robert Thomson since he unceremoniously bundled him out of Pictou eleven years earlier. He had written three or four times a year dispatching the letters when his ships visited the West Indies, to keep Robert aware of what was happening to his family and friends. Naturally William was very careful to mention the tragic shooting of Judge Fogo, father of his wife, Delia, only in the most general of terms. Nevertheless he contrived to ensure that Robert stayed where he was, safely in Jamaica, convinced that it was too dangerous to go back.

Mackenzie's letters were factual, emotionless, business-orientated, but they were a link with life in Pictou which Robert treasured. He had not thought he could become so homesick. When he had been there in his wild youth, he had fought to get out of the little town, had resented the family pressures to tie him to the farm, and to lead as respectable a life as his elder brothers, Alexander and Nathaniel. Now he yearned to return, to see the maple tree grove, ablaze with red in autumn, to watch his mother and sisters working in the dairy, even to round up the cattle himself with his dog, who by now would be grown old and stiff, if indeed, he was alive.

Robert had felt regretful at missing his sister's wedding in July 1828, and inexpressibly sad at the death of his father, William the Pioneer, in 1830. He lamented in solitude when he read an account of the funeral and burial at Antigonish in a letter from William Mackenzie. He could not have been there anyway, for the old man had been buried well before news could have travelled to the West Indies, but he held his own melancholy farewell. He even went so far as to borrow a Bible and read aloud some of the texts from which his father used to read at family prayers.

He would have liked to take ship immediately to pay a personal tribute to his powerful father's pioneering life; he would have liked to comfort his mother, regale Alexander with the account of how he was succeeding in the management of the Jamaican estate – and yet he dared not return.

Robert's mind went back to the first years of his exile, to his acquiring the knowledge of the routine of the sugar-growing plantation, to the decisions demanded of him by the overseers of his slave-labour force, to the loneliness of the nights spent at this tawdry bungalow.

True, in his first year he had found a lively Spanish girl with whom to enjoy a protracted flirtation, but that had come to an end when her father demanded to know his intentions. They were not in the least honourable, for he had no desire to be married to a Roman Catholic wife, who would likely grow as fat as her mother as she grew older, and who would present him no doubt with an annual addition to the family. Lonely as he was, he did not want that. Now had she been like Delia, with poise and wit, it would have been a solution, but Consuela had mere pertness in her chatter, lacking any sense of style.

His next amatory adventure had come to an equally abrupt, but more painful end. Dalliance with the English wife of a soldier in the Garrison had been exciting while it lasted, but discovery by the husband of his wife and Robert "in flagrente delicto" had led to fisticuffs, followed by a duel. He shuddered at the thought of the cold steel ripping into his side, mercifully missing his vital organs, but disabling him for a couple of months. During this time he had wondered about expanding the plantation to grow coffee, as they did on the Craighton Estate in the Blue Mountains, but he had reluctantly come to the conclusion that the soil and the heat lower down made it a risky proposition.

Later in his recuperation he had spent some time at the Harbour. The Navy had two men of war and some smaller ships stationed there. He had sailed on some of William's ships on the Atlantic run, and he was interested in comparing the rigging and construction of the Naval ships with the commercial ones. He got to know the bo'sun, and while they drank together in a tavern, Robert learned what he could about the British fleet and her press-ganged crew. The gulf between Officers and crew was very wide; discipline was severe; patrols were arduous, and piracy still a problem.

When the ships left harbour this temporary amusement ceased and Robert found an interest instead in a boat-building yard. Whenever he could escape from the estate he would gravitate there, offering help, questioning reasons for this or that construction, and getting the feel of a sea-going craft under his feet again. Sometimes they would hoist sail and take a trip round the bay to test the way a boat handled. There were fishermen too, who would take him out for sixpence. The fishing was vastly different, he found, from the cod-fishing he was used to in Newfoundland.

Sadly, his plantation was some distance away, and he could only visit the boatyard when he could be away for three or four days at a time. He searched instead for an interest nearer home. He now knew where he could obtain wood, and how to use woodworking tools. He discovered in himself a talent for wood-carving and made a stool and small table. Then he became more adventurous and constructed a chaise-longue and a dresser. Thus the years passed by.

A tropical storm, in fact almost a hurricane, devastated the estate one winter, and his bungalow was damaged, though not as badly as the workers' quarters, which were picked up bodily by the wind, and hurled in smithereens some hundred yards away. His talents, both for wood-working and organisation, had been called into play to direct and re-build the shelters, improving them in the bargain. There had been little in the way of harvest that year.

However, it had not been a disaster. His wage continued to be paid by William, its owner, who was also true to his word and paying hush-money into an account for him in a Halifax bank. The deposits were accumulating and earning interest. An annual statement gave Robert the reassuring news that he was becoming wealthy – not that there was any opportunity to spend that wealth, isolated as he was in the Indies. Drinks at the

Club, and some occasional clothes were all he needed to buy, and so his wages were accumulating too.

Eleven years like this, however, were more than enough. He developed a capacity for rum, which seemed to make him more morose than merry, and this latest missive from William was fuelling his miserable mood. William Mackenzie's letter, written in a sloping, angular script, was terse as usual:

Pictou, May 1836
Dear Thomson,

Your last report gave me pleasing tidings. I little thought when you took over the Kingsley Plantation with little experience that you would transform its yield to such satisfaction. I commend what you have achieved.

Our news is that we are to move away from Pictou. My son, Gilbert, is now fifteen. He has absorbed most of the knowledge our local Academy can provide, yet is desirous of further study. It may be that he will enter the Law, like his grandfather, Judge Fogo, whose sad death you will recall. Though that event is well behind us now, I have not heard that the case is closed.

As you know, your brother, Alexander, and his wife, Isabella, now reside in Quebec, where Alexander has the prestigious position of Immigration Agent. Your other brother, Nathaniel and his family, I understand, now run the properties Alexander acquired in Upper Canada. Your Mother, who grows quite frail, and your two younger brothers still farm at Maple Grove. Your sister, Gertrude, has been confined, and there is a second daughter to grace the family.

To return to my plans, I have sold Malibou and next week Delia and I embark on the *Albion* sailing to Leith. We shall rent a house in Edinburgh and enrol Gilbert in the Law School as soon as he has obtained qualifications to render him eligible.

My current business interests are therefore changing. You may buy the plantation from me at a price equal to the funds in your Halifax Account if that is what you wish. If it is not what you wish, then arrange to sell the property locally and have the funds placed with my legal representative in Kingston.

This is the parting of our ways. I may never return to Pictou.

Yrs. etc.

William Mackenzie

Having finished his third perusal of this missive, Robert tossed back another jigger of rum and called to the house-boy for limes and a second bottle. His befuddled brain tried to make sense of the carefully crafted letter by reading the implied messages between the lines:

He was not to return to Pictou. The case of Judge Fogo's death remained open!

His younger brothers were prospering, and might well not welcome the disruption of their lives his return would create! They would not want to share the farm's revenues three ways instead of two.

William was washing his hands of him, and did not intend to see him again!

William was keen to get back the hush-money he had already paid him -- in exchange for the plantation in which he obviously had no further interest!  William was always keen on a bargain!

Robert felt a burning sense of anger rising at the thought of his eleven years of exile at William's behest.  It had all been designed to keep him out of the way while William Mackenzie escaped scot-free from the murder he had committed!    If he, Robert, had faced a court, he could have denied that it was his shot that killed Judge Fogo.  It would have been William's word against his.  However, his flight, engineered by William, would appear to people in Pictou to confirm his guilt.

"Hell and damnation!" he swore.  "He's made a fool of me as well as a scapegoat for his own evil act!"

Robert pondered, not for the first time, on how William had shot the Judge.  He knew that William's second shot had come several seconds after the other two.  William must have crept through the trees immediately after firing his first shot; or indeed before he shot the first time.  He had only to waste a shot in the air, while making sure of his second.  He knew why – the devil needed to conceal his law-breaking habits and feared the Judge would expose him.  Robert had gone along with that.  Yet the plan to murder the Judge had been cooked up by William alone.  Older and wiser now, Robert regretted ever getting enmeshed in William's schemes.  They had seemed exciting at the time, but what had he now to show for those years dancing to William's tune?

He began to stumble restlessly around the room.  He had wasted eleven years of his life in this god-forsaken backwater, growing sugar-cane and making furniture.  If he accepted William's offer and saw his precious capital swallowed up in purchasing the plantation, all he could look forward to would be more of the same.

Unsteadily, he collided with the table, and slumped down again hastily into his chair. He was thirty-six, he thought, or was it thirty-seven? Neither he, nor anyone else, had marked each anniversary, and the best half of his life was gone. He'd be damned if he stayed in this hole. What could he do?

The effort of thinking became too much. He surrendered to the soporific effect of the rum, and crashed out on his bed, just conscious enough to pull the sleeping-net over him before passing out.

* * *

The idea of revenge occurred to him only the following morning when the work of the plantation had got under way, and he was riding round the farthest boundary.

His anger remained red-hot. He would not stay here, that was for certain. He would get the next ship to Halifax, cash in his funds and pursue William to Scotland. On the way he would get more detailed evidence of the rum-smuggling, lay information to the authorities, and pay William back for the years in exile.

The poetic justice of the project appealed to him, and he laughed out loud at the thought that William would think himself secure, and presume his victim was too cowed to strike back. He could even tell Delia that William had murdered her father – no, perhaps not. It would cause too much distress to her and the youngster.

He would not be so vindictive – but William was now his sworn enemy and must suffer the consequences!

When he felt calm enough, Robert penned two lines to William, saying he did not want to buy the plantation and had instructed William's lawyer to sell on the evidence of the letter.

He began to wonder how he could re-enter the world. It was all very well to pursue William, but he needed a future for himself. He had allowed himself to be regarded as a black sheep, despite his innocence of any serious crime. He wanted that future to be in North America. His funds would not last long if he did not find himself an occupation and a home of sorts. Perhaps it would be best to forget that he was Robert Thomson. Perhaps he should become Robert Anstruther, or Robert MacBride, or Robert Younger – the Scottish names came naturally to him. Perhaps he could visit his family under a cloak of secrecy. Did he need to change his appearance? Hair, perhaps? Grow a beard instead of remaining clean-shaven? He had been missing so long, probably no-one would recognise him anyway!

His attention was distracted on the boundary line by a broken fence which needed repair. To hell with it, he thought, and rode on.

* * *

The next day he rode down to the harbour. A ship was loading, looking for all the world like the *Mary Ann*, the very ship which had brought him to Jamaica eleven years ago. She was a slow old tub, a work-horse of the ocean, but she would do.

As he hurried aboard, Captain Murchison recognised him. "So it's Thomson," he said. "How are you after all these years, and how's the plantation going?"

"I've had more than enough of it," replied Robert. "Any chance of a berth to Halifax?"

"Not going there," said the Captain. "It's direct to Newfoundland this trip. St. John, followed by Port au Basques. You remember the routine. We're loading now."

He pointed to the barrels of molasses being rolled towards the hold. Robert swallowed and thought rapidly. His plan to check up the illegal *modus operandi* of William's shipping schemes would be equally facilitated by going to the tiny Newfoundland port. He had enough money in Jamaica to see him through, he judged, without touching his Halifax funds.

"Port au Basques will do me," he agreed. "Anything to get out of this heat! I can probably pick up a coastal steamer there. When d'you sail?"

"Day after tomorrow," said the Captain. "I'm not supposed to take passengers, but seeing as it's you . . Mr. Mackenzie know you're leaving?" he queried with careful casualness.

"He's the one who has given me the opportunity," replied Robert equally obliquely. "I gather he's moving to Scotland."

"I think Pictou was becoming dangerous," responded Murchison. "He's given out that it is because of the boy's education, but I've a suspicion the Navy has been getting interested."

"Is Port au Basques still safe?" asked Robert.

"I believe so. It's the Halifax/West Indies link that was causing concern."

The two men had reached the cabin quarters.

"This do you?" enquired the Captain, throwing open the door of a minute cabin.

Robert agreed it would. "I'd better pay," he offered. "As I'm leaving William's employ."

"No matter," said Captain Murchison. "I'll be glad to have your company, and presumably William would have had to get you back home at some stage. What are you going to do instead?"

"Have a vacation first," responded Robert. "Then, who knows? I might even go to Scotland myself. I came to Pictou as a toddler, so I've no recollection of Scotland, and it would be good to track down my roots. I'll collect my baggage and join you the day after tomorrow, then. Thanks for the passage."

Murchison hesitated. "The Halifax boat will be arriving in about a week if this is too much of a rush, and you'd rather wait for that."

"Not on your life! A boat in the hand, as they say – I'll travel with you." They shook hands on the deal.

\* \* \*

By the time Robert had collected his money and his portmanteau, he had also reviewed what he knew of the Port au Basques operation. He had been there before as William's henchman.

The barrels of molasses which were now being loaded in Kingston Harbour, were in fact a mixed cargo of genuine molasses and high quality rum, all ostensibly labelled "molasses", but with a subtle difference in the batch numbers. Customs checks at St. John's, unlike the busier ports, used to be virtually non-existent and the rum barrels had always escaped detection. Once the cargo had been cleared at St. John's, it went on its way to Port au Basques for trans-shipment to Sydney on Cape Breton.

But the quiet little haven at Port au Basques, where dried cod was prepared for the legitimate and profitable trade with Scotland and the West Indies, was also William's transit and sorting point. There the rum barrels were separated out from the real molasses and transferred into a transatlantic fishing vessel bound for Greenock, while the real molasses stayed on the original ship till it reached Sydney, Cape Breton. There was a chance, thought Robert, that he could also transfer to a ship bound for Scotland, if the Master was a Captain he knew. Then his knowledge of the chain of William's operations would be up-to-date and complete. He had only once been to the Greenock end of the chain, and that had been on the occasion when the shipment had been almost discovered, and the off-loading aborted. Thus he would need to know whether Simon Bennett, who had retired from the Navy and become a fish importer as well as a boat-builder, was still handling the off-loading and sale, and how he was doing it?

Robert and Captain Murchison, together with John Campbell at Port au Basques, had no problem with the ethics of evading revenue. The British Government was remote from them and they had few scruples about cheating it of unjust revenues. However, they had every respect for the naval ships, which enforced the

Government's tax policies, and it was only the certainty of huge rewards, which made the game worth playing. Similar smuggling was done, of course, throughout southern England. French brandy found its way into the homes of the well-to-do through the activities of smugglers, otherwise known as the Gentlemen, pitting their wits against the Excisemen.

Robert enjoyed the voyage. The breezes at sea were refreshing after the close and humid atmosphere of the plantation. Captain Murchison and his officers were pleasant companions, and he learned a great deal. The Captain was well-paid for his operation, and the crew also better rewarded than most seamen, thus ensuring that they stayed with the ship.

He learned that the Captain also was hankering after retirement, but trying to build up the biggest fortune he could before calling it a day. Assuming that Robert was still sympathetic to the system of which he had once been a part, the Captain was frank in discussing his work. He also had a fund of stories of narrow escapes and pursuits with which to amuse his passenger. They shared many a bottle as they exchanged tales of their experiences. Robert saw no need to dissemble about the past. Captain Murchison had been well aware of his reason for leaving Pictou. Where he did dissemble was in his attitude towards William. He pretended to have no hard feelings and that he had naturally come to the end of his exile.

After a day in St. John's, a dreary little town, still chilly and grey despite the season, they left it thankfully for Port au Basques, and dropped anchor at the Point, from which they could see the little jetty and the low sheds of the cod-drying plant. Other fishing boats were standing off too. They lowered a boat and rowed into the shore, to be met by John Campbell, who oversaw the operation.

Long time since we met," was Campbell's greeting to Robert. "Hear you had a spot of bother in Pictou and have been looking after one of the Jamaican properties."

Robert assented to this. "Glad to be away from it," he said. "Too humid and too little to do. How are things here?"

"Busy! Always are in this short summer."

"Do you still do the Scottish run?"

Campbell gave him a sharp glance, not suspicious exactly, but cautious. "Why?"

"I've hitched a lift here, and I wondered if there was a chance of hitching one across the ocean. Otherwise, I'll go back to Halifax, but I had a fancy to see Scotland again."

"Maybe we can fix something. Come in anyway, and meet the others."

Some of the workmen Robert remembered from a dozen years ago. Mainly Scots, there were a couple of Irishmen working in the sheds, and a couple of Cornishmen and a Jerseyman belonging to the fishing fleet. Families were not generally encouraged, though the women were as good as the men at filleting the fish and drying it. There was a well-equipped bunkhouse for the single men who formed the bulk of the work-force. Not everyone stayed throughout the winter. Some went off lumbering; others migrated to Pictou or Halifax.

One man sat alone, aloof from the noisy, drinking mob. Robert made a gesture towards him. "A new recruit?" he asked.

Campbell, following the gesture said, "Hardly! Surprised you didn't see him when you were here before. He's actually been around since the early twenties. Tragic, really. He had totally lost his memory. Got picked out of the sea by the Frenchies. They patched him up a bit, then brought him to us. He couldn't speak then and couldn't understand their lingo anyway. Had a cracked head and a busted arm, but those have mended."

"Can he talk now?"

"Yes, he started talking when we tried to get him to crew on one of the fishing boats. He dug his heels in and wouldn't go near the boat. Shouted, "No, no, no" as if we were hauling him to the gallows. He had no idea why he was terrified, but we suspect he'd been on an immigrant ship. He's obviously not a sailor, or he'd have been glad to get on the boat."

"Couldn't you trace him?"

"Well, we asked around, but you know what it's like when we're busy in the summer. We've no-one to spare, and there are so many ships going up the Gulf when the ice breaks. It's like looking for a needle in a haystack. If he could have remembered whether he came from Scotland or England, it would have helped, or if he had known the name of the ship, we could certinly have done something."

"So he's stayed ever since?"

"Sure. He's a good worker on dry land. He earns his keep."

Robert asked, "What is his name?"

"We don't know. We call him Barney on the basis that it was something different from Tom, Dick, Harry and Mick, of which we've got several."

"I'll go over and say hello." Robert was as good as his word. He was intrigued by the story, and felt a strong fellow-feeling for someone exiled from his home, as he had been himself for the last eleven years.

"Robert Thomson," he introduced himself. "I hear you've lost your memory."

"I've lost the first part of my life, if that's what you mean," replied Angus. "I can remember everything since I got rescued by the Frenchmen, but nothing before then. They call me Barney here, so you can do the same. I think I came from Scotland, and I think I used to work with horses. That's all I know."

"You can't recall your family? Did you have a sister, parents, a brother?"

"I can't remember."

"Who was with you on the ship?"

"I don't know. I must have had an accident, because I had a broken arm and a gash on my head."

"One wonders why the ship didn't pick you up. Usually, they're desperately keen not to lose a shipmate or a passenger. Perhaps the ship was damaged or in trouble. Or perhaps they threw you overboard for some reason – you weren't a pirate, were you?"

"I'm terrified of the water. So I think I wasn't a seaman, pirate or otherwise."

"Then you're a passenger, an emigrant from Scotland, who used to be a stable-hand or a rider in some way."

"I had no coat and no boots and  anything that could have identified me has either been left on the ship or I threw them off."

"If you'd been meaning to kill yourself, you'd have left them on!" observed Robert. "I've often felt life wasn't worth living, but I don't think I'd choose to drown as a way of ending it all.  Your family, if you had one, must assume that you're dead.  The Captain would have had to report the loss of a passenger.  It is surprising no-one came in search of you."

"I think the ship must have been going up into the Gulf of St. Lawrence," surmised Angus.  "Whereas the Frenchmen who picked me out of the water were rowing the other way towards Newfoundland.."

"The ship would either be bound for Pictou or Halifax or Quebec," suggested Robert.  "I know Pictou well.  I could enquire there for you – except that I'm not going there immediately.  I'm going to Scotland first – some unfinished business to attend to!"

"It's over thirteen years ago," said Angus  "But if you can find out my real name, it would help me very much.  People here are kind and have given me work and shelter. I'm very grateful – but Barney is not my name."

"I think you need more than a name," said Robert. "I think you need a family – as I do myself.  Perhaps you had a sweetheart, or a father and mother, or brother and sister.  What other skills have you?  Are you educated? Do you read and write?"

"I'm doing both now," answered Angus. "No-one here does either, except for Mr. Campbell, so, as I had no-one to write to, I hadn't bothered. I couldn't talk for years, and then gradually that has come back."

"I think you were educated," observed Robert. "You speak clearly. You compile a proper sentence in your mind instead of uttering phrases. I think you might have come from a good family, or at least from a family that respected education. Have you looked at a map of Scotland to see if any places seem familiar?"

Angus said not, and Robert went away to search for a map. They pored over it together.

"That's Glasgow," pointed out Robert, "And on the eastern side is Edinburgh, the capital, where the cream of society lives."

"E-din-burgh!" repeated Angus slowly, and buried his face in his hands, concentrating fiercely. The Minister had said memory would return, but slowly... "E-din-burgh," he repeated again.

"Does it mean something to you?" asked Robert.

Angus lifted his face. "It could be. I seem to have known cobbled streets and oil-lamps and carriages and big houses with basements ..." His voice trailed away again.

"That's good," encouraged Robert. "You won't have seen cobbled streets and oil-lamps here, but they have them in Glasgow and most probably in Edinburgh too. This must be part of your old memory coming back. Did you have a family there?"

"There was a family in the big house,  but not my family …I don't know …I think I was only there a short time. Perhaps that was where I learned about horses."

"You're doing well.  Think about it some more, and maybe you'll  remember."

Angus was already tracing the map with his finger. "Aberdeen, no, Dundee, no.  Inver-ness …Inverness.  I have heard of Inverness, I think."

"Then  maybe you came from the North or the North-East of Scotland.  Many emigrants did – and still do.  You might have come alone as single men often did. Or you might have come with a family, if you had one."

"I am being welcomed by another  family here," volunteered Angus.  "The Gales in Codroy Valley are being very kind.  Alice has been helping me to read and write again.  Last year I couldn't have read the map."

"I am going to Scotland,"  said Robert.  "Do you want to come too,  if I can get you a passage?"

Angus shuddered.   "It's very kind of you, and possibly it would help.  But I couldn't do it,"   he said. "I've tried to get accustomed to the sea, but even to go out in a fishing-boat is an ordeal."

"Perhaps you could get as far as Pictou.  There are many Scots in Pictou who might have come over at the time you did."

Angus agreed that that was a more practical suggestion.  He had been thinking that he needed to take steps to establish his history if he was to make any headway with Alice's father.

# Chapter Twelve - Detection and Disclosure

Robert had to wait more than a week before he could take passage for Glasgow. There was nothing much to do, and he often joined Angus, after the latter had finished work, for more conversation and efforts to prompt his memory. But the glimpses of Edinburgh that had been aroused were fitful and fleeting, and it seemed that there were neither place-names nor family names that could prompt older recollections.

At last the expected brig hove in sight, creeping through the mist like a shadow. John Campbell set off in a smaller vessel to meet her, with only four of the Scottish workers to help him. Robert surmised that they would be loading the barrels of rum into the lower deck out of earshot and eyesight of those on land. He knew that the illicit cargo would be stabilised with heavy stones, probably already on board from the last trip, and smothered with bits of wood and other ballast. Thus anyone peering in would take the mass below decks for ballast only, and those loading or unloading the legitimate cargo would have no sight of what was concealed beneath. Then the ship would come in to the jetty to have its hold filled with tons of dried cod on top of the ballast, and that would be the only obvious cargo. The quantity and quality of the Newfoundland catch was more than good enough to provide a profit on the voyage, and there were hungry purchasers in the Glasgow markets to buy it. He wondered who would buy the rum – the rich merchants in their splendid houses, or the port innkeepers with customers eager for an inexpensive trip to drunken oblivion?   Probably both!

Normally a fishing brig would carry no passengers. But Captain Frobisher was not averse to Campbell's request to take an old friend to Glasgow.  With both rum and Scotch whisky aboard, he and Robert spent many a garrulous evening together, staggering to their bunks in convivial amity.

The journey was swift for the most part, the ship being pushed ahead by the "roaring forties" and making good speed until almost in sight of Ireland.   The stiff wind gave way to a settled spell of weather, and the ship became virtually becalmed.   The sea was placid and the sky blue with hardly a puff of cloud.

A revenue cutter was spotted in the distance by the look-out man aloft in the rigging.   It altered course to make a leisurely approach, the lighter craft catching what little wind there was, insufficient to move the heavy-laden, deep-bottomed brig.

Captain Frobisher did not seem perturbed. Carrying little sail, he awaited the smaller ship, hailed it cheerfully, and asked if they were coming aboard.  A young Lieutenant, smart in his navy and white uniform with silver buttons and its single epaulette and tricorne hat, was rowed over by four stalwart sailors, and the small boarding-party clambered over the side.   Captain Frobisher produced his papers, "We're Glasgow-bound," he volunteered. "Cargo of dried cod from Newfoundland. Regular run."

"I can smell your cargo!"  agreed the Lieutenant. We'll just take a look in the hold."   The hatch covers were removed by the brig's own seamen, and the fishy smell became even more pronounced. The Lieutenant hesitated. It would take days to shift that lot, he reflected. A case for a port search if anything. But he had no reason to suspect the boat. The trade was legitimate, the way-bill proved the cargo's origin, and past records from the log showed it was the umpteenth time the ship had made the same trip.

"Ye'll take a dram," offered the Captain hospitably. The Lieutenant saw no reason to refuse, and was offered rum or whisky. "All duty paid," said the Captain, producing the refreshment from authentically-labelled bottles, and toasting his visitor. "To your best endeavours, Sir," he said.

It was easy, thought Robert. Legitimate business, strong-smelling cargo, trustworthy Captain, bluffing his way through -- no wonder William had never been caught! Well, he would see about that!

The breeze soon picked up again, the brig crowded on sail, and tied up at Bennett's Wharf less than a month after leaving Port au Basques.

Robert had two sections of the system clear in his mind. He now needed to gain the complete confidence of Simon Bennett in order to understand the mechanics of the operation at the Scottish end. He asked Simon for advice on somewhere to stay, and invited Bennett for a meal at the recommended tavern. They gossiped knowledgeably about the West Indies, Port au Basques and William's surprising move to Scotland. Bennett, having met Robert before, though many years ago, was not suspicious.

"So you've a fancy to see Scotland for yourself?" he asked.

"I was born here," Robert replied, and took out a piece of paper, bearing an address and a sketch-map. "My father came from Morayshire, and left when I was two."

"Aye, well, that's a tidy journey. Ye'll need to take the coach to Edinburgh, and then the Mail northwards, or the coastal packet from Leith."

"If. I've got to go to Edinburgh, I might as well call in on William and Delia," said Robert. "He'll want to know in what state I left the Kingsley plantation. Have you got his direction there?"

Simon provided an address, and Robert led him to think he would catch the coach the following day. Instead of doing that, however, he provided himself with a woolly cap, reefer jacket, oilskin trousers and sea-boots, and hung inconspicuously round the dock-side for a couple of days, picking up a casual labouring job, while he waited for the fish to be off-loaded from the brig. There was no hitch in that operation. Half the crew, their job done, disappeared into the taverns round the dock, but Robert noted that some remained on guard, and with the gangway lifted up.

Simon Bennett's boat-building yard was off Regency Dock in Greenock, and sure enough, the brig moved there at dusk two days later. Robert had trailed her from on land, attracting no attention in his rough, sea-faring gear. It was otherwise when he reached the yard. There was a man on duty at the gate. He could not get too close, but watching from a safe distance, he saw men with pulleys and ropes board the ship.

Some men busied themselves about the decks and the rigging. There was some hammering, but night had almost fallen, and the ship showed only a couple of lights. No serious work of repair could take place till daylight, yet dim figures could be distinguished, moving about the deck by the light of oil-lamps only. The night, which was necessary for the unloading of the contraband cargo, was also helpful to the watcher. Robert could approach quite close to the ship from the seaward side of the wharf without detection, and could gain shelter from the numerous bales, barrels and bulky objects littering it. He was under no illusions as to his fate, if caught. A determined push, and he would be food for the fishes in the murky water of the dock.

A ramp was secured against the ship's side and soon the first of the barrels was rolled down its slipway and into a nearby shed. It was followed by others, as many as one hundred, Robert estimated. In the flare of a flame as a pipe was lit, Captain Frobisher was seen conferring with Simon Bennett. Robert was not near enough to hear what was said, but he observed the handshake before the men parted, Captain Frobisher returning to his ship, and Bennett to the shed.

Robert made a mental note of the time of unloading, and the exact location of the wharf, before creeping away to his tavern, mercifully unobserved. He considered whether to hang around long enough to discover how the rum cargo was decanted from the shed, but rejected the idea. Fortune had favoured him thus far. The cargo's arrival without paying duty was all he needed to know.  It was for the land revenue to investigate the rest.

* * *

Robert's subsequent trip to Edinburgh was uneventful,  although he enjoyed the landscape and the chatter of his companions on the box of the coach.  He marvelled at the extent of the City when he finally arrived, at the tall houses and the noise on the cobbled streets.  It was vastly different from anything in Pictou or Jamaica! Perhaps the sights and sounds would trigger Barney's memory, if he were only here.

Armed with William's address,  he sought out the street, and observed the house with its flight of steps to the front door,  furnished with a brass knocker.    The windows on either side of the door were curtained with lace and he could not see inside.

Eventually a carriage drew up at the door, and a lady and young lad emerged from the house and were handed into the carriage.  Robert recognised Delia, her dark hair confined in a modish hat, and a stylish coat buttoned to her throat.  The youngster must be Gilbert, a slender youth in a grey tail-coat.    There was no sign of William.

The carriage pulled away, and Robert wondered whether to call in the absence of the mistress of the house, and ask for its master.  He had compiled a dossier of the smuggling system, beginning with its origin in Jamaica, detailing the trans-shipments in Port au Basques, and concluding with the double unloading in the two Greenock ship-yards.  He entitled his dossier "The Pictou Triangle."

He could simply post it anonymously to the Revenue, or deliver it to their offices in person. Somehow that seemed an underhand thing to do. He thought of his friends, Captains Murchison and Frobisher, of the upright John Campbell at Port au Basques, honestly working for the most part at his cod-drying plant, and handling contraband rum on the side. Was he justified in betraying them just because of his grudge against William? There was Simon Bennett, too – a respectable fish importer and boat-builder, but topping up his income on the side. He liked them all; they were not hardened criminals, though the law would treat them as such when and if it caught up with them. Could he deliver William to justice in any other way, without betraying his friends and associates?

He knew William was different. He had to be the murderer of Judge Fogo, his own wife's father. Robert questioned the effect on Delia if her ordered world were destroyed? What would be the effect on Gilbert if he hoped to take up the law as a profession? That his own father would be exposed as a smuggler of contraband and a criminal would surely shatter the young man's career.

What would happen to William himself? The authorities would arrest and imprison him, Robert was fairly sure. Then the case would come to trial. Perhaps William would hire one of those clever lawyers who would argue to keep him out of prison. Perhaps William would face a massive fine and be ruined. So too would be his family. Robert could not picture Delia seeking to earn her living as a Governess, and she was surely blameless in all this. She might have money of her own and not be destitute, but her status in society would be ruined.

Robert could feel the resolve, which had burned steadily in his mind throughout two voyages, flicker and falter. He was now in two minds. He could not burst in upon William with his conviction undermined. He would have to think this through more carefully and weigh up the pros and cons.

Robert turned on his heel and trudged back to the inn he had made his temporary base.

Throughout a long night Robert wrestled with his problem and his conscience.

That William needed to be punished, he was in no doubt. The murder of the Judge, and his own enforced exile as a suspect for eleven long years needed to be avenged. Was the divulging of the illicit smuggling trade the best punishment? Should he just execute William himself?

He spent the early hours of the morning pondering how he could achieve this? A firearm would have to be acquired. He knew not where. An accident could perhaps be contrived. Could he push William off the quay to drown, as he suspected he would have been pushed, had he been discovered at Bennett's Wharf? Perhaps not -- it would be hard to lure William to a quayside in the first place, and there could be witnesses to testify against him. Robert shuddered at the thought that he might be convicted of murder and hanged, or at least spend the rest of his life in a stinking jail. No, William was not worth that risk. The more he struggled to solve the problem of William's demise, the more he grudgingly admired the decisiveness and skill with which William had disposed of

Judge Fogo. Two birds with one stone, or one shot, indeed!

Poison? No sooner was this considered than it was dismissed. He knew nothing of poisons, nor how to obtain them. Then William would almost certainly suspect his efforts to be friendly and be wary enough not to drink with him.

Drink! He tossed down some of the brandy he had had the forethought to purchase earlier. Could he fight William? Waylay him in the dark with a strong cudgel and beat him to death? The Watch would be on to him, he suspected, for William would fight back, and then there would be the arrest, imprisonment, hanging as before.

While these improbable ideas coursed through his mind, Robert began to feel that he would be as guilty as William. A murder, even of a murderer, would be entirely wrong. No, his first idea was the best. Ruin William's source of illicit income and make him face the music. He thought he ought to warn Delia. But his warning would not be credible without disclosing the truth about Judge Fogo's death. That alone would ruin her marriage. So it should! She was too good a woman to be tied to that miserable blackguard for the rest of her life.

Another brandy convinced him that he should first see Delia, then tell William what he meant to do, and then do it!

\* \* \*

Thus fortified, Robert set off the following morning, overlooking in his new-found decision what had been the consequences of Judge Fogo making a similar disastrous decision to confront William with his iniquities, and thus give him an all-important warning.

Robert plied the knocker of the Edinburgh house, and the door was opened by a manservant. He had no visiting cards, but had taken the trouble to write his name and business on a plain card, which he handed to the footman as he asked to see Mr. William Mackenzie.

The master was not at home, replied the footman. Would he be wishful to see Mrs.Mackenzie? Robert agreed and asked that his card be taken to her.

As he climbed the elegant staircase to a saloon on the first floor, Robert had time to admire the magnificence of William's Edinburgh abode. It reeked of money and style. Robert felt another surge of fury that all this had been acquired while he had been enduring the discomforts of steamy Jamaica.

Delia was standing by the window. She made a half-turn towards him, but did not advance or hold out her hand. Robert saw a statuesque woman, dark hair piled high on her head, but without the teasing ringlet he remembered she used to wear, descending over one shoulder. Her elegant dress was made high to the neck with narrow lace ruffles – some blue and shiny material, long and full. Her complexion was paler than he remembered, the high bloom of youth having faded. He caught his breath in admiration, and made a formal bow.

She inclined her head in acknowledgment. She saw a strong, tall and well-built man in plain brown suiting, his face clean-shaven and tanned and with the piercing blue eyes that she well remembered. His still brown hair, tinged with the Thomson red, was long but pulled back in a clasp. He had filled out since his days as a twenty-year old, and looked powerful and determined. Was he married now, she wondered.

"This is a surprise, Mr. Thomson," she said. "You have been given up for lost in Pictou. Wherever have you been?"

So William had told her nothing of the Jamaican hide-away!

"Did your husband not tell you …?"

She looked puzzled. "Tell me what? As far as I know you ran away when my father was shot. I know it was an accident. It had to be. I have cursed your carelessness as I grieved for him, but you had no motive for a deliberate act …"

"*I* had no motive, true," he said. "But others had!

"Others? There were no others, save you and my husband."

"Exactly," he said. There was a moment of silence as the word sank home.

Delia's brow furrowed. She motioned him to a chair, and sat down herself.

I think you must tell me more. What is your purpose in coming to see me?"

"To warn you," he said. "I believe William to have killed your father because the Judge threatened to expose his illegal trade in contraband rum. The fortune William has amassed is largely based on this, although he has many other sources of income. When I was a young man, I became involved in the smuggling trade too, for a lark. I know that the Judge overheard an incautious remark that

I made, and I know that he confronted William with his suspicions afterwards."

"Contraband rum!  But William  has estates and shipping.  He does not need to run contraband."

"I  know," said Robert.  "I have puzzled over that myself.  Why?  I think it is in the nature of the man.  He must be so used to courting danger that it is like meat and drink to him.  He cannot do without it."

"But it must be supposition that such a discovery by my father led to he shooting accident."

"It is not supposition that William contrived to spirit me away to Jamaica after the shooting as the only witness, and keep me out there, while he played the innocent!"

Delia looked at him in mounting horror.  "You are telling me that my husband plotted to kill my father to save his own skin, and laid the blame on you …No, No!  Why should I believe you?   William told the court it was an accident."

"You can believe me because William has been paying me all these years to keep out of the way."

She seized on the minor issue.   "Where have you been?  Your brother, Alexander,  has been searching high and low for you?   Your disappearance has caused your family untold distress."

"I am aware …and that is what I find most unforgivable.  No, William found work for me on his Jamaican sugar estate and paid hush-money into my account in Halifax.  He has kept writing to say it was not safe for me to return to Pictou.  He has treated me like a conspirator and a scapegoat – and I am come to settle my account, and bring him to some sort of justice. However, I don't want you and your son to be hurt more than you need be, and so I thought I should warn you in advance of what I mean to do."

Delia was silent, her thoughts in a torment, half of disbelief, half of concern for the future. Robert admired her self-control. There were no hysterics, no tears, but her hands were twisting and turning, kneading the tightly clasped handkerchief in her lap.

For her part, Delia's mind was racing, trying to absorb the shocking accusation she had just been told. .She had grown apart from her husband over the years, but she had no reason to complain of his lack of generosity. He expected her to preside over his mansion, to facilitate their entry into society, to bring up their son as a gentleman. He provided the means to do all this. She had consented to the move to Scotland because it would be best for Gilbert's future. Now was all this to be put at risk by dangerous and malicious charges from a renegade?

Finally she spoke. "I cannot begin to make sense of all this. How do I know that you have not been blackmailing William all this time? You tell me that he has given you money. Are you threatening to expose him because you want more?"

Robert could appreciate her dilemma, though he winced at the accusation of blackmail. He saw that he had to do more to convince her. He produced his dossier from his inside pocket.

"This is the detailed account of William's years of duplicity in cheating the revenue and making his illicit fortune. I mean to lay the information with the Revenue. It is a sort of revenge, if you like, for the years of my life he has stolen from me. It is a means of expiation for the Judge's death. He would have exposed William like a shot – and he died for it."

She held out her hand for the document. He hesitated, unwilling to surrender possession, but arguing with himself that she had the right to look at it.

Delia began to read. It was there in black and white – an accusation of deliberate fraud, stretching back fifteen years and more, the names of the ships, the places, the people involved, the methods used. She was appalled. The daughter of a Judge, with a son who was studying law, she understood now that her husband was operating on the wrong side of the law. He could be convicted as a criminal, could go to jail.

Robert took back the papers as they dropped from her hand. "I am sorry to cause you distress," he said. "Believe me when I say that I thought this a less brutal way than to leave you to discover it when the law officers enter the house."

Delia shuddered at the thought. "Is there no way of avoiding this disclosure?"

Robert was non-plussed for a moment. "You cannot mean that," he said. "The commandment says "Thou shalt not kill." I intend to keep quiet about the killing, for I can prove nothing, although I swear that is how is happened. But the evil must be punished in some way. Would your father have expected you to turn a blind eye?"

"No, of course he would not. But this is too sudden, too overwhelming! What do you think I should do?"

"I wondered if you might wish to return to Pictou," suggested Robert. "You would have friends who could help, and this action would take place in Scotland, which has a proper legal system. There would be fewer repercussions back in Pictou. Some gossip, no doubt."

"I would return to Pictou if I had only myself to consider. It has been my home, and I love it there. But I have Gilbert to think about."

"Edinburgh is surely not the only university where he might pursue his studies."

"True, but it is probably the best. Also, he is enrolled now and would find it strange to be taken away."

Robert rose. "It may be that the law will catch up with William anyway. People tell me that suspicions have been aroused by his trade between the West Indies and Halifax. I think he has closed that down, but I know for a fact that the Atlantic run to Glasgow is continuing. I even travelled on the ship, which ran the contraband. You will hate me for disturbing your life," he said. "I would like to say that I am truly sorry."

"Could you not stay your hand for a while? I might persuade William to stop this stupid illegal trade."

"I should counsel you most strongly not to discuss it with William. I will do that myself. I shall not say I have told you. You may wish to pretend ignorance, but meanwhile you have at least an opportunity to make what plans you may. I hope you prosper in spite of all this. I intend to wait upon William tomorrow if I can. I wish you goodbye."

As Robert withdrew, Delia moved again to the window, and stood looking out unseeingly at the Square where nursemaids and children were taking the air. The scene was peaceful, in stark contrast to her inner turmoil. She did not seriously doubt what Robert had told her, and in a way she was glad that he had, but her peace was shattered. Murder, smuggling – her husband was living a big lie, which was soon to be exposed. How could she rescue her son and herself from this sudden chaos?

Unbidden, the thought crept into her mind that she had faced a similar catastrophe in her life once before, when William had struck her for her childlessness. She had ridden in solitude then, until she had found a solution. She would walk alone and think this crisis through. The image of Judge Fogo's face, as he bent over his treasured grandson sprang unbidden to her mind. His death had been a wicked, wicked act. If he were here, what would he advise?

Choosing a hat with a veil, which she hoped would deter casual acquaintances, Delia left her home to pace alone with her problems through the Castle grounds.

# Chapter Thirteen - An Ignominious Return

If Robert had imagined that his odyssey to Scotland had been unobserved, he was sadly mistaken. Although he had aroused no overt suspicion in his meetings and his wanderings, the bush telegraph had been busy, keeping William informed.

First, Captain Murchison had included in his report the fact that Robert Thomson had taken passage to Port au Basques on the *Mary Ann*. Strange, William had pondered when this intelligence reached him. He had expected Robert to go straight back to Halifax and Pictou, the home from which he had been parted for so long.

Then John Campbell had written from Port au Basques, using a code to indicate that rum had been loaded on to Capt. Frobisher's brig, and gossiping that Robert Thomson had taken passage also en route to Morayshire. The letter went via the same ship that Robert had travelled on, but because he had spent more than two days in Greenock, it sped to Edinburgh before him. Odd, thought William, that Thomson was coming to Scotland, ostensibly to visit his birthplace. He hoped their paths would not cross.

Finally a hand-over consignment bill between Capt. Frobisher and Simon Bennett contained an appended note that Robert Thomson had disembarked and enquired about William's Edinburgh address, which Simon had given him. He hoped that was all right. It was all wrong, thought William. Robert might be seeking a confrontation. Well, forewarned was forearmed, and he would be prepared.

It was not difficult for William to absent himself from his Edinburgh home. He had established an office in the City, and he had many activities to engage upon. He awaited developments, hoping that Robert would take himself off to Morayshire, without them having occasion to meet.

The first intimation that he had not done so came from the footman when William returned home that evening. A Mr. Robert Thomson had called, the servant told him, and had seen Mrs. Mackenzie.

William trod up the stairs to the saloon, in some trepidation, and found Delia busy with some embroidery.

"Ah, so you're back," she observed brightly. "I had a surprise visitor this morning."

"Indeed, who?" he asked, though knowing perfectly well.

"That Robert Thomson, who went missing from Pictou after my father was killed."

"Thomson! What is he doing in Edinburgh?"

"He's going to wait on you tomorrow, so I presume he'll tell you."

William's mind was working furiously, when his wife spoke again in an accusing tone.

"He said you knew where he had been all along – on your Jamaican plantation."

There was no point in denying it. "Yes, well," admitted William. "He escaped via the *Mary Ann.* Naturally I didn't know about it at the time, but he was desperate to get work, and so I told them to take him on."

"Robert said he became your Manager. I never heard you mention his name, or that you kept in touch all the time. Why didn't you tell his family you knew where he was? They were so worried."

"If I'd told them," he answered smoothly, "The Court would have wanted him to come back and explain the accident. It would have re-opened all the old wounds. Better to let sleeping dogs lie, I thought. What else did he say?"

"Oh, by-the-by, I've got the invitations for the Queen's Coronation Ball," Delia said, changing the subject.

"Very good," he commended. "Does that include Gilbert?"

"Regretfully, no. The tickets are scarce as gold dust, and I could only achieve two, by a good deal of persuasion."

"What else did Robert Thomson say?" William persisted.

"Oh, he was asking about his family, and I told him all the news I could remember. I asked him what he was going to do now that he had left Jamaica."

"And what is he planning to do? Why has he come to Scotland?"

"He didn't divulge. Perhaps he'll tell you tomorrow."

"I offered to let him buy the plantation," William said.

"I think he has had enough of Jamaica," replied his wife.

With that William had to be content. He covertly observed Delia's demeanour. She seemed quite serene, stitching away contentedly. Thomson had certainly implicated him in his disappearance, but perhaps had not tried to shift the blame. Why then had he come? There must be more to the visit than social chit-chat with Delia. He sensed that the morrow's interview could hold more danger. He excused himself on the grounds that he wanted a breath of air before changing for dinner, and left the house.

\* \* \*

Robert spent the evening in the only way he knew – making friends with strangers and drinking the hours away. He made a few plans before facing one of the most critical meetings of his life. He paid his shot at the Inn, checked the coach times to Inverness, and packed his valise. He thought it would be best to put as many miles as possible between himself and his adversary, and leave for the North with all speed after seeing William. He procured a large white bag and put his dossier in it, addressing it to the Commissioner of Revenue for Scotland, at an address which he discovered from the Landlord.

What he failed to do was anticipate William's killer instinct.

The next morning, Robert walked towards the Mackenzie's house, carrying his valise. It was a respectable district, and he had no concerns about his safety, but suddenly, however, he was jumped upon by two stalwart rogues, and dragged down the alley from which they had unexpectedly emerged.

Instinctively he fought back, winding one with a sharp elbow to the stomach, and trying to swing his fist to the other's jaw. This failed to connect, and a hefty punch landed on his own cheekbone instead. He remembered the first rule of stopping slaves from fighting. Grab hold of each, and knock their heads together! But the Edinburgh heavies had more skills in rough and tumble than he or his Jamaican slaves. The winded one hooked Robert's feet from under him, and he fell heavily into the runnel in the middle of the alley. The one with the hefty punch also possessed a powerful right boot. Robert could only try to protect his head with his arms while four boots pounded his ribs and his back and his legs mercilessly. He wondered why they didn't just grab the valise and escape with their booty.

This seemed also to be the objective of the winded one. "Come on, Sam," he urged. "Let's scarper before we're sussed."

"Time enough," replied the man with the hefty punch, who seemed to be in charge.

He aimed a mighty blow at Robert's jaw, and seemed to be satisfied that he had rendered his victim unconscious. "There you are, help yourself," he added, pointing his confederate in the direction of Robert's watch. Fumbling in the inner pocket of the unconscious man, he withdrew the large white bag with much satisfaction. "This is what we have to give the boss," he said.

"Then, let's get away before the Watch is on us."

"Nay," said Sam. "We're to take him with us. Do tha get under his left shoulder and I'll tak the right, and we'll haul him to yon barrow and stow him under the swedes."

This programme was soon accomplished, the barrow having been placed ready by the organiser of the attack. The winded one was left to mind the barrow while Sam straightened his jerkin and necktie, and waited on William Mackenzie's house in the adjoining square.

"First part done," he reported, when the door was opened by the owner himself.

"Good!" replied William. "Have you obtained the documents?"

"Reckon these must be them," said Sam, handing over the white package.

William checked it briefly and agreed.

"Well done! Second part. You're to move him to the *Margaret Bogle* at Leith, bound for Pictou. Buy him a passage in steerage, get him aboard with his baggage, and remove yourselves from the area as fast as you can. Here's 25 guineas – and a letter to give the Captain, which will cover the fare. The rest is for you and your mate. Mind, the master of the ship is known to me, and so I shall know if you've done your part right. If you come back to my office in a week's time you shall have the other 25 guineas, making fifty which I promised. Is that clear? No killing. All I want is him out of this country."

"Clear as daylight, yr honour. I want no truck with killing neither."

"Then do what I say."

William turned back into the house, and Sam returned to his mate. "Has he come round?" he asked.

"Not shifted a bit. But I've been through this bag of his, and there's good clobber we can share between us. Have you got the cash?"

"Some of it," said Sam, "But we've got more work to do before we gets the rest. We've got to put him on board ship, and that's seven mile away."

"Dang me, if we ought to bother. Leave him be, and we can go and wet our whistles at the Bull."

"Don't you ever think, man! You'd have him set the Watch on us once he gets his wits back. Nay, there's more good money for us if we do the toff's bidding."

"We'll have to hire a hoss and cart, then."

"You're a market man. Can you find one if we pay?"

"You're a seaman. Can you get him on the ship?"

"I reckon." Sam handed over five of his guineas to his partner, and the deal was done.

* * *

"Who was that?" asked Delia curiously, as William turned back into the hall from the front door.

"Just a fellow Robert Thomson had sent to say he was going up to Morayshire, and would call on his way back instead."

"Oh. Strange. He seemed most determined to see you when he called yesterday."

William shrugged. "People change their minds," he observed, and thought he should try and find out exactly how much Robert had divulged already.

"Did he give you any indication what he wanted to talk to me about?" he asked.

"Not really," Delia dissembled. "Only he seemed to be very unhappy that he had stayed in Jamaica so long.

He said he had missed many years of his life. Perhaps he is making up for it."

"He was well paid!" asserted William, "And it kept him safe."

"He seemed to think that he had wasted all those years. Money isn't everything," she declared.

"It is to a lot of people. Did you get the impression that he wanted more?"

"No ... .Of course I don't know what was in his mind, but I think he had some feelings of resentment."

"Resentment about what?"

Delia sensed danger. There were a lot more questions than the incident warranted. For the first time she felt a *frisson* of fear. She must not divulge to William the suspicions Robert harboured about him. Robert had urged her not to do so. But then Robert had said he would talk to William himself, and he had not kept that undertaking. She did not know what to think.

"He did not tell me," she answered. "Perhaps resentment that we are living well here in Edinburgh as we did in Pictou, and he has relatively nothing."

"I would remind you that I made good money out of my Jamaican plantations," answered William, "And he could have done the same. Did he hint at any secrets he thinks he knows, that could give an excuse for blackmail?" She had turned away from him and moved half-way up the stairs. She was terrified that if he continued to press her, she would give something away. The very fact that the question was asked seemed to confirm Robert's accusations. She could not stay here to be cross-questioned, or the man who was her husband would worm information out of her, and that might spell danger for Robert.

"Secrets!" she achieved a light and slightly amused tone. "Why, no," she answered. "And blackmail! I would not suspect it of a man we have known for most of our lives." She retreated up the stairs, and left William still wondering. He thought Robert must have said something to Delia, but what?

\* \* \*

Since her walk in the Castle Grounds, Delia had reached several important conclusions:

Firstly, that she did not wish to spend the rest of her life in the arid environment of her marriage to William. Secondly, that she must ensure that Gilbert completed his legal training and became settled before she cut the ties with William and that must entail her remaining in Scotland for the time being. Thirdly, that she would probably wish to return to Pictou at some stage, although she would like to see more of the world before she did so. Fourthly, that she must ensure she had enough financial resources to sustain all these ambitions.

A second husband did not feature in these plans. Admittedly she was not tired of men – the interest aroused by the brief meeting with Robert Thomson, now a handsome, attractive man, was proof of this – but her plans were for herself, rather than as part of a couple.

Divorce was so unacceptable socially that she did not consider it an option. However, many people went their own way, and formed their own circle of friends, took lovers even. Though the dissolute Regency period had come to a close and the teachings of a strict Church were re-establishing moral values, the change was gradual, as yet.   She needed an excuse to detach herself from William, to form a separate establishment, to set up her own group of like-minded friends.

Her thoughts turned to her mother's cousin,  the lady who had  chaperoned her in Halifax.  Cicely must be verging on old age now,  but correspondence, though infrequent, had kept the connection alive.  She had not visited her aunt since arriving in Scotland, and it was high time she paid a courtesy visit.  The letter was penned and a fortnight provisionally blocked off in her social diary for such an excursion to take place.  William would not want to go,  which he confirmed when she suggested the visit, and she could not take Gilbert away from his University studies.   Therefore she would need to take her maid for convenience and to conform to custom.

She knew little of the rest of Scotland, but Tain was on the southern shore of the Dornoch Firth, way beyond Inverness.    A coach trip, or perhaps a coastal steamer would be the best way to travel.   She would enquire tomorrow.

Tain would probably be too far from Edinburgh to be a likely place to find a second home, but Cousin Cicely would be able to advise on suitable locations, she was sure.   The idea of a separate establishment could result from the visit.  It could be explained to William in that light, rather than as a consequence of the upset of Robert's intervention.

Delia wondered why Robert had changed his mind and not kept his appointment.  He had assured her twice that he would tell William his intentions himself and he meant to do so the next morning. He had wished her to pretend ignorance. Was that because he was afraid for her safety? Had he indeed considered his own safety? She wondered if she had been indiscreet in what she had told William last night.

She thought not. But why had William gone out unexpectedly afterwards? And why had Robert not come again?

Instinctively she assumed William was lying when he said Robert had sent a message. Who then was the man who had come to the door? Why had William opened the door himself instead of letting the footman do it? Delia shivered. She profoundly hoped that nothing sinister had happened to Robert – and for the second time she felt afraid of the hidden depths in her husband's character. If he had murdered once, could he have struck again, or would he strike again in future? She would have to be very watchful.

# Chapter Fourteen - Close Relations

The *Margaret Bogle* was riding at anchor in Leith, near Edinburgh, when Robert Thomson's comatose body was rowed across to her, and bundled unceremoniously on board. The more articulate of the two miscreants who had attacked him, handed a letter to the Captain, Walter Smith. The Captain opened it, noted the glint of gold coins inside and nodded briefly.

Robert was lowered into the hold and stowed in a spare bunk, amid the bustling pandemonium of excited emigrants, trying to find room for their baggage and possessions in the gloom of the steerage quarters. There were more than two hundred of them in the deep, copper-bottomed hull of the former whaling ship, and each had paid a few pounds for their uncomfortable transit from poverty-stricken Scotland to the new opportunities offered by the wide expanses of North America.

Robert was breathing heavily and unevenly, and more than one of the members of a family near him gave him a wary glance. His clothing reeked of whisky and they assumed he was drunk and would sleep off his excesses, but the breathing became more stertorous and accompanied by groaning of a sepulchral kind. At last a stalwart farmer approached the bunk and shook Robert's shoulder. It was then that the man saw blood on his clothing and drew away. There was a muttered consultation with the family, and the farmer responsibly took it upon himself to report that there was an injured man among the passengers.

"Mortal bad he looks," the farmer told a sailor, after clambering up the ladder to the deck. The sailor told the Second Mate, and, as all emigrant ships carrying more than a hundred passengers now had to have a Doctor on board, medical aid was despatched below.

The Doctor in question was a twenty-year old medical student from Edinburgh, working his passage back home to Upper Canada after three years of study at the Medical School. Until he came to Edinburgh Neil Thomson had been lodging in Quebec with his Uncle Alexander and Aunt Isabella, herself a Scottish lady who had married Alexander in 1831. Neil's own father, Nathaniel, oversaw and farmed his brother, Alexander's land in the Huron Tract. The talented eldest son had been sent away for schooling and abroad to learn a profession, as such skills were much needed in the emerging territories.

Neil descended into the dim hold, and picked his way through the melée, escorted by the concerned farmer. He asked for an oil-lamp to be brought closer so that he could examine the extent of Robert's injuries. He did not like the uneven sound of the breathing, and on removing his patient's coat and waistcoat, he could feel the rib-cage compressed and possibly damaging the lung. There were contusions on the head too, though both legs seemed whole. He was not sure about the right arm and shoulder. Having felt the injuries, Neil and the farmer laid Robert gently on the floor of the hold, the better to allow attention. Released from the cramped middle bunk, six feet long, but only eighteen inches high, Neil saw his patient to be a white man with reddish-brown hair, clean-shaven except for side-burns, and well-dressed in clean, but blood-spattered clothes. His hands were not roughened, as the farmer's were, by constant manual work in all weathers, but smooth and strong with well-tended finger nails. He was a gentleman or merchant, concluded Neil, an unusual occupant for a steerage bunk. Such passengers would have been more likely to book a cabin for the voyage.

Attempts to revive the man were initially unsuccessful, but eventually Robert swallowed a little water and opened unfocussed eyes to his new surroundings.

"You have some broken ribs," diagnosed Neil. "What happened to you?"

"Attacked …two men . ." muttered Robert.

"Were you robbed?"

"Dunno …papers…money…" the injured man managed to utter.

Neil gave him more water, and felt in the pockets of the coat.

"No papers," he said. "No money. No watch. You must have been set upon by footpads. But it is not usual for them to treat you quite so brutally. Also, who brought you here?"

However, Robert had relapsed again into a stupor and could not respond to questioning. Neil made him as comfortable as he could, left him in the care of the farmer and his guidwife, and reported to the Captain.

Captain Smith was not much interested in what Neil had to say. Absorbed as he was in the preparations for leaving port – getting visitors ashore, hoisting sail, shouting instructions, paying heed to the port pilot, and a dozen other simultaneous actions – he had to concentrate on departure while the tide was full. To Neil's suggestion that the passenger be off-loaded and the Watch contacted, Captain Smith re-acted with a brusque "Nay, his passage is paid," and "Tend him as best ye can."

* * *

Among the cabin passengers on the *Margaret Bogle* was a youngish lady called Elizabeth Ritchie. At long last Elizabeth was going to North America to be re-united with her family, who had emigrated fourteen years ago. By now the disaster, which had overtaken the family, the loss overboard from the *Ruby* of Elizabeth's brother, Angus, had been reluctantly accepted by all. The surviving members of the family, father, mother and younger brother, Matthew, had gradually prospered and kept urging Elizabeth to join them. She, however, having served seven years with the family who first appointed her their governess, had been offered another prestigious position with a titled family, at double the salary, to educate their three young daughters at their country castle. By then convinced that her favourite elder brother, Angus, must be dead, Elizabeth had accepted the opportunity.

The titled family had proved congenial. They did not dismiss their governess purely as a paid servant. Elizabeth was invited to parties as a duenna to her charges, and expected to instruct them in manners and genteel behaviour. If there was a balancing female needed for a dinner party, Elizabeth was distinguished by a request to join the family circle.  She could appreciate the difference in attitude between her former employers, who were merely genteel, and her subsequent ones, who were of the nobility, and had no need to puff off their consequence.

Thus Elizabeth had been reluctant to undertake the arduous journey to a strange land while she was treated with such distinction at home in Scotland.  Latterly, however, her mother's letters had become desperate pleas to see her only daughter again.  As the time of her usefulness to the daughters of the peer was drawing to a close, Elizabeth determined to take a vacation from education.  She obtained a glowing reference, which would stand her in good stead if she were to return in future, and took passage on the *Margaret Bogle*, which was sailing to Pictou and Quebec.

She found her cabin restricted and confined after her spacious quarters in the castle.

The sailors were hearty, uncouth and bawdy.  She shrank from talking to them.  The stream of emigrants coming aboard was from the Scottish peasantry.  Unlike most gentlewomen, who would have brought a maid, Elizabeth was travelling alone.  She found herself the only female at dinner.  While Captain Smith politely did his best to make her feel welcome, she felt that his other officers were embarrassed by her presence.  Their conversation was mainly with a trio of merchants, who seemed to be travelling on business and were used to the ship's customs, drinking freely and laughing at one another's jokes.

Elizabeth kept her eyes on her plate. The food was good and fresh, as they were still drawing supplies from the harbour. Only a very young man, who joined the table late, did she feel drawn to as a travelling companion. Neil addressed the Captain first, "Your passenger is still unconscious," he said. "I cannot get a word out of him as to his name or status."

The Captain shrugged, "I must make our Doctor, Neil Thomson, known to you, Miss Ritchie," he said.

Suddenly the ship, which had been moving forward slowly, pitched and rolled as it hit a substantial wave. "It's a bit rougher, outside the harbour bar," commented the Captain. "Hang on to your plate, madam!"

Elizabeth felt she needed to hang on to her stomach, which was behaving strangely.

"It takes a while to find one's sea-legs," observed Dr. Thomson, as her countenance whitened. "You may prefer to lie down if it gets rougher."

Elizabeth pressed her handkerchief to her lips. "I am not used to the sea," she replied.

Neil sympathised. "Nor are most of our passengers. We shall have wailing and lamentations for a couple of days, while we sail north round the Cape, but in a couple more days, they'll be as right as rain, and begin to enjoy the voyage."

"Are you a good sailor?" she asked.

"I was not ill on the voyage to Scotland," he answered, "And therefore I hope so. I'm sure I'll be kept busy by those who think their last hour has come. Keep sipping water," he advised her.

Elizabeth thought him kind and charming. Her experience of men was limited, but she liked the way his auburn hair flopped forward over his brow. He was fair of skin, and had a firm mouth beneath a long nose. She thought his eyes an unusually piercing blue, and his lashes were darker than his hair, a pleasing feature, for gingery brows and eyelashes tended to spoil the average Highlander's appearance, particularly if combined with a florid countenance. Dr. Thomson was pale, youthfully slim, and undoubtedly handsome, but much younger than herself."

The Captain excused himself from the company, "We shall be dropping the pilot soon," he explained, and as he did so, there was another alarming lurch from the elderly, converted whaling ship.

"Have you been qualified long?" asked Elizabeth of the young Doctor.

"I'm half-way through my training," answered Neil. "Most of the medical work is under my belt, but there is surgery and any special studies ahead of me."

"And where will you go when you qualify?" she enquired.

He hesitated. "There's so much scope in the New World. Hospitals are few and far between. My Uncle Alexander would like me to work at Grosse Ile, which is in the Gulf of St. Lawrence, and a busy quarantine hospital for immigrants. Maybe I will, but general medicine is also much needed in the growing communities. People die when they need not, partly because our medical skills are so imperfect and there are too few of us. There's scope for research and there's a need for better surgery. Our population is expanding with every ship that braves the Atlantic crossing, and with every bairn that's born to the mainly young people who make the crossing."

"My family came over to Pictou," volunteered Elizabeth. "At first it was very difficult for them, because my elder brother was lost on the voyage out, but my younger brother is now a grown man, and has shouldered much of the work of the farm."

"Is this just a visit, or will you stay?" asked Neil.

"I do not know. I am a governess, and I do not know what scope there may be for employment in North America."

"It's quite good, I believe, in the towns," Neil replied. "There is a growing society in Quebec, where my Aunt Isabella lives. She is the wife of my Uncle Alexander, and she plays an active role in society, and does a lot of charity work. He is the Government Immigration Agent, which is why he wishes me to work at Grosse Ile."

"Will you need to return to Edinburgh to complete your course?"

"Yes, this is but a three-month vacation. I must return in the autumn, probably on the last trip of this ship, if I meet with Captain Smith's approval."

The ship's irregular motion was causing Elizabeth's head to swim. She was grateful for Neil's hand beneath her elbow as she retired to her cabin. Such a nice young man, she thought, as she tottered to the tiny booth, hanging on to her bunk for dear life, as the swell rolled the ship again and again.

Neil meanwhile went below to check on his patient. He seemed to be sleeping more normally, his head raised on one of the farmer's baggage rolls, and Neil did not disturb him, merely covering Robert's body with a spare blanket brought from his medical cabin.

He occupied one of the larger cabins, able to accommodate some basic items of medical equipment, including a bench and a basin, a shelf with a deep rim, to contain any bottles or potions he might need. There was also a tilting looking glass. Neil felt Robert would benefit from being brought up to the fresher air of the upper deck, and went in search of the steward to ask whether a spare cabin was available. Mercifully there was, and Neil sought the Captain's permission for its use.

Captain Smith had returned to the state-room once the Pilot had been dropped, and he could safely leave the ship in charge of the First Mate. Now well into a second bottle, he was feeling benign and gave the requested permission, no doubt reflecting that the gold coins in his envelope adequately covered the cost, with a slice left over for himself.

Thus next morning Robert was hoisted up the companion-way in a canvas sling by two brawny seamen, and installed in the spare cabin, where Neil could keep a close eye on him. He told Elizabeth of his success in getting the man moved, as he mixed a draught for her to try and help settle her unruly stomach. She offered to sit with the invalid as soon as she felt better.

Robert's bruising was coming out, and turning livid and purple. Neil cautiously felt the right arm and shoulder. He felt no bones were broken, other than the collar-bone and the cracked ribs, but he would have to keep his patient as still as possible for these to mend properly, and that would not be easy if fever developed. A cool compress on the temple, which had suffered the most bruising, could help. Some of the spattered blood seemed to have come from a torn ear and a gash on the chin. These he cleaned up, and Robert opened his eyes during Neil's ministrations.

"Where am I?" Robert asked the classic question as he became conscious of the movement of the ship.

"Aboard the *Margaret Bogle*, out from Edinburgh and bound for North America," replied Neil. "The question is who are you?"

"I'm Robert Thomson, once of Pictou," answered the patient.

"Strange! My name is Thomson too," commented Neil. "I'm glad you can remember anyway. That crack on the head hasn't harmed you as much as it might have done."

Robert tried to shrug and winced as the pain washed over him again. "Are you a Doctor?" he asked. "What's the damage?"

"Yes, I'm the ship's doctor for this voyage, working my passage home to America. You've got some broken ribs, four or five probably, a broken collar-bone, a lot of bruising, particularly on the right side, some superficial facial cuts, and I need your help to check what else."

Robert groaned. "There were two hefty fellows who jumped on me in an alley-way."

"You may tell me the whole story later. What we have to do now is check for other problems and make you comfortable. This is a four or five week voyage, depending on what weather we meet, so there is plenty of time to get you fit before we see land again."

Apart from a twisted and strained knee, no further injuries were discovered. Exhausted by having the rest of his clothing removed, and a strapping wound round his chest, Robert again fell asleep. When he awoke, the steward had made some broth which he was urged to sip. It tasted good and Robert began to feel human again – so much so that he asked for whisky or rum.

His youthful medical adviser prohibited this.

"It will help dull the pain," urged Robert.

"It will likely give you a fever," countered Neil. "Tomorrow, perhaps."

Tomorrow brought a new distraction. Elizabeth, fulfilling her offer to help, was sitting by the bunk when Robert next awoke. He blinked, not sure if this was a dream! She spoke softly with a lilting Scottish accent, "Are you feeling any better, now?"

"I hardly know," he replied. "I must be dreaming, or else I've died and gone to heaven. Who are you?"

"Elizabeth Ritchie, a passenger, not a real nurse. Actually I'm a governess. Would you like me to get youp anything?"

"Just some rum ..." asked Robert provocatively.

Elizabeth looked very doubtful. "I'm not sure that would be good for you."

"It probably won't, but it would deaden the pain."

"Is it very bad?"

"Sore, and it screams when I move."

"Then you must just stay as still as can be, and give your ribs their chance to heal."

"Why are you going to America?" asked Robert, after a short pause, while he surveyed her neatly braided hair and slender figure beneath a smooth grey silk dress. "Are you travelling out to get married?"

Elizabeth felt herself blushing. "No, I am going to somewhere near Pictou to join my family, who emigrated fourteen years ago. My mother is in poor health, I fear, and is very anxious for us to be together again."

They continued to chat in friendly fashion. Elizabeth could tell that Robert was well-educated, and he was obviously well-travelled, as he mentioned the Indies. He was a little evasive about his work, but talked freely enough about his family in Pictou and the neighbourhood there. He painted a pleasing word-picture of the harbour at Pictou and its thriving trade in timber and people; he described the hunting available and he spoke of the town's farming hinterland and his family's beef herd; he commended the excellent school for boys, which he had attended. She warmed to the town, which he obviously knew well, and felt that she might like Pictou. It would not be as cultured as Edinburgh with its long traditions and its elegant buildings. Robert had not had time to see much of the City, and so, prompted by his questions, she told him what she knew of its public buildings and landmarks, and promised to show him sketches she had made while she lived there.

When Neil returned from sorting out the scratches and cuts occasioned by a territorial scrap between two female steerage passengers, patient and "nurse" were getting on famously. Elizabeth withdrew while Neil attended to his patient. He promised to help him dress, and take a stroll round the deck next day if the weather was fine.

"Why this obsession with drink?" Neil asked, when Robert for the third time demanded rum.

"I've always drunk …no, not true! We drank very little when I lived at home, but I got a taste for it on the voyages I've done, and in Jamaica of course it was safer than water. I was there for eleven years."

"Just a seaman's tot, then."

"That's stingy!" retorted Robert. "Find me a bottle, there's a good chap!"

"Certainly not!" said Neil, outraged. "Do you want to undo all my good work by getting drunk again?"

"What do you mean, 'again'?"

"Your clothes reeked of drink when you were dumped aboard."

"I swear I was stone-cold sober. I was on my way to meet a gentleman I knew when I was attacked, and at that time in the morning I had all my wits about me."

"You mentioned 'papers' when you first came round."

"The papers were to discuss with the man I was going to see."

"Were they sensitive and important?"

"You could say so – enough to put him in jail."

"Then, conceivably they could have been the reason for the attack," suggested Neil.

"Almost certainly so," concurred Robert. "And the thugs took money and my watch as well to make it look like just a street robbery."

"You are in something of a hole," said Neil. "No funds, and being transported against your will!"

"If this ship is going to Pictou, it isn't against my will," said Robert. "I've family there and can start afresh. But what I don't at present understand is why I have been 'transported' as you put it, when I could easily have been killed outright."

"Bodies raise questions," suggested Neil. "Also, autopsies can yield answers; and bodies have to be identified. Simpler just to make sure you go a long way away. Is your enemy wealthy? Could he bribe the thugs, and perhaps square the Captain, to take you."

"He has shipping connections, yes," replied Robert, turning this proposition over in his mind. Was the Captain in William's pay? If so, he might not be entirely safe, even on the ship.

"Then that is probably what happened and why."

"I've been a complete fool," said Robert bitterly. "I've known this man strike before potential trouble hits him, once before in my life. Stupidly I gave him the opportunity to do it again."

Neil kept silence for a while. He judged Robert to be potentially a decent man, but was concerned at his involvement with some seedy negotiations and resultant crime. He forebore to ask for more details, but returned to the question of the surname they shared.

"My father's family are still based in Pictou," he said. "Dad's name is Nathaniel Thomson. Are we connected, perhaps?"

"Nat! The preacher!" exclaimed Robert, sitting up with a yelp of pain. "My older brother!"

"Then … can you be the long-lost Robert?" queried Neil in astonishment.

Uncle and nephew stared at one another in total amazement. The tilting mirror reflected their likeness, as the two shook hands.

"Do you know Maple Grove?" asked Robert.

"Indeed. I've stayed there with my grandmother."

"Tell me how they are. It's many years since I was last at home, and there will have been many changes, not least that my father is dead, but that's where I'm going now. Nephew, this calls for a celebration! How about that bottle of rum you promised me."

"I promised you a tot! No more – but I'll have one with you to celebrate this astonishing meeting!"

"Lend me some cash, Neil. I don't scruple to borrow from a relative! Then I'll buy my own."

"I'll lend you none for liquor. Enforced abstinence will do you good!"

Robert frowned. "You sound just like Nat and Alexander."

"It's not surprising!" retorted Neil. "Since they brought me up between them.

Robert managed a laugh, but grimaced as the movement racked his damaged chest.

"You win," he said. "We'll do our big celebration when we reach dry land."

# Chapter Fifteen - An uncanny Coincidence?

Elizabeth was excited and thrilled by the discovery that her two new friends, Robert and Neil, were in fact related. It seemed to her an intervention of the Almighty that Robert and Neil had been brought together coincidentally on the same ship, both having come from roughly the same part of North America, and both for differing reasons having gone to Edinburgh. She said a little prayer of gratitude on their behalf, since she thought neither man would be inclined to do so!

She also included in the prayer a wish that her own missing brother, Angus, might be be re-discovered in similar fashion! True, Angus had last been seen in desperate circumstances, while Robert had been unmistakably alive when he had disappeared. She had discovered something of his story, while chatting to Neil at dinner.

Robert's injuries continued to mend rapidly, and as he got better, he became restless and difficult to keep quiet.. Neil urged Elizabeth to spend time with him and keep him amused, so that he did not unwittingly hinder recovery by too much early activity. While not averse to spending time with an attractive lady, Robert felt the games with which she amused her employers' children were hardly suited to him. He taught her piquet instead, an ideal card game for two, and much enjoyed by the bucks and gamblers of the Regency. Since this was no fun without a stake, and Elizabeth refused to play for money, he instituted a system of forfeits instead. When she lost, which she frequently did, he claimed a forfeit, and these gradually became more and more outrageous!

The two greasy packs of cards borrowed from a sailor became their daily battleground.  Neil was too busy to join them,  having to set a seaman's broken forearm and help a woman below decks deliver twins, among other medical chores.

For forfeits Elizabeth suffered the loss of a lock of hair without complaint, and parted with a handkerchief cheerfully, but could not think that the removal of her shoe so that he could tickle her toes at all the thing!  What was worse, her more serious nature meant that she could not respond in such flippant kind. Demanding that he abstain from rum for 24 hours was an impossibly difficult forfeit to police, or asking him to recite a prayer from memory could only be used once.  She was running out of ideas.  Luckily she did not win too often.

He was flirting with her,  she knew, and it made her uncomfortable.  Although it was no business of his, and she told him so, Robert had asked why she was not married.   She had occasionally been the subject of unwanted gallantry while at the Castle, but she could depend on her employers to protect her.  Here there was no-one to turn to.  She much preferred the handsome, uncomplicated, but much younger, Neil  to the disturbing Robert.   She acknowledged his magnetism and decisive character, but she feared that he was an adventurer.  Neil had told her of Robert's missing years and the "accident" which had driven him away.  She could sympathise with that, but could not feel that he had lived a "good" life.

"I wish my elder brother was here to look after me," she confided in Neil.

"Where is your elder brother?" he enquired.

"He was almost certainly drowned," she replied sadly. "He fell overboard from an emigrant ship when he was trying to free a sail. We have really given up hope of finding him, but the way Robert has been re-united with you, gives me a glimmer of hope again."

Neil urged his new-found Uncle not to tease Elizabeth. "She feels very alone in the world," he said. "And she has a missing brother too, so it is hard for her."

Immediately Robert felt remorseful. His next "forfeit" that they should sing a duet together at the shipboard concert was considerately watered down, and instead he extracted a promise that she would sing if he did. All young ladies had a repertoire of songs or recitations, and this presented no great difficulty to Elizabeth. Her performance was applauded warmly, particularly by Robert, who urged an encore. Neil offered a selection of mystifying card tricks and Robert composed an original monologue. So the time passed quite swiftly until the ship passed the Banks of Newfoundland and entered the Gulf of St. Lawrence.

This, Elizabeth knew, was where Angus had most likely perished. She became quiet and withdrawn. She haunted the rail, peering out to sea, looking for the rocks on which the *Ruby* might have all but foundered. However, since the *Margaret Bogle* was steering a more prudent course, she saw nothing of the rocky shore. The image of a familiar figure climbing the rigging was only in her imagination, though she tried to deduce from observing the *Margaret Bogle's* mast what might have happened.

Here Robert joined her. Strangely for him, the least obvious of his injuries was causing the longest lasting trouble. His strained knee, which had stiffened while he was lying still to recover from the rib damage, still gave way from time to time, causing him to limp and sometimes lose his balance. He stumbled quite heavily against her. She was not hurt, but the tears which had been brimming, now noticeably overflowed.

"I'm sorry," he apologised instantly. "Clumsy of me! Why, whatever is the matter?"

Elizabeth's sobs grew more uncontrolled. "We might have fallen overboard, like my brother did," she managed to say eventually, extracting a handkerchief from her sleeve, and mopping her streaming eyes.

"Your brother?" Robert questioned. "When did your brother fall overboard?"

"When my family were emigrating, in 1823," she said. "There had been an accident to the *Ruby* and the women and children, including the rest of my family, were rowed over to the *Harmony* for safety. But the able-bodied men were kept behind to help save the ship. That is how the family became separated. The Captain of the *Ruby* told me Angus was trying to free a sail and had climbed up a rope ladder, when the ship pitched and he fell overboard. Angus must have drowned, for we have not been able to trace him since, and it would have been near here, I think."

Robert frowned, and in his mind, he pictured "Barney" at Port au Basques. He tried to recall details of his conversation with the man. The encounter had troubled him at the time, and "Barney's" piecing together of the events of his accident bore an uncanny resemblance to what Elizabeth had just told him. He looked at Elizabeth's face. Could he detect any facial resemblance? Could "Barney" possibly be Angus, he wondered? One man missing – and one man found, but with no memory of his past!

"In 1823, you say?" he asked. The dates would be about right, he thought.

"Yes, in early June, probably."

It would not do to raise Elizabeth's hopes too high, in case there proved to be no connection. He excused himself, and approached Captain Smith in the cubby-hole where the charts were kept, just below the bridge.

"Where are we exactly?" he asked. "Can I see the local chart?"

Captain Smith, who by now approved of his unexpected guest, gestured to the chart and pointed out the present position of the ship. Robert saw that Cape Breton lay to the south, and Newfoundland to the North-west. The spit of land on which stood the fishery station at Port au Basques jutted out into the Gulf. If Angus had entered the water near here, and been picked up by a fishing vessel, that was possibly where he would have been taken, though St. John's Island would have been nearest.. "Barney" had suffered a complete memory loss. He had no recollection of his sister or his family. He could easily be Elizabeth's missing Angus. Not only the dates, but the location seemed to fit.

Robert thought back to his several conversations with "Barney", seeking for clues, which might lead to a more definite identification. "Barney" had said that bits of his memory returned in flashes. There was the flash of recognition that he had once worked with horses; the flash that he seemed to remember houses in a big city.

Robert thought he must establish a few more facts if he was to give Elizabeth any cause to hope that her brother might still be alive. He sought her out in the state-room where she had become more composed, and was bending over some stitchery.

"Please tell me some more about your family," he asked. "Particularly about your elder brother; that is, if you feel able to talk about it."

"There is only a thirteen month difference in age between us, and therefore we were always close. He and I were both good at our studies when we were at the village school together. The family thought we should seek our fortunes in the city rather than stay on the small-holding in the strath, where there was no real future. So, when Angus got a job at the big house, and they took him with them to Edinburgh, he made enquiries and found a job nearby for me too. I looked after the little children in a neighbouring mansion. We used to try and get the same times off so that we could be together, and we would go to concerts and fairs together. That is why I have missed him so much."

It was beginning to tie together. Now for the crucial question! "What job did Angus do?" asked Robert.

"He was a groom, but he fell out with the young ladies, who were teasing him, and so their father sent him back to Kilcalmkill, and we couldn't be together any more. That is when Angus persuaded my father and mother that the only way forward to seek a better future was to emigrate."

Robert had heard the words he wanted. The man had worked with horses. He took a deep breath. "I think I must have met your Angus," he said quietly.

Startled, Elizabeth raised questioning eyes to his face, which was grave, rather than flippant, the mood she distrusted so much.

"You have met him? Recently? He is alive?" she stuttered, with mounting excitement.

"I think so. The man I met was badly injured in a fall from a ship. He had completely lost his memory. The only thing he could remember, and that was after a couple of years, was that he knew how to handle horses. And, when we were talking together, we established that he had probably worked in a big city. He could not remember his name, or whether he had a family."

"So that could be why we have had no word – not that he had died!. Are you sure the man you met is Angus?" Elizabeth became flushed and animated. "I can't believe that he can be alive after all this time."

"I think it must be him. He goes by the name of "Barney". But there can hardly be two young men, one of whom was lost, and the other found in this precise sea area in 1823. Can you describe him a little?"

"Fairly tall ..." Robert nodded. "Reddish hair, fairly dark red, like your own ..." he nodded again.

"Was he afraid of the sea?" asked Robert.

"We had only once seen the sea. I don't think so."

"This man was terrified of the sea. But that would not be surprising after the ordeal he had been through. Besides, that was a present fear, not a past one. He told me that he had lost his coat and his boots, and had nothing on him, which could identify him. He had no money, but a British penny in his breeches' pocket."

Elizabeth was breathless with delight, and added another confirmation.

"My parents wrote to me that they were given Angus's coat and boots and the other luggage he had with him, which had been left on the *Ruby*. It must be him! How was he found?"

"He was picked up, more dead than alive, by some French fishermen, from Port au Basques. They were on their way home with a full catch. They hauled him out of the water and did what they could for him. He showed no ability to speak, nor understand what they said and so they thought he must be English, and when he was a little recovered, they took him to the nearby cod-drying station, run by Scots. He's been working there ever since."

"Thirteen years, drying cod!" she exclaimed. "My poor Angus!"

"You must remember he had no memory, and therefore no expertise. He had to earn money wherever he could.. They were kind to him, and gave him a wage."

"How is he now? When did you last see him? Can you take me there?" Her questions tumbled forth. He answered the last one first.

"I can't take you there, for I don't think the Captain would trust me with a boat, but I can show you on the chart where I believe him to be.   And yes, he was very well when last I saw him a few months ago.  He will be thirty-three perhaps now, and he has no signs of injury – his damaged shoulder has mended well.   There is only the memory loss, which troubles him greatly. Yet ..."

"What?" she asked sharply.

"I fear he may not remember you!  He has excellent memory of events since the accident, and things he has learned since, but he knows virtually nothing of what went before.  It might be rather daunting for you, if you remember him as once he was, but to him you are just a stranger."

"Yes," she agreed slowly.   "That would be very difficult.  Will he want to see us?"

"It was his dearest wish.  He has been spending years and years trying to remember whether he had a family, and who he really is.  I also think he has now found a new family to make friends with.   There's a girl called Alice -"

"How lovely!  And how nice for him!"

"Alice's father won't approve of any marriage until "Barney" discovers his true identity, and knows who his family are."

"Then we must waste no time in finding him, and filling in the missing years.  Surely meeting us again will restore the memory loss?"

"I wish I could be wholly sure of that," said Robert, who remembered his many attempts to jog Barney, or

Angus's memory. "Memory is a very tricky thing. You have your mother to see first," Robert reminded her.

"Yes, but she will be delighted too. I do not precisely know what her illness is, but joyful tidings must lift her spirits."

Neil, when told of the discovery, was incredulous. "To find two missing brothers on one voyage is quite amazing," he said.

"The Good Lord must have meant this to happen!" was Elizabeth's heartfelt belief.

"You and I were always going to be on a ship, going to America, and we would have been bound to pass this place," said Neil, more prosaically. "The wonder is that Robert was here, too, and through no design of his own. That must be an astonishing coincidence!"

"Not so astonishing as all that!" declared Robert. "I happened to have a piece of knowledge. Elizabeth had a piece of knowledge. All that happened is that we were here to exchange it. I was going to make some enquiries about Angus in Pictou, but the problem was I didn't have a name to go on."

"You make it sound prosaic, but I think it is a miracle!" insisted Elizabeth.

She was very grateful to Robert, not only for giving her tangible news of Angus, but also for his consideration in breaking the momentous news so gently. She saw him in a new light – not so much a rake, but more as a benefactor. She thought that, even if he did drink too much rum, and transgress upon her dignity, he was still a splendid friend for potentially re-uniting her with her long-lost brother.

Neil was a little more sceptical. "And what were you doing in an out-of-the-way place like Port au Basques?" he wondered audibly.

"Oh, this and that," said Robert airily. "It was on my way back from Jamaica."

Neil remembered that the missing Robert had once been the black sheep of his own family. He was sure there was more to the story than he had been told. Elizabeth, detecting mysteries beneath the surface, made a mental note to probe a little further one day. For the moment, she was happy in the anticipation of at last seeing Angus again.

# Chapter Sixteen - The First Reunion

Meanwhile Angus was suffering great frustration in his romance with Alice. His beloved was as warm and affectionate as ever, but her father's position was hardening. Alice, young and inexperienced, did not have the strength of mind to go against his wishes.

Mr. Gale was blunt with Angus. Puffing on his pipe, he leaned back in his rough-hewn chair, cushioned with quilted duck-down pads of bright material. He said, "I like you well enough, lad, but y're more than fourteen years older than Alice if yr reckoning is right, and even if ye knew the real date ye was born. We don't know what's in yr past, though likely it's pure enough. But we canna be sure."

"My last thirteen years have been clear enough for anyone to see," urged Angus desperately. "I've not been a drunkard. I've saved what money I could. I've been a good workman for the company at Port au Basques. No-one could say any different."

"All that," agreed the older man. "But we Scots like to know a man's background, where his loyalties lie, what is his clan. Though you've taken the name Macdonald for convenience, it's a pound to a penny ye're not one of them."

"I have racked my poor brain until it's bruised and battered," replied Angus. "Robert Thomson has helped me. We're fairly sure I must be from the North of Scotland, and that I probably worked with horses for a while in Edinburgh,. It doesn't sound like a life of iniquity," he added with some bitterness.

"Nay," soothed the farmer. "It's hard for you that ye canna recall yr roots. And ye're more than welcome here, and to share in my family. The wife and I can offer ye comfort, the boys and Alice can give you friendship, but marrying our only daughter is different. Ye mun offer her a home and security. Young MacArthur is mad after her and already has a house half-built and a flock of sheep to be proud of. 'Tis true that at the moment Alice wants you and not him, but she's young and could change."

"I love Alice very deeply, and she has said she loves me, " repeated Angus, as he had done many times over the past months.

"I know that," replied Mr. Gale. "But I'd not be doing my duty by her, and her future family if I let her go to the first young fella she sees and fancies. She'll make some young man a wonderful wife and mother to his children and our grandchildren. I'll not be giving my consent. That's my last word for now."

Angus took the blow with near despair. Alice was not of age. All of his instincts were honourable, and he owed the Gales so much already. He could not try and persuade her to go away with him, even if he had anywhere to take her. Nor, he knew, would she consider such an action in defiance of her father's wishes.

The two walked hand in hand towards the upper meadow. She cried a little, but was sanguine that, if they waited a while, her father might change his mind.

"When I'm nineteen," she said, "He must realise I can't wait for ever. I'll coax him, and knit him a new waistcoat, and make his favourite dinners."

"It won't be enough," answered Angus gloomily. "What about your mother?   Could she take your part?"

"My mother has always done as he said," replied Alice.   "She says there can only be one head of the family, and that's her man, and she must obey."

"The Minister?   Could he help?"

"He would marry us, of course, if my father said 'yes'.   But I don't think he would interfere otherwise. Also, my older brother, Euan, agrees with Dad.   He thinks I'm too young to settle down."

The next weekend things were even worse.   Angus could not get Alice on his own to talk.   Either her mother or John would be around if they sat together or went for a walk.   It was obvious that Alice was being protected from anything he might persuade her to do.   The attention of neither was on the book they were trying to read together. Though they sat close and touching, there was no real comfort in the contact – merely a shared misery.

Angus made up his mind.   He had been mulling over the prospect all week, and he could not let the situation go on as it was.   He declared at the family dinner-table: "I have come to the decision that I must go away for a while.   I shall go to Pictou, and try and find out more about the ships that were going through the Gulf before I was rescued.     There should be records of passengers who died or went missing."

Mr. Gale's brow lightened.   "Mebbe ye should have done that afore,"  he said.

"I didn't think it mattered very much before.   Now I do.   I was destitute then.   Now I have a little money.   I was afraid of the sea crossing. Now I know I must conquer that fear."

Euan said, "Good man! You've got to take hold and shape your own future. I wish you all the luck in the world!"

"We shall miss you," volunteered Alice's mother. "You've made us your family, and it is to us you must come back, when you've found out what you can, and when you feel the time is right."

Alice's tears fell on her plate. "If you do come back," she sniffed.

Angus seized her hand. He felt a new sense of empowerment. He was dictating the action, instead of passively accepting his fate.

"I swear I'll come back," he said. "A year from today I'll come back, with either success or failure, and I pray it will be the former. Please may I write?" he asked Mr. Gale. "Then I can tell you how I'm getting on."

"Of course ye can write," said Alice's father. "And of course Alice or any of us can write to you, when you can give us a direction. Ye're going the right thing, lad. Time and effort sorts out most problems."

Alice was tearful as they said good-bye "Wait for me!" urged Angus. "Go out and see other folk, and enjoy what offers in the way of amusement. I don't want you to sit at home and be miserable. Also, it will do me good to see some more of the world. I'll always be thinking of you. Don't do anything final till I get back to you. I promise faithfully that I'll come."

She promised she would wait, and they clung together for a long embrace before Angus swung away down the track to Port au Basques, turning every few yards to wave until he was out of sight.

Over the past weeks he had talked over with Euan and his father the prospect of buying some acres and starting to farm. Both had been fairly discouraging. "To farm successfully takes a lifetime to learn," said Euan. "What crops can be grown on which soil, for instance. When you need tree shelter, and when to cut the wood down; when the lambs are born and how to rear them. It's work that tires the muscles. I doubt ye"ll get all that experience before ye'll be too old to manage it."

"Though land is cheap, you'll need to buy stock and seed and tools," added Mr. Gale. "What we have here has taken twenty-five years to build up, and my worth is still all tied up in the farm. Ye have to have some brass to make a start, and then it's a hard row to hoe, with many mistakes, before you can say you've succeeded. Every mistake can set you back a year or more."

What else could he do to earn money and make a home? Angus had lost twenty years of experience to limbo, and had spent thirteen years confined to cod-drying ever since. In one way he felt useless; in another he felt the surge of a new excitement. He had health and strength and some learning. There must be some opportunities for him in this land of promise.

His mates and John Campbell at the fish-drying plant wished him well, and found him a berth on a packet bound for Pictou. His few possessions were packed in a canvas bag and he bravely took his place in the row-boat, holding fast to both sides and staring fiercely at the boat's bottom, rather than the heaving sea around. His mates went fore and aft to propel him up the rope ladder until he was safely on board, and he scurried down below to the safety of a saloon.

Angus survived the journey, although he took no pleasure in it, and disembarked on to the quay at Pictou, taking in the sloping hard, the houses rising up the hill, the three churches, and the bustle of a busy port. He had no memory of being in such a crowd of people, and he felt alone and lost as he walked towards the town, his canvas bag slung over his shoulder. A shop selling bread and a kind of sausage provided him with a meal, and he made his way to the shipping office to see what records they kept of thirteen years ago. He was doomed to disappointment. The records went back three years only. All the ships' logs and such passenger lists as existed were now housed in Halifax, he learned.

There was a livery stable in the town, the very one patronised by Delia before she left Pictou for Scotland. Angus asked about the possibilities of work. They had as many grooms as they needed, they said, nor could they suggest any likely private employers who might want a man. Try Halifax, they said.

Angus spent the night at a lodging in Pictou and found out there was a mail-coach travelling to Halifax the next day. There seemed little more he could do in Pictou, but he needed to pursue the trail to the larger town. He booked his seat on the coach, and ironically left Pictou only s couple of days before his sister, Elizabeth, and Robert Thomson landed from the *Margaret Bogle*.

\* \* \*

Elizabeth, of course, had no idea that she had missed seeing Angus by a mere forty-eight hours. She had said good-bye to both Neil and Robert on board. The former had reports to prepare before sailing on with the ship to Quebec, and Robert had his own problems with immigration, because of the absence of papers with which to prove his identity. He thought he might have to send to Maple Grove for a witness, but luckily was granted temporary admittance, pending the formal signing of an affidavit.

Peering anxiously over the ship's side, Elizabeth had identified her father, little changed from thirteen years ago, but was that burly young man at his side really Matthew? And where was her mother? She almost tripped on the gang-plank in her haste to meet and greet them. They exchanged hugs and kisses, picked up her luggage and walked to a waiting pony and trap, tethered to a hitching-post.

"It's a new trap," said Matthew proudly. "We felt you would think us very shabby if we had the old cart."

Her father warmly clasped her hand in his. "Your mother did not feel well enough to come," he explained, "But she's that anxious to see you after all this time."

The homestead was a few miles out of Pictou to the North-West, and the pony laboriously pulled the trap, passengers and luggage up a long hill from the estuary. Matthew sprang out to lighten the load and urge the animal forward. Then they were entering woodland, which eventually gave way to more open ground, and fields, rectangular for the most part, undulating away from the marked-out road, just as they had been allotted to the settlers.

"The soil is really good here," said her father. "Once we had cleared the land, it cropped well for us." A low wooden house came into view, and the pony turned into its narrow drive. Half-barrels of flowers flanked the doorway, but the house looked hardly large enough for three people, never mind four! Elizabeth's mind went flashing back to the huge and spacious Castle where she had been governess. It was such a contrast, but she put the thought away once she caught sight of the small, shrunken, black-clad woman who was her mother, obviously frail..

Elizabeth dismounted, with Matthew's help, and went to enfold the old lady in her arms. "Mama, Mama," she cried, and they were both choking with tears, and trying to talk through them, overcome with emotion at this long-awaited reunion. Elizabeth was drawn into the house, made comfortable in the rocking-chair and plied with tea and scones, while the chatter was all of Scotland, the voyage, their former home, and eventually of how Angus should have been here.

"I have news of Angus at last," Elizabeth told them in excited triumph. "I met someone on the voyage, who thinks he may have seen him. He may not have died after all, but have been living all this time at Port au Basques in Newfoundland."

"After all these years!" marvelled Mr. Ritchie incredulously. "We never dreamed he had been picked up, though we made as many inquiries as we could. Why didn't he try and find us?"

"He'd been badly hurt and lost his memory," explained Elizabeth. "He couldn't remember his name, and he had nothing on him which could identify him. However, this friend I met on the ship says a man he knows as 'Barney' could easily be Angus, for he was rescued at very much the same place and at the same time of year that we lost Angus. We must go there as soon as we can to find out."

"It'd be a miracle," said her father. "Don't put too much faith in it, Mother, in case it turn's out to be a mare's nest. I hope, of course, we do find it's true."

"I've never felt certain he was dead!" exclaimed Margaret Ritchie, "Even though the rest of you did. He's never been dead in my mind."

"The loss of his memory has been a big handicap," warned Elizabeth. "My friend says he may not remember us at all. Robert said that this Barney could remember the last thirteen years perfectly, but nothing at all, except his love of horses, of what went before. He will look different now – not our slim, handsome Angus. He will have grown older and filled out, like Matthew here has done."

"He'll be a grown man for sure, I know, but he'll still be the same loving son we once had," declared her mother with confidence.

"Robert says this man has been doing his utmost to remember his past, because he feels lost without an identity. His coat and his boots and his luggage were all on the boat, and I think were given to you from the *Ruby*, so there was nothing salvaged to suggest where he had come from, and who he was."

"There was an advertisement put in the Pictou newspaper," said her father. "Couldn't someone have read about it and put two and two together?"

"Apparently not. The people who found him were French fishermen. It was some time before he was well enough to be taken to the Scottish settlement at Port au Basques, which is in Newfoundland, not Nova Scotia as you are here. We must find out how to get there."

"In a day or two," suggested the older woman, surveying her daughter, elegant in grey gown and fur pelisse. "Give us time to welcome you home first, so fine as you've grown, and hear all you've got to tell us. A day or two more, after thirteen years, won't matter to Angus."

"I'll tend to the cows and the pony. Then I can show you the farm," volunteered Matthew.

Elizabeth thanked him. The house was humble, true, but better by far than the little croft they had occupied in Scotland. Her family had done well to emigrate, but she was glad she had not gone with them. There must have been hardship aplenty before they had achieved all this.

She wondered at Matthew's reaction if Angus came back to the farm. Would his nose be put out of joint? She recalled Matthew's clumsily written letter telling her Angus was missing. The lad had lost much of his education. Would help with writing and reading be resented, if she offered it?

She was conscious of a gulf between herself and the rest of her family. That gulf might be worsened when Angus returned? Would he, particularly, as well as herself, find the gulf difficult to bridge?

# Chapter Seventeen - Return of the Prodigal

Robert's welcome home was less ecstatic than Elizabeth's. He had eventually disembarked, having obtained letters of explanation for his lack of papers, signed by Captain Smith and Neil. Unencumbered by luggage, he walked up the long hill to Maple Grove, and let himself in through the gate into the drive. He stopped to let his eyes feast on the well-remembered sight of the fine maple trees in a semi-circle near the house, now touched with their autumn colour, and then turned back to gaze at the spectacular harbour view. The white-painted farmhouse was as he remembered it, with wooden shutters ready to keep out the winter storms. A herd of bullocks grazed in a nearby field, fat, sleek and hintinpg obviously at prosperity.

He shrugged. His father's death had left his younger brothers, Reuben and Paul, sitting pretty on a fine estate, he thought. His sisters were married. His two elder brothers, Alexander and Nathaniel, were well established in Quebec and Upper Canada respectively, the latter with a family of six, of whom Neil was the eldest. Where would he, the black sheep, Robert, fit in now?

As he trod up the drive, a man of about his own height and build emerged from an outhouse and stood looking down the drive. Brother met brother a few yards from the house. "Hullo," said Robert casually. "Reuben, I presume?"

"Robert! Can it really be you?" Surprise and shock, even doubt, mingled in his brother's voice.

"Really me – returned home like a bad penny, broke and penitent. Do I get a welcome?"

"Of course you get a welcome!" said Reuben, pumping his hand. "Mother will be overjoyed to see you. Paul, too. Where've you been, and what have you been doing all these many years?"

"I'll tell you all in good time. It's a very long story. How I've dreamed of this place for the last eleven and a half years!"

Robert followed Reuben into the house.

"Let me prepare Mama," suggested Reuben. "She's none too strong, and this will come as a big shock – a pleasant one, of course, but still a shock!"

Robert concurred, and waited in the sitting-room. The two iron dogs still guarded the fireplace, imports from Scotland when William the Pioneer first emigrated. The fireplace was empty of logs, as the room was often unused while the family congregated in the big kitchen. He wondered if family and servants still assembled before supper for prayers, as they always used to do in his father's day. There were sounds of light footsteps as his mother, upright still, but with snowy white hair, came into the room with a beaming smile and warm embrace.

"Robert, my dear, dear son! How lovely to have you home!"

Robert felt tears prick his own eyelids. So generous, so loving, as always! He kissed the top of her head, and then her cheeks. "Mama, I am so sorry I have stayed away so long. I should never have run away like I did, and left you without a word."

"Why ever did you go?  And wherever have you been?" she asked.  "Reuben, tell Betsy to light the fire and bring in some tea."

"No, " Robert protested.  "Let's go into the kitchen. Then it will really feel like home.   This is the Sunday parlour!"

They went back to the kitchen, made warm by the wood stove, and sat round the scrubbed pine table, where Paul, the youngest son, joined them, to hear talk of Jamaica, ship's voyages, and briefly, of Scotland.

At length Robert turned to Reuben.  "The Judge's death,  remember? Has the case been officially closed?"

"Of course!    They brought in Accidental Death. Closed eleven years ago.  Why did you leave?  It caused some to suspect there might be something wrong."

Robert buried his head in his hands.  All those wasted years!

"I shouldn't have left, of course.  I see that now. But in the heat of the moment, I let William Mackenzie put pressure on me to run.  He said one of us would be blamed, and if they accused him, he'd accuse me!  I swear I had absolutely nothing to do with the Judge's death. We were after deer, and I got a buck, while I believe now that William shot the Judge."

"Accidentally?"

"No.  I  believe it was deliberate.  William was a smuggler on a grand scale and feared the Judge would expose him.   They'd quarrelled and the Judge said he'd sleep on the matter and decide what to do the next day. So William wanted the Judge dead.  He told me as much To be honest, I'd got myself involved in William's schemes, which made me a pawn of his. He's been paying me to stay out of the way, and run his plantation in Jamaica."

"Could you not have written, dear?" asked his mother. "We have been so worried."

"I wanted to. My God, how I wanted to! But William kept writing to me by every boat, saying the case was still open, and it would be dangerous to return, or to let anyone know where I was. I thought of Father and that awful eighteen months when he had been put in jail for debt. I couldn't face returning. He'd have been so ashamed if I went the same way as he did, and for such a reason. To lie low seemed the safest policy. And it wasn't all bad. William had been buying my silence with money in the bank, and I was earning a generous salary. Then, eventually I found out William had been lying to me, and was going to move away to Scotland. That decided me. I went to Edinburgh after him to make him pay for some of the wasted years he'd caused me."

Robert passed his cup and saucer for another helping of strong farmhouse tea, and continued the story:
"Again I was so stupid. William got in first, as he always does. His network and intelligence are so sharp. Before I could even get to talk to him, he set a couple of thugs on me. To do him justice, this time he didn't mean them to murder me – just incapacitate me enough to get me transported back to North America, and batter me enough to teach me a lesson."

"Were you badly hurt?" asked his mother anxiously.

"Bust a few ribs and had a sore head for a while. Maybe my pride suffered most. Did I tell you I met young Neil on board the *Margaret Bogle*, working his passage as the Ship's Doctor.  It was he who patched me up, and as our names were the same, put two and two together and recognised who I was."

"Neil is a good lad," said Robert's mother.  "A credit to Nat, and to Alexander too, for he and Isabella won't have children of their own, and more or less adopted Neil while he was studying in Quebec.  You've many more nieces and nephews, Robert, for the girls have two each, and Nat has five more younger than Neil."

"Quite a dynasty!  I must start contributing to it," he commented flippantly.  "Meantime I need a bath and some clothes.  These are all I have left, and they're filthy."

"You won't get into your old ones," said his mother, surveying his broad frame.  "Reuben will have to lend you some."

"If he will, please.  Then in a day or two I must go to Halifax and draw some funds.  I haven't a bean with me, but there should be cash in the Bank there."

"So you're not really destitute, then?" queried Reuben

"I hope not, after sweating it out for eleven years on a Jamaican plantation. Just now, I've either spent my Jamaican funds or had them stolen, and so all I've got left is in a Halifax bank – enough to start a business, I hope."

"You've changed," observed Paul, entering the conversation for the first time. "How does it happen that the devil-may-care adventurer has decided to become a sober businessman?"

"He wasn't an adventurer," protested his mother.

"No, it's fair comment. I did want adventure. I didn't want to stay here, raising cattle. I wanted to see the world."

"Are you still against raising cattle?" asked Reuben. "You've a third share of this property. Father didn't change his will when you left."

"I wondered. He would have been quite justified in doing so, but no, this is your home, not mine."

"Reuben," said his mother disapprovingly. "Robert has only just come back, and you are quizzing him about shares. While I'm alive, Robert, this is your home."

"Maple Grove!" said Robert dropping into a reverie, "You'll never know how enticingly it beckoned when I was out in Jamaica's steamy heat. I'm deeply sorry I was not here for Father's funeral. I didn't know anything about it, till one of William's letters arrived months later."

"Alexander arranged everything beautifully," said his mother. "You must go and see Alexander and Isabella in Quebec. Alexander spent weeks searching for you after you disappeared. William Mackenzie had said he thought he saw you making for the Halifax road, and so Alexander enquired there, and they searched the copse; then they thought of the harbour, but no one had seen you, and several ships had left that day or the next."

"I'm sure Alexander would have done his best to trace me, but that was just one of William's devious tricks. I actually left Pictou on the *Mary Ann* that same afternoon. I got aboard by the skin of my teeth, and by dodging from cover to cover. The Captain, of course, was one of William's trusted men. I'll write to Alexander and explain, now that I'm back in the real world."

"Reuben, take Robert upstairs and find him some clothes," Bella Thomson insisted. "I'm going to kill the fatted calf, or else the fatted chickens, and we'll have a celebration dinner. Prayers at 6.30 sharp, Robert!"
He was home.

\* \* \*

It was the youngest brother, Paul, who was most resentful of Robert's return. As the youngest son, perhaps he had had a life-time of being at the end of the queue for hand-me-downs from older members of the tribe, and he had always had a rather sulky outlook on life.

Robert remembered him slouching along the path to school, kicking a stone in front of him, instead of running and jumping to catch a branch of an overhanging tree, as the more extrovert boys liked to do.

It had been a pleasure to Paul when one by one, his seniors had left the family circle, and a source of pride when he and Reuben, were left alone with their mother, to run his father's farm. Robert suspected that it was Reuben who did the managing, while the slower-witted Paul did the donkey work.

Next day he was a little surprised when, inspecting the beasts, Paul handed him a pitchfork. Accepting it without comment, Robert tossed straw with a long-practised, if almost forgotten, skill, but he thought the gesture seemed to indicate that, if Paul were to allow him back home, he was expecting him to work for the privilege. Perhaps he was refining too much upon it, but another incident on the third day confirmed his impression. When Paul handed him the stick and rope and indicated that he was expected to release the bull from its stall and guide it to the herd, he was certain he was again being put to the test.

Paul sat morosely, saying little when the family gathered at meal-times. He asked Robert no questions, while the others were curious about his life in Jamaica, or his voyages on the high seas. His mother was nostalgic to hear about Scotland, and Robert regretted that he had not been able to get to the north, to see the country where she used to live.

"I must go to Halifax," Robert insisted, after he had been down to Pictou to obtain some proof of his previous existence from the Parish register. He would need something to show he was entitled to the money in the Halifax bank. "Can you lend me a horse, Reuben."

"You could go on the coach," suggested Paul grudgingly.

"I'd rather ride and enjoy the journey in my own way," Robert countered.

"Take Pretty Polly. She's good-tempered. Meg Merrilees' fourth foal," offered Reuben.

Robert remembered the old mare. He had done a lot of riding on her back, after he outgrew his first pony.

"Ye'll come back soon?" enquired his mother anxiously, as if unwilling to let him out of her sight.

"Give me a fortnight. I'll need to get some money, buy clothes, look around for some business opportunities. Then I'll come back," he reassured her. "By the way, I've written to Alexander. Asked him if he can suggest any openings in Quebec or Upper Canada."

"Will you farm again?" asked Reuben.

"Unlikely," said Robert. "I thought I'd like to try my hand at boat-building. I enjoyed it as a hobby in Jamaica. Or I could manage an enterprise. I did well enough for William Mackenzie, damn him, when he put me in charge of his plantation."

"Don't swear, dear," said his mother automatically. "Didn't I hear old Farquhar was selling out, down the West River?" she asked Reuben.

"Farquhar's built some neat vessels in his time," observed Reuben. "However, the word is that he's finding the physical work too hard. I'll make some enquiries while you're away. It might be just the thing."

Robert thanked him for his offer, and went off to get acquainted with his new mount, Pretty Polly.

* * *

It was a long, but pleasant ride to Halifax. Robert followed the erratic coach road as it wound its way through the hills, and he lodged at wayside inns overnight to rest the mare. He met Scots and Irish settlers in the tap-rooms of the inns, and learned more about the changes which had taken place in this rapidly developing land. He passed native settlements, homesteads of new settlers with freshly-cleared land, and sometimes rode through dense forest for mile upon mile. There were thickets of pine, but mostly deciduous trees, with saplings self-set, cramming the little road on either side.

Halifax he found to be a rapidly growing port. Although Pictou was the nearer landfall to Britain, Halifax had the advantage of a sheltered waterway, free of ice most years, and was open nearly all the year round. Robert made his way down to the main harbour, the ancient hub of the town, but his country horse took exception to the crush of carriages and carts in the narrow streets. He found the road out again, deciding to procure a room for a night or two, and stabling for the mare.

Then he walked back towards the waterfront. The warehouses were thronged with buyers, hoists and cargo. He walked slowly along Water Street, found his Bank, established his credentials, and withdrew enough money to pay for some tailoring, re-pay Reuben's loan, and leave himself cash in hand. A valise was urgently needed to contain his new purchases. A bottle of rum was a long-felt want, as tea was the more usual tipple at Maple Grove.

He had thought he knew no-one in Halifax, and indeed he did not, but, on returning to the stables to check on Pretty Polly, Robert thought he saw a familiar figure carrying fodder cross the yard in front of him. He recollected his last visit to Port au Basques.

"Barney!" he shouted, amazed at the chance meeting. The figure checked, spun round, and stared in surprise.

"Mr. Thomson. Robert!" he said. "How come you here?"

"I believe Providence must have sent me," said Robert. "There's many people trying to find you now. We have discovered your name and your family."

Angus blinked in disbelief. "I thought you'd gone to Scotland," he said. "How did you find out after all this time? Who am I then?"

"You're Angus Ritchie from Sutherland in the north of Scotland, missing, believed drowned, from the *Ruby*, bound for Pictou with a cargo of emigrant Scots."

"Angus Ritchie," repeated the groom slowly, savouring each word of the name he had long been desperate to know. "Angus Ritchie," he repeated. "Do I have a family?"

"I know where your mother and father and younger brother are living, and I've met your sister, Elizabeth. How do you come to be working here, rather than at Port au Basques?"

"I went first to Pictou, then came to Halifax to find work," answered Angus. "I've been meaning to check the shipping records. I can't marry Alice, her father says, until I can prove who I really am."

"Then your troubles are over," exclaimed Robert blithely. "Come back to Pictou with me, meet your family, and we'll soon prove who you are."

Angus suddenly looked concerned. "How will I recognise them?" he asked..

"No matter, if they recognise you!" The two men repaired to Polly's stall together, fed the mare and led her out for exercise round the stable-yard.

"I'll come back tonight, when you've finished work, and tell you the whole tale," offered Robert. It struck him that the homecoming, which had been simple and straightforward in his own case, was going to be much more complex for Angus.

# Book IV

## Chapter Eighteen - Leaving Home

Still reeling from the shock of Robert Thomson's visit, Delia recalled a maxim of her father, Judge Fogo. "If you decide on a course of action, take your time," he had said. After Robert's disclosures, she could no longer stay with her husband. They already lived largely separate lives under the same roof, but a murderer and an international smuggler could not be tolerated. Mindful of Robert's warning, she had tried to act as though nothing had happened.

Delia researched her forthcoming separation from William with care. Her aunt, with whom she planned to take refuge, lived in a small town called Tain on the Dornoch Firth. It helped that Gilbert after all could escort her on the journey there during his long vacation, and so they took passage on the coastal packet from Leith. She remembered that her friend, Isabella, had taken the same journey in reverse while she had been travelling throughout Scotland raising money for building churches on Cape Breton island. William had raised no objection to her declared intention of visiting the aunt who had been her chaperon before her marriage. He knew it was something she had been seeking to do ever since their return to Scotland.

The packet hugged the coastline, putting in at various ports, and Delia enjoyed the leisurely pace, the changing scenery, and her observations of their fellow passengers.

Gilbert had his nose stuck in a book for most of the time. He had conceived a passion for Sir Walter Scott's monumental novels, and read them in succession. Just now he was ploughing his way through "Guy Mannering", a diffuse tale of a lost heir, restored to the ancestral home after a series of improbable adventures, featuring some wild and fanciful characters. From time to time he regaled his mama with lurid summaries, or asked what some of the Scottish or Gaelic words and phrases might mean. She herself became re-acquainted with the novels of Jane Austen, more feminine and eminently re-readable. She amused herself also with a volume of Alexander Pope's witty poetry. Occasionally she took out her sketch-pad and attempted to record some of the harbour scenes, or the striking light and shade effects of the hills and clouds.

She knew she must discuss her situation with Gilbert, but refrained from doing so until she had a clearer idea of how to accomplish her next step. She made a lightning sketch of Gilbert too while he was not looking. The youth had grown to be tall and fair, with a distinct resemblence to the Naval Officer she had briefly known so long ago. That some of his features could well have been inherited from Judge Fogo, she was grateful for. What was certain was that he was nothing like William!

Aunt Cecily was pleased to welcome both her relatives. Twenty years older than when she had chaperoned Delia in Halifax, her grey hair was pulled back with a comb, and enclosed in a net bag, an easy style for gnarled and twisted fingers to manage. The cold North-East must have been a trial for one with arthritic tendencies. Aunt Cecily's home was neat enough, a grey stone, five bedroomed house on a hill overlooking the market square of Tain. An elderly retainer and his wife lived in and looked after the house, as Aunt Cecily now progressed only from bedroom to parlour, and that with the aid of a stick. The hill on which the house was situated meant that she could only with difficulty go down into the town, even to the kirk. The letters she used to write to her niece had become less frequent, and sometimes almost unreadable as her misshapen fingers struggled to control the pen.

"You'll find it quiet here," the old lady said, but, directing her gaze to Gilbert, added "If it's walking you want, then the heather and the hills are free, and if it's riding you fancy, the livery stables can mount you, no doubt, while you're here. It's a long time since we kept a horse."

Delia made it her business to find out how her ex-chaperon was situated, whether financial or any other support was needed, but it seemed that the old lady's demands were few. It was companionship she craved most, for time lay heavy on her hands, and many friends and acquaintances had been lost to her as the Grim Reaper gathered them in.

Delia tried to divide her time between her son and her aunt, accompanying Gilbert on some of his rides, and buying little cakes and pastries in the town to share with her aunt over afternoon tea. She discovered that Tain had a tiny library, and she chose some books, which she could read to her aunt, or leave with her to read for herself. She found a nurseryman who could supply some plants with which to re-stock the neglected garden. She also attended a service at the nearby Presbyterian kirk, and made an effort to get to know some of the congregation. She found, as others have discovered, that it was a closed community, and strangers were not embraced with enthusiasm.

It was very quiet. She did not think Tain a big enough town to afford her sufficient stimulus for long. But would it do as a bolt-hole for the present? She owed something to her aunt in return for those years of chaperonage. Could she survive comfortably here until Aunt Cecily died, and then perhaps find a larger house in a larger city? There might be seven years to wait before Gilbert completed his studies.

On one of their country rides, she broached the topic of separation to Gilbert.

"You are old enough for me to seek your advice," she said. "I have determined not to go back to Edinburgh to live with your father any more. You must not think I am deserting you, or want to deprive him of your company, but he and I have grown so far apart that I am acutely unhappy there, and want us to separate and live our own individual lives, rather than live as a family in future."

"Mama!" Gilbert's sense of shock struck him temporarily dumb, save for the single, sharp interjection.

Delia went on: "I know it is not done in our society. I don't seek a divorce, for I have no firm grounds. Neither has he. It is just that we no longer have that respect for one another which is needed to sustain the appearance of marriage.  I thought if I could live quietly here with my aunt, on the understanding that I would look after her in her old age,  you and your father could continue living in Edinburgh, you occupied at the University, and he with his businesses.   You could come up here and see me during your vacations, and later on, if Auntie dies, I could move closer to Edinburgh, and it would not be noticeable if I do not re-join William, for people will have forgotten that I was once his wife.   I could not have succeeded in doing that in Pictou, but we are not yet so entangled in society here."

"Have you quarrelled with Papa?"  asked Gilbert in an anguished tone.

"Not quarrelled in any major sense," replied Delia. "But we do not see eye to eye."

"Is this because that man came to see you?"

"That man was Robert Thomson, an old friend of ours.  You knew him when you were a small child.  Yes, perhaps his visit unsettled me a little.   I miss our many friends in Pictou. I did not want to come to Edinburgh in the first place, but William insisted, and I wanted to see you start your life here.  Pictou would have been too far away from you, my darling.   And so, I acquiesced, without a fuss."

"But it doesn't make sense. You will be away from me here, up in Tain."

"Letters will reach you in a few days, not a few months. We can meet in the long vacation. In term-time you will have your own friends, and your studies.   A housekeeper can run the town house as well as I can."

"I shall miss you terribly if you're not there to talk to. Papa is not so easy."

"Yes, you will miss me. But you will adjust to having me at arms' length, rather than at your beck and call. Think about it, dearest, and we can talk again when you have had time to digest all the implications."

"My father will be very, very angry."

"Yes, he will be very angry, but maybe he will be relieved as well. I don't fulfil many of his needs. I am his hostess, but not his intimate. I run his house more or less to his liking – but sometimes less, as we don't share the same tastes any more. Do you remember the battle royal when I ordered the new covers for the drawing room chairs? I daresay he will spend more time at his Club. I would not deprive him of you, because you are his only son, and it would be too cruel. Equally he must share you with me from time to time. You must insist on that, dearest, if he proves difficult."

"How can I insist, Mama? He is my father. He pays my allowance."

"You insist, sweetheart, by being your own man. You say you have a duty to me, as well as to him. He can be a bit of a tyrant, as I know to my cost, but he will agree in the end because he does love you more than anything, and he will not want you to be unhappy."

"Mother, I wish you will not do this," urged Gilbert desperately.

"Are you thinking of yourself, Gilbert dear, or are you thinking of me?"

Gilbert's glance fell before her eyes, and he flushed at the implied reproof. "I suppose I am thinking of myself," he muttered.

"Then you must be wise and strong and think of me too. Do you remember how we have often discussed the unnecessarily inferior place of women in our society? You remember our agreeing that women's brains were as good as men's, but we never get the chance to use them properly? We concurred that women are always the dominated sex, because men have the money and the vote? Well, my father ensured that I retained control of his money through my Trustees, and I have my own income, if not full control of my capital, and so have the means to do this."

"I am only sixteen, Mama. Can you not wait for a year or two?"

"It is very young," Delia agreed. "I intended to wait a year or two more, but events have forced my hand. Believe me, Gilbert dear, that a crisis has been reached that will not be resolved. It is better that I do not go into detail, but what has happened is so profound that I cannot even meet William again. It has been difficult enough acting a part for the last few weeks. I want you to instruct our servants to pack up all my personal things --I will give you a list – and send them here by carrier."

"Does my great-aunt agree with this?"

"I have not discussed it with her yet. I will do so today, but I think she will like the idea. She gets very lonely, and is quite ill, you know. I wanted to talk to you first."

Gilbert was silent for a few momwnts. He looked at her in puzzlement, then looked away. "Can I have some time to think about it?"

"Yes, dear, of course. I won't speak to her until we've talked again."

The boy suddenly kicked his horse, and trotted, then cantered, away from her. She understood his desire to be alone, and turned her own mount to go slowly back the way they had come. The deed was done.

Delia had arranged to take Gilbert to a small evening Assembly, where she hoped he would meet some young people, and form friendships in the neighbourhood. He had been sullen and withdrawn all day, but he brightened up in the evening at the prospect of amusement. Dancing was very much the main social entertainment; he was confident of most steps, though he thought he would have to sit out the reels.

The chandeliers glittered in the Town Hall, and a red carpet had been laid up the steps to protect the young ladies' dresses from the mud and dirt. Delia joined the mothers and chaperons on the chairs at the side, after presenting her son to the Master of Ceremonies, and asking that he be introduced to some partners. A little gaggle of young men stood at the far side of the room, and she watched as Gilbert bowed in formal greeting to several of them. She was again reminded of the time when she had similarly surveyed a group of naval officers in Pictou, before choosing one of them to be her lover. Gilbert's colouring and the way he moved were a younger version of that dashing Naval Lieutenant. Ah, he had found a partner, and was leading her to join the set.

She herself began to chat to the matrons on either side. They were curious about her status, but Aunt Cecily's name seemed to establish respect and acceptance. She found the heavy Scots burr a little difficult to comprehend, especially as the sweating bandsmen were thumping out the tune with might and main, and there was a competing high-pitched drone of conversation, as people screamed to make themselves heard above the noise.

One of the matrons she met proved to be a Mrs. Gordon, wife of a retired Vice-Admiral.

"Could your husband's name be Richard?" wondered Delia.

"He is, indeed. How did you know?" queried the lady.

"Only that I met a naval officer by the name of Richard Gordon sixteen years ago in Pictou."

"He has been in North America, and indeed all over the world," responded Mrs. Gordon. "He's in the card-room now, but I can introduce you again when the dancing is over."

Delia expressed her thanks, and asked which of the delightful young ladies was Mrs. Gordon's daughter.

A dark-haired vivacious girl was pointed out. "Anne-Marie is my youngest," confided Mrs. Gordon. "Her two older sisters are creditably established, and my son followed Richard's example and joined the Navy."

"She is very pretty," complimented Delia. "Do you think my son could beg the favour of a dance?"

"If her card's not full already, certainly," agreed Mrs. Gordon.    "Anne-Marie is a popular little puss. Which is your son?"

"Gilbert is the fair boy in the second set," Delia pointed out.  "He's only sixteen, but will be studying law at the University in Edinburgh, and will be spending vacations here, I hope."

"Are you a widow?" asked her new acquaintance, although it was obvious that Delia was neither in deep nor semi-mourning.

"No.  I am Mrs. William Mackenzie.  My husband and I came over last year from Pictou, but he is away a good deal with his business interests, and has agreed that I spend some time here with my Aunt Cecily, as she is becoming frail, dependent and lacking company," explained Delia mendaciously.

"Your Aunt being …?"

"Mrs. Cecily Forfar.  She has been widowed many years, and was my chaperon for two of them."

"Yes, I think I remember her talking of you when she returned to Tain after your marriage.  Is she well?  I think I have not seen her lately at the Kirk."

"The rheumatism is affecting her very badly," explained Delia.

"It is the climate here.   Richard says a warmer climate is very beneficial, or indeed a colder one, as long as the air is dry."

They continued to chat until the call to supper separated them.  Having already committed herself, Delia profoundly hoped her aunt would agree with her plans.

She must talk with her before gossip reached her from another source.

Gilbert was enjoying his evening, she could tell. A fresh face was usually welcome in country circles where young men were rare. Younger sons for the most part left the land and entered one of the Services. Tonight the numbers were better balanced by brothers home on leave or down from University.

The evening wore on, and Richard Gordon eventually joined his wife from the card-room and was introduced to Delia. He remembered her immediately. "Pictou," he recalled, "My ship stopped there many years ago, but since then my interest in it has been reinforced by the work I'm now doing in connection with Alexander Thomson's agency to recruit Scots to migrate to Upper Canada. Many emigrants choose to go to the fertile land there, but some have relatives in Pictou or Cape Breton, and settle for the shorter journey."

"I am part of the counter-flow," said Delia. "My husband and I have brought our son back to study law at Edinburgh."

"One wonders how long English or Scots laws will hold sway in North America. The recent small rebellion shows the colonists resent the dominance of the old country."

"Yes, but the unrest was quickly put down," countered Delia. "I am much in favour of the colonies developing their own systems, and cutting some of the dependence on the Mother Country, but I trust it will not happen as happened in America, and will rather evolve naturally. The basis should be the best of English and

Scottish law. My father was Judge Fogo, whom you may remember. He wrote a legal text-book which is still well regarded."

Richard Gordon nodded. "Is he still alive?" he asked.

"No. My father was shot in a hunting accident about twelve years ago."

Richard Gordon commiserated. "I offer my condolences," he said. "I believe it was reported at the time, but I fear I had forgotten."

"You mentioned Alexander Thomson. I am honoured to claim his wife, Isabella, as a friend," said Delia. "We got to know one another when she visited Pictou, and I was a guest at her wedding. She is a most energetic and capable lady."

"They are happily settled in Quebec," responded Richard. "As we have mutual friends, perhaps you and your son would care to visit us. Mrs. Gordon …"he called to his wife. "Can we arrange lunch for Mrs. Mackenzie and her son?"

The two ladies compared notes in a search for suitable dates. Just then Gilbert came up to join them, and was presented to the Gordons.

"Mama, this is a very jolly party," he said.

Delia caught Richard Gordon regarding Gilbert closely. "Well, young man, have you met my tease of a daughter yet?" he asked.

"I have just been dancing with her, Sir. She is a beautiful dancer."

"And you are a very tactful young man," approved Richard. He glanced at Delia as he spoke, and she thought he raised a quizzical eyebrow at her, but the impression was very fleeting. She might well have been mistaken.

* * *

Gilbert had come round to think more favourably about her proposition the following morning when they went walking and talked again. Whether it was the jollity of the previous evening convincing him that Tain was not such a bad place after all, she did not know. He had acquired a couple of invitations of his own, in addition to the projected visit to the Gordons.

"You want me to say 'yes', Mama?" Gilbert said, when they were clear of the town, and walking alone.

"I should like your approval, darling, if you can give it."

"It is very unconventional, Mama, but then you are a very special and unusual person."

"I do not mean to turn into an eccentric, I assure you," she responded. "I shall ensure that everything I do observes the proprieties, and I shall not lead anyone to think that I have deserted my husband."

"Yet desertion, if it were established, would be a cause for divorce, would it not?"

"I do not think William will take that course. He will eventually value his freedom, as I value mine, and you could persuade him against it, if he did threaten it, and if you wanted to."

"He will be simply furious."

"He may throw things!" she agreed. "He's that sort of a man! But the storm will pass. He may question you, and you will need to say that you think I have made up my mind, and am quite determined. I will give you a letter for him. You must ask that you make your main home with him, and that will give him reassurance. Do not be seen to take my part. Just let him rant, and agree that it is very bad. Do not try to defend me to him, except in your heart and privately, you must understand that I have to do this."

"I think I do understand now," Gilbert said.

"Remember, to everyone else say that I have gone on an extended visit to look after my aunt. The ties of family are much respected here, and no-one will think that particularly strange. If I can leave her, or should she die, then I may want to travel, as I used to do when I was a girl. I should love to take you to Paris, for instance, but it all depends what happens. If I am still based here, there would need to be a little white lie and I would let it be assumed that I am travelling with my husband."

"You've got it all worked out, Mama," observed Gilbert with a hint of admiration.

"Darling, we women have to do that. Without power, we can only persuade. Without money, we can only manipulate. Some of us have become quite good at it."

"All very well, Mama, but where does love come in? We are supposed to love our wives or husbands, surely."

"The fortunate do love one another – very much. I hope in your time you will be attracted to a young lady, and she to you, and I hope you will marry and have children and live happily ever after, but never suppose, Gilbert, that attraction alone is enough for a happy and lasting union. Our Church decrees that marriage is for life, and so tolerance and understanding, compatibility in temperament are all important if the marriage is to last. Then marriage is also a social condition; arrangements are often made between families of a similar class. Fathers need to ensure that their daughters will be kept in the manner to which they are accustomed. Between the two people themselves, there has to be give and take – not too much of the one, and not too little of the other – in day to day matters. Marriage does not have to be a gamble, if these things are carefully considered in advance."

"Did you marry for love, Mama?"

"No, my darling. My marriage was a mutually convenient arrangement, and for many years, it has worked very well."

"Were you ever in love, Mama?" asked Gilbert, chancing his arm with an intrusive question.

"Only briefly once! And I hope not to be again. It is a very turbulent state!" Delia declared.

# Chapter Nineteen - The Bird had Flown

Elizabeth Ritchie and her father soon set out from their homestead near Pictou, full of excitement, and yet trepidation, on their journey to Port au Basques, to search for Angus at the cod fishery where Robert had reported seeing him.

They were not entirely sure, after all, that the man rescued in Newfoundland was indeed Angus, though it seemed a real probability. If he were not, then such a disappointment would be hard for them all to bear, particularly so for Margaret Ritchie, worn down by illness. She and Matthew were to keep the work going on the farm until the others returned. Few ships seemed to be bound for Port au Basques, and father and daughter were held up for some days in Pictou until they secured passage on a sister ship of the *Mary Ann*, part of William Mackenzie's fleet.

To Elizabeth, whose experience to date had been on the busier emigrant ship, life on a cargo boat was much less interesting. Elizabeth compared it with her voyage on the *Margaret Bogle* with Robert and Neil, when the time had sped by. She and her father whiled away the hours with backgammon, and with speculation about Angus, until they saw the rickety jetty, jutting out from the cod fishery on the peninsula. It was warm in the autumn sunshine, and the Newfoundland shore, so cold and inhospitable in winter, presented its most attractive face to the visitors.

As they were rowed ashore, the Ritchies eagerly scanned the faces of the workpeople busy with the boats and the drying platforms, but none seemed even vaguely familiar. It was with a feeling of growing disappointment that they asked to see John Campbell, as recommended by Robert. The bluff Scotsman was taken aback by his lady visitor, smart in her Edinburgh gown.

"Angus Ritchie?" he repeated in puzzlement. "Nay, there's no-one of that name been here."

"You wouldn't have known him by that name," explained Elizabeth. "Robert Thomson told us that a man who had lost his memory worked for you here, and that you christened him Barney. We think he might be my brother."

"Yes," agreed the Scotsman. "We had Barney here for a long time, but he's been gone a few weeks now."

"Gone, oh, no!" Elizabeth buried her face in her hands. "How cruel! Do you know why he went, and where he might be?"

"He didn't know himself. He was going to start at Pictou to try and trace the ships that sailed through the Gulf in Spring 1823, in a quest to find his family and his ancestry."

"But we've just come from Pictou to try and find him!" exclaimed Elizabeth despairingly.

"He said he'd write when he found something out, but we haven't heard yet. I tell you, though, he had friends in the Codroy Valley. Mebbe they had a letter."

"Where can we find them?"

"Up the Codroy Valley. Twenty miles perhaps. They were farmers by the sound of it. Name of Gale, if I remember right."

"Oh, thank you! We'll go and see them."

"It's a long walk, Missy."

"Never mind. Just tell us the way."

John Campbell pointed: "Well, it's down past the French fisher-folks' shacks, and turn right up Little Codroy Valley – keep the mountains on your right. More than that, I can't say."

Father and daughter looked at one another, dismayed by this further extension of their task. "We've come so far, we must go on," said Elizabeth.

"He won't be there, Mr. Campbell said," argued her father.

"But they might have heard from him, and could give us a direction."

"I'll go," offered Mr. Ritchie. "I'm more used to tramping hills than you are, lass."

"No, we must stick together. Let me see if I can buy some food to take with us."

They found the cook at the bunkhouse, and explained that they were Barney's family come to look for him. That earned them bread, fruit and much good will, together with a few reminiscences of Barney's trouble with his memory, and how he had found himself a sweetheart in the Codroy Valley.

It was as well the sun shone, for the ground was rough and treacherous to Elizabeth's feet, though her father fared better in serviceable boots. He cut a stick to help her progress, just as Angus had done to assist his. Together they struggled on.

The first houses they called at gave them overnight shelter, and the tidings that the Gale family farmed in the next little village.

Elizabeth was almost fainting with exhaustion, and her shoes and the hem of her gown mired with dirt, when the three farms came in sight.

Alice's mother came to the doorway, as her son shouted that he could see visitors.

"We're Barney's family and we've come to see if you've heard from him," said Elizabeth, sinking on to the porch seat.

"Well, now, that's a big surprise!" exclaimed Mrs. Gale. "Just you sit yourselves down while I call my daughter. Alice had a letter from Barney only yesterday."

Elizabeth exchanged a glance of triumph with her father. It had been worth the long march, after all. A fair, pretty girl came out of the house to greet them. If this was Angus's love, he had chosen well, thought Elizabeth. Alice herself gazed at the visitors with a mixture of welcome and apprehension. She clutched in her hand a single sheet of paper.

"This is the letter Barney sent me," she said.

"Does he tell you where he is?" asked Elizabeth.

"He's reached Halifax," replied Alice. "And he says he's got a position in the stables at the King's Head Inn." She studied the visitors anxiously. The lady's dress was the finest she had seen outside a magazine. Could she detect a hint of likeness to Barney in the older man's face? Elizabeth had got her breath back now. "My brother used to be a groom in Edinburgh," she said. "That sounds very like Angus, and very much what he would have sought to do."

"Angus!" Alice savoured the name that had eluded them for so long. "That suits him much better than

Barney," she said. "He always hated that, and was desperate to find out his real name."

"You'll stay and have a meal with us, I hope," intervened Mrs. Gale. "We shall all have a great deal to talk about."

Indeed they had. Around the supper table, the two older men discovered a farming tradition in common. The two younger women already had a bond through Angus and his welfare. Elizabeth formed a strong liking for the younger girl's modesty and sweetness of disposition, while Alice admired Elizabeth's style and assurance, though holding her a little in awe. Mrs. Gale bustled about, making her unexpected guests welcome, and the Gales kept trying to find ways to prove that the Barney they knew was in truth the Angus the Ritchies sought.

Height and colouring were right, they agreed. Eyes, yes; voice, not sure. Handwriting – no. Alice explained that he had learned to write again, and he may have copied her style. Hope and flickers of doubt alternated as they compared their distant memories with more recent recollections.

"I said he'd got to find out his background before I let him marry my lass," confided Mr. Gale to Mr. Ritchie. So this romance is serious then, thought Elizabeth.

"My Angus is very thorough in what he does," offered Mr. Ritchie, anxious to support the man he thought to be his son. "He was a good scholar at the school, like Elizabeth here, and he gave us no grief. But it was he who wanted to emigrate. He complained that there was no future left in Scotland, when the Lairds could do what they liked with our land. He talked us into packing up our chattels, and taking ship on the *Ruby* with Mr. Dudgeon's emigrants in 1823."

"That was the year when Barney so nearly drowned," said Alice excitedly. "He was rescued from the sea by the French sailors, in only his shirt and breeches and with one British penny in his pocket."

"We've still got his coat and boots, that he took off when he was working to help save the ship," said Mr. Ritchie. "Praise the Lord. They must be one and the same!"

"Tell us more about his loss of memory," suggested Elizabeth.

Euan Gale replied: "He knew nothing of his life before this last thirteen years. Even the skills of writing and reading were lost, though they soon came back when Alice took him in hand. The only skills he seemed to have kept were knowing how to handle horses, and I remember he fashioned a shepherd's crook to help him walk over the hills."

Mr. Ritchie silently produced the crook he had made for Elizabeth's use. The others looked at it in stunned amazement.

"That's it!" shouted Euan. "He made one just like that! He must have remembered how you used to do it. The skill was still in his hands."

Elizabeth, tense with emotion, burst suddenly into tears. "Oh, thank heaven," she said. "I hoped so much it would be Angus!"

\* \* \*

The next task was to find him again. They wrote down the name of the King's Head Inn in Halifax. Alice would not part with her precious letter, but she read bits to them. He said that he was well, that the Innkeeper had said he could stay, because his work was good, but he had been so busy that he had not had time to go and search the shipping records.

Alice kept saying that Barney … no …Angus had promised to come back in less than a twelve-month now. She was counting the days.

"So he will," Elizabeth assured her. "What Angus says he will do, he surely does. Still, he must go and see his own mother first. She has waited thirteen years for him to come back to her, and she's far from well, just now."

"Indeed, he must," agreed Mrs. Gale, and discovered for the benefit of all that they had the same type of family – father, mother, older brother, sister and younger brother. Indeed the two families had much in common, including the urge to emigrate and to own their own land. Only there were those thirteen years lost from Angus's life – the one family knew the first nineteen, and the other family knew of the last thirteen. "Which makes him thirty-two!" they said triumphantly.

"We don't even know how he'll feel," said Mr. Ritchie. "Whether he'll want to join me and Matthew on my farm, which he first intended to do, or whether he's planning to make his own way. Thirteen years is a long time out of a man's life."

Mr. Gale agreed. "Perhaps we can make it up to him a bit for that loss – give him a start, like."

Mr. Ritchie agreed, but doubtfully. He had little money to spare, and he owed Matthew an inheritance.

"I can earn money," interposed Elizabeth, "I have some savings put by, and so I can help Angus."

"I can help too," offered Alice. "I've no money, but I don't need much, and I can bake and sew and keep hens and pigs. We can all help Angus."

The two Ritchies stayed overnight with the Gales, becoming firm friends, and were driven part of the way back to Port au Basques in the cart before taking the hill track down to the coast. The two families liked what they had seen of each other, and while they waited for another ship to call and take them back to Pictou, the Ritchies confirmed to John Campbell and his workmen that the lost sheep had been found.

When Elizabeth and her father landed at Pictou once more it was with a confident sense of "mission accomplished."

* * *

Meanwhile, Robert and Angus arrived back in Pictou shortly after Elizabeth and her father returned from Port au Basques.

Angus had worked out his week's notice at the Inn and received his meagre wages. Between them, they traced and found shipping records, which listed the arrivals from the *Ruby* and the *Harmony*, and there was proof that a man named Ritchie had been lost at sea.

Pretty Polly could not carry both men and their bundles, and so Robert used part of his funds to buy a gig to transport them back to Pictou. He paid for a room at the inns along the way, and shared it with Angus, who looked after the mare as his part of the bargain. In order not to embarrass his impecunious friend, Robert refrained from drinking all evening, save for a half-pint of porter before retiring. They explored each hamlet they rested at. Robert was the elder and the leader, but he found Angus an intelligent and congenial companion. He would offer him a job, he thought, if he founded a business of his own.

He painstakingly described Elizabeth as she was now to Angus, her face, her hair, her clothes, and the little he had learned of the two positions she had held as governess. "Very much a lady," he commented. "A little straight-laced as a governess has to be. She fears her mother is not in good health, which is why she undertook the journey here. She believes the family has prospered since they came to North America. She told me you have a father who used to be a shepherd, and a younger brother, Matthew, who has been the mainstay of the new home. He and your father built it between them, I understand."

Angus drank in all this information eagerly, but it did not lead to an enlightening recognition.

Robert also counselled Angus on possible jealousies after such a long absence. "My younger brother, Paul, wasn't too pleased to see me back," he confided. "Reuben was fine. I don't think he saw me as a rival, but Paul certainly did."

Angus became increasingly nervous as they neared Pictou. "I have wanted this meeting so long and so much," he confided. "Only I'm terrified I won't recognise them, and I'll be meeting them as strangers."

"Don't let that show," urged Robert. "You can't mistake them after all – one father, one mother, one sister, Elizabeth, one younger brother, Matthew. They will do all the reminiscing. All you have to do is nod and agree. Then gradually you will build up the knowledge of what was in the past, even if you don't remember it yourself. You noted that there were four members of the Ritchie family from the *Ruby's* passenger list, and only three arrived, and so there can be no doubt you are the fourth Ritchie – and they will remember you."

"I feel ashamed I did nothing about tracing what happened at the time."

"You couldn't. You had no memory. You were ill. You didn't know where to start. It was a slice of luck that I shortened the discovery time by meeting Elizabeth on the ship. You would have got there in the end."

"I owe you so much," said Angus, with diffidence, but real gratitude.

"You owe me nothing. I have a fellow feeling for you, you know. I was away from my home for eleven years, and my family must have thought me dead, or at least a graceless scamp who hadn't the decency to let them know where he was. It's a wonder I got a welcome at all. At least you were deeply mourned and almost deified in your absence."

They were by this time nearing Pictou. Robert thought it best to drive Angus directly to his home, the direction of which he obtained by calling at the local store. He could return with the mare and gig to Maple Grove, his own home, afterwards. Quite soon the little homestead came into view. By chance Elizabeth was in the garden, watering the flower-tubs and taking the air after returning from her Port au Basques adventure. She looked up at the sound of the horse's hooves.

"See who I've brought you!" called Robert. She came running to the gig.

"Angus!" she cried, recognising him immediately, and reaching up to embrace him. Angus felt stiff and awkward. He should kiss this excited girl, he knew, if she was his sister, which she seemed to be. He leapt down, then hugged her back, and followed as she led him quickly into the homestead.

There were tears of joy as his mother rose from her chair and clasped him to her. "My own dear Angus," she wept. "I knew we would find you one day."

Robert followed more slowly, hitching the mare to the fence, and standing in the doorway surveying the joyous, but chaotic scene. He could just have driven away, but he felt he had played such a part in the reunion that he wanted to see the outcome – and besides he experienced quite an intense desire to see Elizabeth again, and share her pleasure in her brother's return.

Elizabeth called Mr. Ritchie and Matthew in from the field.

"Welcome back, son," choked Mr. Ritchie, wiping his eyes with his sleeve, as emotion overflowed. Matthew slapped his brother's back and shook his hand, his beaming face evidence of his sheer pleasure and delight.

Elizabeth busied herself with the fire and kettle. "Stay to tea," she invited Robert. "How did you find him to bring him to us? We were intending to go to Halifax to look for him tomorrow, after failing to find him at the fish-drying station, or at the Gales' farm."

"I went to Halifax a fortnight ago, and ran across him at the stables where I lodged my horse. Not too surprising to find him at stables, I suppose. Did you meet the fair Alice?"

"Yes. She had had a letter from Angus, which told her where he was staying. Oh, isn't this wonderful, Robert? It is quite the happiest day of my life!"

He squeezed her fingers. "Take it gently," he urged. "It will seem strange to you all at first. There's a lot of adjusting to do. I won't stay now. This moment belongs to you and your family, but I'll ride over next week, if I may, and find out how you're getting on."

He was fairly sure from Angus's stiff and rigid demeanour that he did not remember them at all!

# Chapter Twenty - The Absent Mind

Robert's concern for the next two weeks was, with Reuben's help, to negotiate with old Farquhar to buy his boat-yard as a going concern. The business appeared sound and profitable, with a loyal band of workers and forward orders. The foreman was a knowledgeable Scot, who had served his apprenticeship with Alexander Hall & Co. of Aberdeen.

The smell of timber and varnish was, as it had been in Jamaica, a delight to Robert's nostrils. He took a turn at the lathe, and showed he knew something of the practicalities. Farquhar approved. He was old now and tired, but he did not want his yard to go to some investor who had no personal interest in it.

"They say the future's in iron and steam," he complained. "But I believe there'll always be room for the traditional boat. You can't beat wood, and there's a plentiful and cheap supply of it round here."

Despite his Halifax savings, Robert thought he would need a loan from the Bank to fund the purchase price.

Farquhar's figure was more than he had available. Nevertheless, he could see it was a sound business, and it was what he had enjoyed doing in Jamaica. He could make a small fortune if he invested wisely now.

"I don't want to do you down," he said frankly to Farquhar, "But it's more than I expected. What about extended terms?"

The older man shook his head, disappointed also. "Nay, I'll not be staying round here. I'll want to see

Scotland again, and then decide where me and the missus will live. I need all the capital I can build up. But I'll shave fifty off it if tha wants it."

Robert made up his mind. "Done," he said, "I'll raise the money somehow."

He was on the point of seeking an appointment with the Bank, when Reuben made his helpful suggestion.

"You've got your one-third of Father's legacy you could claim," he reminded Robert. "We'd need to get the farm valued, of course, but if you wanted to realise that, and sell your share to Paul and me, you could put the money into your boat business. Or we could take shares in your business, if you wanted to do it that way round."

"That's an extremely generous offer," said Robert. "But would Paul agree?"

"He would probably agree to the first idea," responded Reuben. "That is, if he can be made to understand it. He might not agree to the second, but his passion has always been the ownership of the farm, and if it meant he had a half share rather than a third, he might well think it a good idea."

"Well, I think it's a good idea! Also I'd rather manage my own company, than have to be answerable to shareholders, however closely related, so that first alternative would suit me."

"I'll suggest it, then. Mother has a life interest in the property, and if she wants to invite you to go on living here, I wouldn't object."

"It might not be for long," confided Robert. "I'd like to marry and build my own place if I can, and the probable profits on the yard mean I can likely do that in a year or two."

"Anyone in mind?" asked Reuben, with a curious glance..

"I might have," replied Robert cautiously, but offered no further confidences.

* * *

With all he had to do, it was ten days before he found time to visit the Ritchies. He saw Elizabeth first. He thought she looked pensive and a little sad.

"How are you finding things?" he asked, as she took his arm to walk in the garden.

"It is difficult, as you thought it could be," she admitted. "Angus treats us with a sort of resigned acceptance, but with no real recognition. His personality seems to have changed. I remember him as always eager to do things, passionate about discovering new experiences, lively and fun to be with."

"Does he remember his life with you in Edinburgh?"

"I think not," she answered. "He pretends. He agrees with me when I talk about it, but he doesn't initiate any memories of his own. He is good with Mother, and he talks farming comfortably with my father and Matthew. I think it is only with me that he is not at ease."

"The brain is a complex thing. Maybe bits of memory are coming back, but not all at once."

"I don't think any of it is really coming back. I think he needs more to trigger it. This is a new home and a new country. I think if he were in Scotland, it might come back, but not here. He can't visualise our former home, and our former life, and that, of course, cuts him off from so much we once had in common."

"Is he happy with your family?"

"I think he would rather be with Alice."

"Well, that's understandable," said Robert. "He's in love with Alice. He'd naturally rather be with her. Just as I would naturally rather be with you."

It was said casually, but there was no mistaking Robert's meaning. Elizabeth flushed bright pink, and snatched her arm away from his. He was teasing her again, she thought. Really it was too bad!

"Now don't get cross!" Robert pleaded soothingly.

"You have been very kind," said Elizabeth stiltedly. "We all owe you a deep debt of gratitude."

He was about to explain that no debt existed, and he meant what he said, when Angus joined them, and Elizabeth seized her chance to make her escape.

"How are you getting on?" Robert asked Angus..

"I've done as you advised," Angus replied. "I've listened, and taken in what they've told me about life in the strath. They have talked about the school I used to go to, and the big house, where I used to work. They have explained the rent crisis, and described the McAndrews, whom I seem to have befriended on the journey, and who are settled near here, and I accept that all this happened in the past, but I don't really remember. It's like a story that I'm hearing which applies to someone else."

"Elizabeth says you need more to trigger your recollections."

"I get a glimpse now and then, but it doesn't last. Last week, when Father was showing me his few sheep in that green field, he was talking about the vast numbers of hill sheep grazing amongst the heather.   Then my imagination painted a background of purple heather in a sort of haze, and then the picture dissolved again, and we were back in the green field.  It's very strange."

"I came to offer you a job," said Robert, changing the subject.  "I'm buying a boat yard on the West River, not too far from here, and I thought you might like to work for me there, and earn more money than you will ever do here.   Also it will give you some independence from the family."

Angus's eyes brightened.  "B . .But I don't know anything about boat-building," he stuttered.

"Well, you can learn.  It would be an opportunity -- unless you want to stay and help on the farm, or find a job in stables somewhere."

"I don't know. I think Father might be expecting me to help around here, and I have been doing that, but there isn't enough work for three.   There were no vacancies at the Pictou stables when I last enquired."

"I think you should branch out on your own.  Live here, but work in the boatyard.  Earn some money and save some of it before you go back to the Codroy Valley, which you've promised Alice you will.  Come down to the yard, anyway, and take a look around.   Here's where you'll find us.  I've drawn a little map.  Then talk to your father, and to Elizabeth!"

"I wish I could remember things, and be more comfortable with the family.   It's all a bit of a strain.  Perhaps it would be better if I did have something else to do, rather than depend on them."

"I'm sure that is right, though I expect it will get easier," comforted Robert. "Neil Thomson will be passing through soon on his way back to Scotland on the *Margaret Bogle*". He might have some advice on memory recovery. I'll ask him. I want him to take a letter to Scotland for me anyway."

In truth Robert had been growing increasingly worried about Delia. He had acquainted her with facts that could put her in danger. He had under-estimated William Mackenzie's ruthlessness twice. He must not do so again. He judged William capable of contriving an accident to his wife to save his own skin, and Delia might inadvertently reveal her newly-acquired knowledge, particularly in the heat of a quarrel between them.

Robert had contemplated going back to Scotland himself and offering her what protection he could. That it would put himself back into danger again, he discounted. Forewarned is forearmed, and he would not give William another chance., but he had become too involved with his new project here in Pictou, and as his financial future depended on that, he could not risk an absence now.

Moreover the ice would soon close in and a journey become impossible for six months. He determined to write instead.

"Dear Mrs. Mackenzie," he began
"It concerns me greatly that the intelligence I gave you about your father's death and its consequences could cause you harm if a certain person knew that you had become privy to it. I thus warn you to be very careful that you do not disclose, particularly to Mr. M. that you have

come by this knowledge. Please do not discount this warning."

He paused, and underscored the last six words.

"You may be surprised that I did not call again to take my leave of you. I was in fact on my way to your house, when I was set upon by two rough villains, who kicked in my ribs, and robbed me of my money, watch, and the dossier I had prepared about your father's death and the reasons for it."

He continued, trying to write in a way, which she would understand, but not to be too explicit in case the letter fell into the wrong hands.

"I would have thought this mere coincidence had they left me in the gutter, but I was conveyed to a ship in the Port of Leith, bound for North America, and the ship's Captain bribed to take me there, with no questions asked. The certain person I ascribe this to, has to my certain knowledge, acted decisively in advance of any threat to his position, and it is therefore of the utmost importance that you be on your guard. I shall ask a thoroughly trustworthy person, my nephew, to have this letter conveyed to you personally.

I intend to set up a boat-building business here in Pictou, and to put down some roots at last. May I wish you also a safe and secure future.

Your sincere friend,

Robert Thomson

PS – It would ease my concerns if I knew that you had safely received this letter, and you may wish to reply to me, care of Maple Grove in Pictou."

The letter written, he sought his mother's permission to invite Neil to dine at Maple Grove when the *Margaret Bogle* next berthed in Pictou.

* * *

Robert had not long to wait. Neil's intentions had been to call and pay his respects to his grandmother anyway. When he received Robert's note, via the harbour-master, he hurried to make his way to Maple Grove, while the ship was disembarking passengers from Quebec, and taking on a few other cabin passengers at Pictou. The sailors and stevedores would also be packing its hold with freight, mostly timber, and provisions, in preparation for the autumn return Atlantic crossing to Scotland.

Neil gave the Maple Grove dinner group recent news of his father, Nathaniel's family at their farm near Lake Huron. His own brothers and sisters had grown mightily since he last saw them, and there was much news to talk about.. Then everyone wanted to hear about Alexander and Isabella in Quebec. Alexander had written that he was delighted Robert had returned, and bade him visit them if he could before the Gulf became impassable.

"And when are Alexander and Isabella coming to visit me?" asked Bella Thomson, in an aggrieved voice.

"Next summer, perhaps," Neil replied, for they were all aware that the busiest time for Alexander as Immigration Agent, was always the summer season, when trans-Atlantic voyages from Scotland, England and Ireland were embarked upon by thousands of economic migrants seeking their fortunes in the colonies. He could rarely get away for long. "Isabella's very busy with

Quebec's preparations for Queen Victoria's Coronation celebrations too," added Neil.

When the meal was over, and Neil and Robert able to withdraw for a private chat, Neil first wanted assurance that his uncle and former patient had fully recovered from his injuries, before asking about Elizabeth.

"We found her brother, you know," said Robert and told the story of the journeys and mishaps, which had eventually restored Angus to his family. "I wanted to ask your advice," he continued. "This blow on the head and partial drowning he suffered have severely confused his memory. He has perfect recollection of the last thirteen years, but no memories of the first nineteen. We have established his name, his family, his birthday, and got him properly registered now as an immigrant, who should have arrived on the *Ruby*. The trouble is that he looks upon his family as strangers, and doesn't feel at home and comfortable with them. Can we give him any medical help to restore his earlier memory?"

"The brain's a very complex thing," responded Neil, unconsciously repeating Robert's own conclusion. "It would be the blow on the head that caused the damage, rather than the drowning or the fever he suffered. We simply don't know much about brain injuries, but the damage may be irreversible, and he will have to live with it. At least he is lucky to have a memory that works now, even though it has shut down on previous experiences. Many head injuries can cause permanent confusion, and changes of personality."

"Yes, Elizabeth says he is not the same outgoing Angus that she remembers. He seems more passive, less eager and enthusiastic."

"Growing older and more responsible, perhaps."

"It could be, but it seems that his hands remember some things that his brain has forgotten – instinctive movements, but not recollections of experiences."

"Interesting!" commented Neil. "I'll do some research into amnesia as some people call it, and see if there are any similar cases written up, which would help to identify Angus's problem. There's no treatment I know of which can be given, but I will mention it around."

"Do, please, -- and there's one another mission I want you to undertake for me. Can you find Delia Mackenzie, and give her this letter from me?"

"That's a coincidence. I am also carrying a letter from Isabella to Delia."

"This one is very important," stressed Robert. "It has to be kept secret, and given into her very own hands. On no account must it fall into William's clutches."

"Aha, I smell a rat," teased Neil. "An illicit correspondence with a married woman, without her husband's knowledge!"

"It's no laughing matter," said Robert soberly. "And it's not what you might think!"

"All right, I promise. If it's a love letter, I shall divulge your faithlessness to Elizabeth."

"Much damage that would do," retorted his uncle. "Elizabeth doesn't take me seriously."

"And are you serious?"

"I might be. It depends . . " .Robert evaded the question, as he had done with Reuben.

\* \* \*

When Neil arrived in Edinburgh, and went to deliver his letters to Delia, he found, of course, that she was away in Tain. The servants at William's house provided him with her direction, and he determined to entrust both letters to the mail coach service.

Delia duly received Robert's warning, and was grateful for it. Despite having taken her own steps to remove herself from danger, she was glad that he had cared enough to make sure she was forewarned.

Her reply had no hope of reaching Canada until Spring thawed the ice and the ships began moving again. Thus she had time to think about her response.

"Dear Robert," she began. The familiarity was justified, because she had known him in Pictou as a young man, and used his christian name, if only as a way of distinguishing him from his older brother, Alexander.

"I am touched that you should have taken the trouble to write. I have indeed taken my own steps to safeguard myself, and have determined to separate from my husband, and continue to stay with my aunt in Tain. I would ask you to keep this fact confidential, for I do not wish any of my friends in Pictou, nor my acquaintances in Scotland to know of that decision. They will understand that I am acting as companion to my aunt , who is far from well and needs my company. My son, Gilbert, knows the true situation, but will keep his own countenance, and I do not believe William will want to spread such news.

I was very sorry to hear of the attack upon you, and I do hope you are fully recovered from the injuries my husband must have arranged to be inflicted upon you. We must thank God that he was satisfied with returning you to North America, rather than kill you as he must have killed my father.

My main concern is for my son – that he should complete his legal training and become independent, with a secure future. I do not seek to alienate him from William, nor have I breathed a word of the secret we share. I can only hope that William will himself conclude that his illegal trading is not worth the candle, and will bring it to a close.

I was interested to hear that you will be setting up as a boat-builder, and I trust you will prosper. You have certainly lost much through association with my husband, and deserve every success. I can only be glad that you lost the dossier! I must be much less courageous than you and my father, for I would not have been happy for myself, nor Gilbert, had the true facts become known.

Should you have further occasion to write, the above address will find me, and perhaps we shall meet again, if I return to Pictou some time in the future.
Yours sincerely,
Delia Mackenzie.

It would be wrong, thought Delia, to offer him any recompense for the personal loss he had suffered. The Thomsons were a proud family. Nevertheless, she would like to remain in touch with Robert. His manner had impressed her greatly. It was a pity the whole Atlantic Ocean had become a gulf between them.

## Chapter Twenty-one - Adventures Beckon

Margaret Ritchie did not survive her son's home-coming by more than a few months. Her husband, daughter and two sons laid her to rest in the little cemetery on the shore of the estuary, and erected a headstone in her memory. Her remains lay in company with many early pioneers, their names synonymous with those of Highland and Island clans.

Angus and Elizabeth found their options improved and restricted respectively by her death. For Angus the emotional tie to the Ritchies was loosened. For Elizabeth it became tighter, as her father and brothers depended on her to keep the homestead functioning. Her skills were educational, rather than domestic, and she fretted at the enforced household duties in a far from well-equipped home. The winter had been colder than she had ever known, and its length bore down her spirits.

For Angus the year was almost up when he had promised to return to Alice in the Codroy Valley. He had hammered and varnished and knotted rigging with his mates in the boatyard, and put by a sum enough to take him to Port au Basques, with something to spare. He parted from Robert with regret, and asked him to look after Elizabeth, for he thought she would be lonely when he had gone.

"My mother will invite her to visit us at Maple Grove," promised Robert. "Don't worry. Just sort out your own future with Alice, and we may be able to advance you some cash to get started."

It was to prove unnecessary. Euan's marriage and move to his own farm was imminent, and Mr. Gale decided that, now he knew Angus came from good Highland stock, and Alice remained of the same mind, he should give his consent to their marriage also. More than that, he was prepared for his new son-in-law to replace Euan for labour on the farm, and look to expectations from it, if he were willing. Angus jumped at the chance. He asked permission to add a mare in foal to the farm's stock of animals. He would buy, feed and look after her, and any profit from the horses would belong to him and Alice, while he gave his labour on the farm in return for a home for them both.

Thus it was settled that a double wedding should take place in the summer of 1838, shortly after the Coronation in June of Queen Victoria. Robert and Elizabeth received their separate invitations, but joined forces to travel to the Codroy Valley. Robert argued that it would be ridiculous for them to go in two separate parties, and indeed, as Elizabeth had unfavourable recollections of their previous attempt to get there, she was urged by her menfolk to accept, despite some reluctance.

Elizabeth had by then been introduced to the family at Maple Grove. Mrs. Thomson welcomed her warmly, and seemed to like what she saw of her. Elizabeth herself was less nervous of Robert when she saw him in the natural surroundings of his home. However, she still wondered what had been the dark secret in his past, which Neil obviously knew about. One day something the jealous Paul said gave her a clue.

"Watch what you're doing with that gun!" had shouted the youngest brother, as Robert lifted a hunting rifle from the wall, in preparation for a day's shooting.

"How dare you, Paul!" hissed his mother, while Robert himself stood frozen for a second, and then broke the piece to show it was unloaded. He refrained from making any comment.

Elizabeth looked from one to the other. There was a mystery here, she was sure. Could Robert have caused an accident with a gun – even killed or injured someone, perhaps?

She rode her pony home again with her mind in a ferment. Was it unreasonable of her to want Robert to tell her the truth? He had disappeared from his home for eleven years. Why?

Her doubts and puzzlement were not lost on Robert. He sought guidance on the way women's minds work from his mother.

"What do you do, mama, if you've been playing carefully to land a fish. You think you have it hooked and you start to reel it in, but the fish panics, and it darts this way and that, looking for any means to escape . "

Bella looked her son straight in the eye. "Robert, if you mean what I think you mean, Elizabeth is not a fish! You don't deserve to catch her if that is the way you talk! If you want her, ask her! Don't play around like this!"

"Mama, I think she might reject me – and I dare not risk that. Elizabeth is a very strong-minded young lady, and she would not easily change her mind. She is convinced I have a shady past, and would not make a dependable husband."

"And would you be a husband she could depend upon?" asked his mother.

"I wouldn't have been once – but I believe I would be now."

\* \* \*

Robert had still not dared put his question to Elizabeth. He rode over to see her at least once a week, and she began to look forward to his visits as highlights in the dreary existence. One day he found her pegging out shirts, socks, trousers and sheets, and waited patiently while she finished the chore and came to sit beside him on the garden seat. He took one of her hands in his.

"Once this hand was smooth and white ..."

And now it's rough and red with scrubbing working clothes," she interrupted. "I hate it – but what can I do? They depend on me to do my share and run the house, just as Mother did."

"You have a choice," he said. "Try for a post as governess, or consider marrying me! I wouldn't expect you to wash even one set of clothes. We could afford a scullery-maid at the very least!"

"I think you're joking me again."

"I was never more serious. Why won't you trust me, little one?"

At the term of endearment, Elizabeth first snatched her hand away, then brushed it across her eyes, and a lump arose in her throat.

"Once an adventurer ..." she choked on the implied accusation.

"Always suspect, you think? Will it do any good to tell you I haven't looked at another woman for ten years or more.  Also I'm quite willing to give up rum if you insist,  though I'd much rather you won't . ."

"Just a sailor's tot, then!    Truly I hadn't thought of marrying.   If anything I had thought of taking a teaching post over here, but my mother's death means it is difficult to leave just now."

"We must hope that Matthew will bring home a bride, and that would  release you, wouldn't it?"

"Yes, I would then be free to make up my mind what I should do."

"You need time, I know.  I don't mean to rush you. Still, you deserve better than this.   You've been a governess.  Were you fond of children?"

"Fond is perhaps not quite the right word.  I liked bringing up children and teaching them good manners and good behaviour as well as their lessons.  However, I've done that, and would welcome a different challenge."

"I could well be described as a challenge," laughed Robert ruefully.   "Perhaps you'll find the idea of your own wedding more attractive after we've seen Angus and Alice married."

\* \* \*

Their excursion to the Codroy Valley threw Robert and Elizabeth together again, but in the company of Mr. Ritchie and Matthew.   McAndrew, their neighbour, with one of his boys, had agreed to look after the stock while they were away. The four of them squeezed together in Robert's gig to go down to the boat, and they hoped Angus would find some sort of transport to meet them when they got to Port au Basques. If not, they would have to walk, but this event was not to be missed.

The tiny church was full of friends and neighbours from the parish in the Valley. Euan's bride was a homely girl, but Alice looked slender and ethereal in the white dress she had made herself, with her mother's lace veil and a coronet of white June lilies grown specially in their own garden. Simplicity was the key – for there could be no lavish display in pioneer country, but the three nearest families shared their best crockery and linen, and their baking skills to make a wedding feast all would long remember.

The fine weather made it possible to hold the party outdoors, and two fiddlers played for country dancing long into the night. Home-brewed ale and fruit cup kept the dancers refreshed until sheer exhaustion drove the girls indoors and the men to sleep in the barn. The two married couples had stolen away to their bed-chambers long before.

Mr. Ritchie and Mr. Gale puffed away at their pipes, and agreed that all the bad times had now passed, and the young people could look forward to a happy life. Mr. Ritchie hoped Matthew would find as lovely and good a bride as Alice was, for he had done the family proud while his elder brother had been missing, and he deserved the best. Matthew, himself, was having the time of his young life, dancing with abandon in company with one of Alice's school-friends. Young John Gale was keeping the glasses filled and stuffing himself with goodies from the table.

Robert and Elizabeth had taken their part in the dancing, both with one another, and in sets with the others, but with less exuberance than their juniors. As the light faded, they drew away from the throng, and strolled arm in arm to a quieter part of the lane that led to the church.

"I've had enough, I think," said Robert. "Merriment is all very well, but it palls in the end, and one prays for a few moments of peace."

"Matthew absolutely loved it. He hasn't had much fun," responded Elizabeth. "But we're older than most young people there, and perhaps it shows."

"Life's a great adventure," declared Robert. "For Angus and Alice it has begun today. For Euan and Joan too, of course, but that has been more predictable in that his mind has always been set on working his own farm. Matthew has had one side of his great adventure, when he plunged into sudden responsibility in this new world of ours, but his great romantic adventure is yet to come."

"And what has been your great adventure?" asked Elizabeth, hoping for his confidence.

"I've had lots of them. Once for me it was sailing on the high seas. Then it was to make my plantation in Jamaica succeed. Now it is in building boats fit to sail upon the high seas. Shall we find an adventure for you, Elizabeth?"

"I don't think of adventure. Perhaps that's where men are different. I think of duty, and of family, of course."

"But this is a land of adventure you're living in." Robert pursued his theme. " This is a new country. People are taking risks all the time. We have to forge our own future and establish our own Government, break free from the English system, like the United States have done, but more peacefully I hope. Perhaps my next adventure when the boat-building is going well, might be to involve myself in politics – after marrying you and founding our family, of course! That could be your next adventure, my love."

"Oh, I don't know. It is such a big step. To stay always in Pictou . ."

"We might not stay in Pictou for ever. Alexander is in Quebec, which is quite a big city, like your Edinburgh, and growing all the time. Pictou would have to suffice, for a while, of course, but it's not a bad little town – better than being in the wilds of the country, as we are here. Are you coming round to the idea? Shall I ask your father for permission to pay my addresses to you – whatever those might be!"

She had perforce to laugh. "I have been independent so long and am so much older, that it is not like Alice, having to wait for Papa to say 'yes.'"

"All I want is for you to say 'yes'! I've been falling deeper in love with you ever since I woke up and found you sitting by my bunk on the ship – it crossed my mind then that I had reached heaven already, but luckily not so."

"You were a very difficult patient – always wanting to be up and doing, or demanding your bottle of rum."

"You were a very severe nurse. I'll not live under the cat's foot, you know. I'm a free spirit. You can keep your discipline for our children. But I promise to share, and not to dominate, if you're prepared to do the same."

"I'm not prepared to do anything – yet."

"Playing hard to get? Well, I shall claim a kiss. It's the least I deserve after all this prevarication!"

Elizabeth did not refuse. It was a very special kiss, long, lingering and lasting. There was no need for a second. The message had been conveyed. Elizabeth felt distinctly light-headed as, with arms around each other's waists, they turned and wandered back to the farm.

\* \* \*

Elizabeth's next visit to Maple Grove was a longer one – she stayed two nights, as she needed a break from domestic servitude at the Ritchie farm, said Bella Thomson, refusing her offer of help with the dishes after supper. In reality over the two days there would be more chance of a heart-to-heart chat between the two women, while the men were out. It was also a rare opportunity for Elizabeth to do some shopping in the little town.

Elizabeth wanted to find out the story behind Robert's long exile in Jamaica, and Bella also was determined to ensure that she knew it from a reliable source, and was steered away from any feelings of unease or condemnation.

"I don't know what I've done to deserve to suffer with three grown men still hanging round at home," said Bella. "Of course, I'm glad to have Robert back again, but Reuben is taking for ever to fix his interest with his girl – if he's been courting her for a year, I swear it's nearer three. I don't expect Paul to marry – he's too selfish and too slow – but the other two should."

"Perhaps Robert had little in the way of feminine society while he was abroad," suggested Elizabeth. "Why did he stay in Jamaica so long?"

"He needn't have done, except for that dratted William Mackenzie he had taken to going about with. William and his wife, Delia, had a big estate in Pictou. She was the daughter of a Judge, and they had pots of money. Then one day there was a shooting accident and the Judge was killed. The next thing we knew Robert went missing. My eldest son, Alexander and his friends searched for him everywhere, but William said he'd glimpsed him running away near the Halifax Road.

"Robert tells us since that he was forced to go, that William said he would accuse him of shooting the Judge, if he didn't get away ...I don't know about that, but I do know that Robert was very much under Mackenzie's influence at the time. William swore it was an accident, and the inquest brought in accidental death, but Robert did not come back, and some people have always wondered what was the truth of it. William, who was the only one who knew where Robert was, did not tell him it was all right to come back, and didn't tell us where we could find Robert. Robert now says Mackenzie paid him hush money to stay away."

"That was very wicked of this Mr. Mackenzie," commented Elizabeth. "You must have been extremely worried, not knowing whether Robert was alive or dead."

"We were very worried," Bella assured her. "I did not really think he was dead, but I couldn't understand why he didn't contact us. Even a brief letter would have done.   As it was, he never saw his father again, because my William died four years later."

"Why did this Mr. Mackenzie keep Robert in Jamaica?"

"I suppose he was useful to him, running the estate. He was paid quite well, but I always think it was because Robert knew too much about what William Mackenzie was doing, and how he made his money – or it might have been that William shot the Judge himself and wanted Robert as a convenient scapegoat."

"Has Robert said that?"

"Yes.   Robert said he thought William had shot the Judge, deliberately."

"But that's murder!" exclaimed Elizabeth.   "Did he have a motive?"

"Robert thinks the Judge had found out about William's illegal smuggling rackets, and was threatening to expose him.   Robert knew all about William's methods and he compiled a dossier, called "The Pictou Triangle to give to the Customs people.   As soon as he knew that William had left Pictou and was living in Edinburgh, Robert left Jamaica and went after him, to bring him to justice.   But William was too smart, and you saw the result.   Robert was kidnapped and the dossier stolen. Then he was put on the ship you travelled on to come back to North America."

"So William is living in luxury in Edinburgh!"

"As far as I know.   I think Robert takes the view that he has tried to get some justice for the Judge, but was outwitted, and he'd better leave things alone, and live his own life now."

"But Robert was involved in the smuggling?"

"He was very young!" his mother excused him. "And many years ago, lots of people were involved with contraband in one way or another. It was thought of as good sport to get a keg of whisky past the excise officers. Things are much stricter now, and I'm sure Robert wouldn't dream of doing it now."

"He was talking the other day about perhaps going into politics."

The older woman glanced quickly at the younger.

"Robert of all my children is the most like his father, who was called "William the Pioneer", you know. William liked adventure, too. He would take risks, and even found himself in prison once, for debts that were no fault of his. But William was a really good man and did a lot for this neighbourhood. Robert is basically a good man – not quite as good as Alexander or as saintly as Nathaniel – but with a bit more of an enterprising nature. I have been blessed with some wonderful children – as perhaps you will be one day."

Elizabeth blushed, and changed the subject. She was glad to have had her questions answered. The mystery had at last been explained.

\* \* \*

Elizabeth felt reassured and contented this time as she rode her pony home. The nagging doubts she had felt over Robert's past were laid to rest, and there was the memory of that sweet kiss to thrill her also. She was humming a little tune, and a smile was playing round her lips as she opened the door. Her father was sitting in his rocking-chair and greeted her, "You look cheerful, lassie."

"I am," she replied. "I think I'm going to seek your blessing to marry Robert Thomson."

"Aye, I always say that one wedding breeds another, and I canna say I'm surprised."

"My only worry is what will happen here, if I say I will. How will you and Matthew go on without me?"

"Dinna fash yersen. There's McAndrew girls a-plenty we can hire to cook and wash. Their homestead's only up the road, and they'll be glad of the work."

Elizabeth heaved a sigh of relief. "Then you would give us your blessing?"

"Aye, he's a handsome man, and has got himself a good business too. I reckon ye've done well for yersen, and it'll mean ye'll bide in Pictou, and we'll see the more of ye than if ye went back to Edinburgh. I liked the way he came over and talked wi' me when we were at Angus' wedding feast. Kind and considerate, like. I wondered why ye was takin' so long to make up yr mind."

"Oh, I had to be sure," replied Elizabeth. "Marriage is a great step for a woman to take, but Mrs. Thomson Senior is a lovely lady, and I think she'll be pleased too. Just think, I might never have met Robert if William Mackenzie hadn't kidnapped him, and put him on board the ship on which I'd booked passage."

"Kidnapped …what are you talking about, lass?"

"Oh, I shouldn't have said. Please forget it, papa. It's an old, old story, known as "The Pictou Triangle", apparently, and now it's best forgotten. Let me get your tea!"

# Chapter Twenty Two - The Wages of Sin

Delia found life in Tain extremely tame. She had received no reply from William to her letter announcing that she was leaving him. Mindful of Robert's warning, she had given no indication that she knew he had been responsible for her father's death, nor that she was cognisant of the illegal operations of "The Pictou Triangle", but she had made it quite clear that this was the end of her married life. Obviously, he did not care. The explosion of anger feared by Gilbert had not materialised. The boy continued with his studies at the University, and saw his father only at the evening meal when both were at home. Gilbert wrote that he missed her, but that he looked forward to spending the long vacation with her, after visiting a University friend in Yorkshire.

He also told her in the letter how William had filled her place. "My father has brought in a new housekeeper. This is a black lady, called Marie-Louise. I think she once worked for him in Jamaica, and he then offered to get her a post in Halifax. She talks about that town as if she knows it quite well. She is a cheerful lady, rather stout, and I quite like her, but the servants do not want to do her bidding. Two of them have left, and I think others may go as well. I do not know how to tell you this, Mama, but she seems very familiar with my father. She does not dine with us, but I hear her giggling voice often coming from his study, and sometimes even from his bed-chamber. He orders her about, which she does not seem to resent. Of course, he does not take her about socially. You were right in thinking that he would spend time at his Club, going there after our meal most nights, and I believe he lunches there often as well.

He has raised my allowance, and says that I will need more as you used to give me clothes, and now I will have to buy them myself. I will need your advice, please, which shops I should go to. I have shot up another two inches, and some of my coats are looking skimpy ..." The rest of the letter went on to describe some of his University lecturers and the views the students held about them. The Age of Enlightenment had meant that Edinburgh was held in high esteem throughout the rest of the world – but students are never respectful of eminence.

Delia began to think she would have to go to Edinburgh for a little while in the autumn. Apart from Gilbert's clothes, she desperately needed some for herself. Then there were Exhibitions, which she would like to see. She had dispensed with the services of a maid, but she needed someone to trim and style her hair, and she thought she would buy up most of the stock of the main bookseller to help her get through the long winter nights. She could find a concert to enjoy, she was sure, and if she bought some sheet-music, she could try out Aunt Cicely's pianoforte.

She determined to go back with Gilbert for a week before his term started in September, and she would stay a further week for her own amusement. There was a lady in reduced circumstances taking in paying guests in the square where her former house was situated. It was perhaps too near to William, but it would be equally near to Gilbert to enable him to squire her about. They would have to be very careful that William did not see them, but his habits were regular, and she was sanguine that she could avoid any confrontation. She wrote to reserve rooms, using the name Forfar just in case her name was recognised, and the gossips got busy.

It would have been nice to go as far as London, but it would take an age to travel, and she did not wish to leave Aunt Cicely for so long.

*　*　*

Edinburgh proved just the stimulus Delia needed. She enjoyed the shopping and the visit to the Art Exhibition, and she viewed the latest delicate designs, which Spode had produced in their blue Italian ware. It was expensive china to be sure, but she would have loved to furnish her dining table with it – had she still possessed a dining table and the house in which to entertain. She dared not look up the few society friends she had made in the City, but she enjoyed writing a long letter to Isabella describing her activities in the city that lady knew so well. She also made a new acquaintance of a genteel and well-read lady she met while eating a nuncheon in one of the smaller eating- houses, and the two ladies took pleasure in walking together in the Castle grounds.

In the first week after her return to Edinburgh, she had not encountered William, although she could see from the parlour window of her lodgings across to his house, and she had perceived the black housekeeper once on the front steps, and once at one of the downstairs windows. She had also seen William once or twice leaving the house or returning to it. She marvelled a little at the lack of concern this gave her.

Then, one day, her careful plan to avoid a confrontation came to naught. Returning from an early evening stroll around the square, she turned a corner, and came face to face with her husband. Delia stood frozen to the spot.

"Right, my lady!" snarled William. "What are you doing, snooping round here, when you are supposed to be in Tain?"

Delia tried to pass, but he stood four-square in her path, and side-stepped when she did, blocking her way forward.

"I am here only briefly on a shopping visit," she answered. "I had not meant to contact you, or advertise my presence."

"Do you think I'm blind," he said roughly. "I saw you from the window days ago – and if you want to remain discreet, why in the world are you wearing that hideous purple hat?"

He had never liked it, she knew, but it had a useful veil! "Please let me pass," was all she said.

"No!" he refused. "There are matters to discuss and arrangements to be made. We can't talk here. Come back to the house."

"No!" Delia was afraid to be alone with him. "I cannot invite you to my lodging," she began …

"Are you mad? As well publish the situation to the whole of Edinburgh!" He seized her elbow and turned her in the direction of their former home. "Step out smartly," he urged, "Or we'll attract attention."

It would not do to make a scene in public. Delia reluctantly allowed herself to be escorted towards the house and up the steps, mindful of an iron grip on her arm. The footman opened the door.

"See that I'm not disturbed," commanded William, pulling her from the hall into the dining room. He picked up a sheaf of papers. "I presume you know of this nonsense," he said, waving them at her.

Delia fought for time. "What are they?" she asked.

"Robert Thomson's rubbish! He showed it to you, didn't he?"

Robert had said it would be dangerous to let William know that she knew his secret. Delia turned her head away. William pursued his advantage. "He's lying!" he declared, throwing the dossier on to the table, where the pages spread around.

"Why should he lie, and about what?" she queried.

"The Pictou Triangle, as he calls it – he's out to ruin my business."

And why would he want to do that?" If she could get him to commit himself to what had happened in the past, she would know better how to react.

"He has some grudge against me …"

"Robert told me he wanted to talk to you, but he never came back, did he? Then how did you get hold of that dossier?"

This time William became defensive.

"Never you mind! I've got it! And I've scotched his mischief-making! What else did he tell you?"

"He told me that you had helped him get to Jamaica after my father's death – that he did not want to go, but you insisted, making it look as if he were to blame."

"They brought in 'accidental death'. You know they did."

"Yes," she said, "But only because Robert wasn't there, and they heard only your side of the story."

"I never blamed him."

"But you made it appear that he had something to hide. Moreover you let him think that everyone else would blame him ..."

"I paid him well."

"Paying him to conceal the truth!"

They were fencing now, thrust and parry – she wanted him to admit his part in her father's death, but William was too wily.

"It was his word or mine," he said.

"Was it really an accident – or did you murder him?" demanded Delia directly.

"Did Robert tell you it might be murder? Is that why you left me?"

"He told me you had a motive – that my father would have exposed the Pictou Triangle."

"Motive doesn't mean anything. It was an accident," insisted William.

Delia looked at him long and hard.

"I accept it can't be proved, but I don't have to live with the uncertainty," she said. "I told you in my letter. It is time to go our separate ways."

"What about the boy?"

"I have not told him. I have no desire to undermine his respect for you."

"You don't want to deprive him of my funds for his legal studies, more like!"

"Unjust!" she retorted. "I have removed myself, and left you his company."

"Generous!" he mocked. "I've no guarantee you won't poison his mind in the future."

"No guarantee," she agreed. "Only my word of honour – but you wouldn't understand that!"

William raised his fist as if to strike her. Delia was reminded of his attack all those years ago, and prudently dodged round the table end and made for the door. William lunged after her, but caught his sleeve on the candelabra. He stumbled and panted

"You're not to see the boy again!

"What do you mean! He's my son!"

"He's my son! I'm his guardian, and I say you are not to see him."

"I shall see him. I bore him. He's mine, mine, mine!" Delia was screaming now, frantic with fear. The stumble had given her a split second in which to turn the door handle and escape from the room. There was no footman in the hall – drinking tea below stairs, no doubt. She wrenched open the front door, and bunching her skirts, hastened down the steps.

William stood threateningly at the front door, but thought better of pursuing her.

"Mind what I say!" he called.

Delia turned, too frightened and upset to guard her words. "You have no right to my son. You're impotent and a bully. Thank God he's not tainted by you!"

She walked rapidly away across the square, having said much more than she meant to. A screech of "Jezebel!" from William told her that final shaft had hit home!

\* \* \*

Shaking and scared, Delia stumbled back to her lodging. She sat down a little way back from the window to try and compose herself. The ugly breach between them was now complete. William knew that she knew that he had murdered her father. He must now know, too, that she had played him false, and that Gilbert might not be his child. What would he do now? What could he do? For herself she need not be concerned. She could go straight back to Tain. But what of Gilbert? Would he throw Gilbert out too? Perhaps not. He loved the boy, and he would be left with nothing. Perhaps he had not believed her, and put that final declaration down to hysteria. She could not guess how he would react. He would seek to punish her, without doubt, but would he want to revenge himself on the boy? It was a conundrum she could not untangle.

She tried to concentrate on normal things. She was glad that Gilbert had a convivial evening at the invitation of a fellow-student, and so had not dined at home, nor been a witness to that vicious argument. He might look in and see her on his way home, he had said, provided the evening had not been too convivial. She was glad he was settling well into college routine.

The night was mild, and the window sash was open at the top. A light now glowed in the upstairs saloon of the house opposite, where William was probably pacing the floor or drinking. He would certainly fly to the bottle as a restorative after their quarrel. She could do with a drink herself. She poured a small glass of ratafia and raised the glass to her lips. The curtains of the downstairs dining-room opposite had been closed, though there was still a chink of candlelight. Delia pulled her work-box closer, and looked for some tapestry on which she was working. She brought her own branch of candles nearer in order to select a thread. When she looked up again, a few minutes later, the chink of candlelight seemed much brighter, and was flickering too.

She dropped her work and gazed more intently; it was definitely now quite bright, more like the glow of a wood fire, than merely a candle. But it was only September. Surely they had not started lighting fires already!

Then a tongue of flame licked the curtain edge, and shot upwards. Good heavens, there was a conflagration in the room! Her mind raced back to William's effort to intercept her. Surely he had picked up the candelabra when he knocked it over! Perhaps he had not! He had rushed after her. The ensuing altercation must have driven it out of his mind. He had thrown the dossier on the table. Could the overturned candles have set fire to the paper?

For a few seconds she was mesmerised, not knowing what to do. Then two figures rushed up the area steps; she could hear screams, and a commotion as bystanders gathered round. Someone called for the fire engine, and the flames grew more menacing. In what seemed a very few minutes, they suddenly took hold.

She recalled that the room was panelled, and it would be tinder-dry after this warm summer. Someone had opened the front door, and the rush of air fanned the fire. It seemed to leap from the dining-room into the hall, and from the hall to engulf the wooden staircase. The light was fierce and there were sparks, and a crackling sound, which she could hear from across the square.

Delia stood up, irresolute. What could she do? She was not even supposed to be in Edinburgh. Another servant – the black lady, she thought – struggled up the area steps from the basement, and was helped away from the scene of the blaze. But there was no sign of William. Surely he must have heard the commotion.

A clatter of hooves and wheels heralded the arrival of assistance in the shape of a fire-wagon. Men grabbed its buckets, formed a chain and hurled water into the hall, having little or no effect. A ladder was erected against the wall of the house furthest from the seat of the fire. Now a figure had appeared at an upstairs window. It was a thickset figure – it must be William, though she could not be certain at this distance. The ladder would not be long enough to reach him; someone lashed another length to it; more men unwrapped a tarpaulin, and held it at each of four corners. Screams and shouts created pandemonium. Delia gathered that they were urging the figure to jump. A fireman started to mount the ladder, others holding the base of it steady. If the stairs were ablaze it would be the only way William could escape.

Delia could bear it no longer. She had to know what was happening. Wrapping a shawl around her head, she left the lodging-house and joined the throng in the street.    Someone else was pushing past her, and a slim, grey-clad figure elbowed his way to the front, and she saw that he was even trying to enter the house.

Gilbert had come back.

This time Delia joined in the screaming.  "No, no, you can't;  its's madness!" she sobbed, as her son rushed up the stone steps.  A burly man was right behind him.

"Nay, ye'll kill yersen," he yelled, and pulled the boy away from the burning door.

The little drama had distracted everyone's attention, but when Delia looked again, there was no figure to be seen at the upstairs window, only the red glow of the fire in the room behind.   The fireman had reached the top of the swaying ladder and broke the glass of the window with a mighty crack    He tried to lift the sash, but it resisted his effort.   There was no help from the other side of the pane.   The drapes in the room caught alight, and the fireman's fellows urged him down.   There was no sign of William.

Delia pushed past the many onlookers and reached Gilbert, clinging on to him, to prevent any further ideas of rescue.   The flames had reached the roof, and the stench of smoke hung heavy in the air.  "It's gone!"  Delia said, woodenly.  "I could never have believed it would burn so quickly."   Neighbours had been streaming out of their homes, and urging the firemen to damp their houses down before they caught alight too.   Luckily the Edinburgh granite was of some protection.

Gilbert seemed shell-shocked and pale as a ghost.  "My father,"  he said, weakly.  "He didn't get out!"

"If he was upstairs, and I think he was, he couldn't have done," Delia sympathised. "The stairs caught alight very quickly.  It started in the dining-room; the window was open;  possibly the lace curtains blew on to the candelabra, or a candle fell to the floor.  How it happened is of no consequence now.  What we have to realise is that your father must be dead."

"Such a dreadful death!" shuddered the boy.

"He may not have been conscious of it all," comforted Delia,  wrapping her arms around him. "Breathing in the smoke is what kills, I believe.  It is the choking and the fumes more than the flames.  Or he may have had a heart attack at the exertion and the fright.  He may even have drunk enough to be a little befuddled and not thinking straight.  Come back to my rooms, dearest. I'm afraid you may have lost all your possessions, too."

"No matter," he answered.   "But the servants? Are they all right?"

"If there were only three, then I saw them come up from the basement.  Do look for them, dearest, and make sure they have suffered no ill effects."

"I  must see what they can do for tonight.  Have you any money, Mama, if they need to find somewhere to stay?"

"Yes, yes," she stuffed some coins from her reticule into his hand.  "Come back to me, when you have done what you can for them," she urged.

\* \* \*

They got precious little sleep that night.   Gilbert assured himself that the three remaining servants, including the black housekeeper, who had succumbed to an attack of hysterics, were all safe.   He went over to the fire crew and thanked them for their help.   The building was red-hot, and crashing sounds as timbers fell into the smoking hall below could be heard for hours.    There could be no possibility of recovering a body or possessions until it all cooled down.

When eventually it did so, William's body had fallen, with the floor-boards into the hall below.   There was the melancholy task of arranging a funeral.  Gilbert was genuinely deeply upset, and needed all the consolation Delia had to offer.   She wrote hastily to Aunt Cicely,  postponing her return and conveying the dreadful news.   It was ironic, she thought, that the dossier of the Pictou Triangle, which had been written to bring about William's downfall in one way, had succeeded in destroying him in another, as its pages flared from the flames of the candles fallen on top of it.

William's affairs had been shrouded in such secrecy that it was difficult for the widow and son to know where to start to unravel them.   Luckily,  many of his personal papers had been kept at the office he had established in the business quarter of the City, and once they had located this building, William's clerk was able to find some of the papers they needed, including a Will.

All William's possessions were left to Gilbert, and Trustees had been appointed in case William's decease preceded the boy's attaining his majority.   There was no provision for his wife, for the Will had been drawn up only six weeks earlier. Delia had been swiftly punished for her defection.   She was still Gilbert's mother, however, and the Trustees recognised this in the arrangements they proposed for the interim lodging and maintenance of the heir until the estate could be settled. This might take years, the Trustees thought, for William's interests were far and wide. Many of them were also illegal, Delia thought, and she was alarmed to think the frauds and the smuggling network might still come to light.

She thought that she should let Robert Thomson know what had happened. Perhaps a letter might reach him before shipping was disrupted by the winter ice. It was an extraordinarily difficult letter to compose.

Dear Mr. Thomson, she wrote eventually,
I feel I must inform you, and my friends in Pictou, that we have suffered a shattering loss in the recent death of my husband, William, in a fire at our home in Edinburgh.

Fortunately my son, Gilbert, was out of the house at the time, and I had been on a lengthy visit to my Aunt in Tain. The servants escaped from below stairs, but the upper part of the house, including the staircase, was engulfed in a fierce fire from which William was unable to be rescued.

I am somewhat concerned that, in winding up the estate, which has all been left in trust for Gilbert, some of my husband's business interests may attract unfavourable attention. From the conversation we had in Edinburgh, I believe you may know of some people who ought to be informed of his death, so that it is quite clear that trading via The Pictou Triangle is at an end. If there is unfinished business, it must be forgotten.

You were good enough to confide in me some matters of many years ago. You may feel, as I do, that this recent event has been a judgement, ending that episode also.

My son, grieving for his father, needs my company, but I hope one day that I shall be able to return to Pictou, where I was once a happy member of a thriving community.

Yours sincerely,

Delia Mackenzie

\* \* \*

However, the letter did not reach Pictou until the first shipping of 1839 reached the Gulf of St. Lawrence. Robert recognised the writing from its outer cover, and postponed opening it until he could be alone.

He climbed the hill towards Maple Grove, and sat on an outcrop of stone overlooking the estuary. The sky was blue overhead, though the grass had still the greyish hue of its long winter sleep under the snow. Lingering in the inlets of the estuary, there was still some ice, glinting silver in the bright sun. Soon this would disappear, as would the grimy hillocks of compacted snow cleared earlier from the Pictou streets.

Another summer was coming and towards its end would be a threesome instead of a twosome in the new house he had built for his bride, Elizabeth.

He turned over the letter and was reluctant to open it. Lately, life had been good to him, and he was far from sure that he wanted to be hauled back into troubles in Scotland. That the letter would contain bad news he surmised, for why would Delia write to him otherwise? With a sigh, he opened it and perused the lines Delia had penned.

William was dead.

That much was satisfactory, though Robert could feel it in his conscience to be sorry for William's grim end. Hellfire in the after life was to be expected, but ordeal by flame in this present life was a cruel justice. He glanced across to the big mansion William had built on the opposite hillside to Maple Grove. He had sold it well to one of the legislators of the state, and its lavish furnishings, chosen by Delia, were still in situ, and augmented by the taste of its present owner. That house had been the centre of an empire of deceit, with tentacles reaching half across the world. It had played host to murder and the concealment of murder. Was a burnt and blackened corpse any worse a fate than swinging on the end of a hangman's rope?

Delia was alive, but he thought her life would be an emptiness – exiled as she now was from a country and society she had made her own. Perhaps she would marry again – she was an attractive widow, after all, provided no-one knew of her late husband's chequered history. What would Gilbert make of his future? If he had inherited Judge Fogo's aptitude for the law, rather than his father's aptitude for criminality, then he could do well, with a substantial inheritance to set him on his way.

Well, Robert determined no-one should know of William's past from him. The price had been paid, and he would stay silent.

From this moment forward, Robert also resolved to forget his own wasted years. They had gone, and it was too negative of him to dwell upon them any further; indeed in some ways, he could see that he had benefited from them.    His expertise in management had been gained because he had had to manage the plantation.   His hobby of boat-building had now become his livelihood.

That might never have come about without the experience of Jamaica.    Even the voyage of revenge he had embarked upon had resulted in his joyous meeting with Elizabeth and the founding of his family.  It had been an unexpected blessing too, for the Ritchie family.  He felt great satisfacrion at the way he had helped Angus in his predicament.

He had huge dreams for the boatyard.  Yes, it was true that the new iron ships would hiss and pound their way across the Atlantic, but his wooden ships would still glide smoothly and silently round the coastal waters. Only yesterday he had secured an order for another of the boats he was currently building.   Once his income was firmly established, he might give back more to his community – to stand for election to the legislature might be an option.  He was, after all, the son of William the Pioneer.  The image of his father seemed almost tangible beside him -- a powerful man, bearded and with piercing blue eyes, rigid in principle, but with a Christian's forgiveness.  What his father had done for this new land, and what Alexander was doing for immigrants in Quebec had made Thomson a respected name in the country. Robert felt that he, with Elizabeth at his side, could make a valued contribution too.  His wild oats had been sown, and he had reaped a miserable harvest.   But no-one outside the family knew about that.

He could start afresh -- and he would.

Turning over again the letter in his hand, Robert decided that he wanted nothing more to do with Delia or Gilbert. He hoped they would not return to Pictou. She seemed to him to have an aura of disaster -- first her father, then her husband had died violently. He hoped her future would be kinder to her than the past had been, but it was time to cut the connection, or it might return to haunt him.

She had asked him to try and cover up any echoes of William's illicit empire. He did not think it necessary. From what he knew of the captains and operators within the Pictou Triangle, he believed they too would feel it time to retire with their ill-gotten gains. The news of William's demise would be bound to have reached them by now. He saw no need to intervene.

Robert tore the letter into tiny fragments, and flung them aside to be caught by the breeze and carried he knew not where. The distant harbour, the nearer hills, fields and trees were serene and beautiful. Adventures were all very well, but he could now live in harmony with the peace of home.

A beloved figure was treading across the grass in search of him. Looking far ahead, he could see an attractive future for Elizabeth too. Unlike his mother whose centre of interest was only the family, Elizabeth might want to share in his vision of advancement for the colony. To found an academy for girls to join the excellent boys' school which Pictou already had, would be a dream she would be capable of turning into reality.

The new world was stirring, and would soon shake off the shackles of the old. In the old world, Delia sat, patiently reading to her aged aunt, anticipating only Gilbert's next visit, reflecting perhaps that the best of her days were fading into memory.

## THE END

ISBN 1425120079-2